Praise for the work of Susan Mallery

Delicious

"A tasty new series....Using her patented blend of wit and humor, Mallery explores deeply complicated family relationships that are laced with love and loss. Outstanding!"
—*Romantic Times BOOKclub* (4½ stars, Top Pick)

"Susan Mallery has written a winner with *Delicious,* and the series looks to be a knockout group of books you won't want to miss."
—*Romantic Reviews Today*

Falling for Gracie

"More than a romance, Mallery has crafted a fine tale of small-town life, family relationships, and forgiveness. At times funny, at times bittersweet, this story will appeal to a broad spectrum of readers."
—*Booklist*

"Diverting."
—*Publishers Weekly*

Someone Like You

"When you think of passion, drama and heartwarming stories, think Susan Mallery. As always, she delivers a top-notch story."
—*Romantic Times BOOKclub* (4½ stars, Top Pick)

MORE RAVES FOR SUSAN MALLERY

"If you haven't read Susan Mallery yet, you must!"
—Susan Forster, author of *Unfinished Business*

"Smart, sexy entertainment."
—Christina Dodd, author of *Some Enchanted Evening*

Also available from
Susan Mallery and HQN Books

Delicious
Falling for Gracie
Someone Like You

And look out for the next installment in the
Buchanan family saga

Sizzling

Coming soon!

SUSAN MALLERY

Irresistible

HQN™

ISBN-13: 978-0-373-77117-2
ISBN-10: 0-373-77117-7

IRRESISTIBLE

This edition published by arrangement with Harlequin Books S.A.

www.HQNBooks.com

Printed in U.S.A.

One of the most frequent questions I'm asked is how I get my ideas for my books. In truth, they come from everywhere. This particular story was born while I was driving to the grocery store, listening to National Public Radio.

The news had come on and the reporter mentioned how many soldiers had died the previous day in Iraq. Their names were withheld, pending notification of their immediate families.

I remember pulling over, suddenly wondering what happened if the soldier in question had no family. Who would be notified and who would mourn?

In that moment Walker Buchanan was created, and through him, Ben. A hardened solider and a young man with the heart of a soldier. A young man with no family.

This book is dedicated to those who have given the greatest gift to their country. May you live on forever in the hearts of those who have loved you.

Irresistible

CHAPTER ONE

THE GREAT UNWELCOME truth is that there are times when a woman needs a man…or at the very least, an unnatural level of upper body strength. Unfortunately for Elissa Towers, this was one of those times.

"Something tells me you won't be impressed by my to-do list, or the fact that Zoe has a birthday party at noon. Birthday parties are very important for the five-year-old set. I don't want her to miss this one," Elissa muttered as she leaned all of her weight into the lug wrench.

She'd been lamenting the extra ten pounds she carried for at least three years. One would think they'd come in handy now, say for leverage. But one would be wrong.

"Move!" she yelled at the lug nut on her very flat tire. Nothing. Not even a whisper of budging.

She dropped the lug wrench onto the damp driveway and swore.

This was completely her fault. The last time she'd noticed the tire getting low, she'd driven to Randy's Brake and Tire Center, where Randy himself had patched the nail hole. She'd sat in his surprisingly tidy waiting room indulging herself in gossip magazines—a rare treat in her world—not even giving a thought to the fact that he was using some stupid *machine* to tighten the lug nuts. She always asked him to tighten by hand, so she could take off the flat herself.

"Need some help?"

The question came from nowhere and startled her so much, she wobbled and sat down right in a puddle. She felt the wet seeping through her jeans and panties. Great. Now when she stood up, she would look as if she'd wet herself. Why couldn't her Saturday start with an unexpected tax refund and an anonymous chocolate delivery?

She glanced at the man now standing next to her. She hadn't heard stealth guy approach, but as she looked up and up farther still, until their eyes met, she recognized her semirecent upstairs neighbor. He was a few years older than her, tanned, good-looking and at a casual glance, physically perfect. Not exactly the type who tended to rent an apartment in her slightly shabby neighborhood.

She scrambled to her feet and brushed off her butt, groaning as she felt the wet spot.

"Hi," she said, smiling as she carefully took a step back. "You're, um…"

Damn. Mrs. Ford, her *other* neighbor, had told her the guy's name. Also that he had recently left the military, kept to himself and apparently had no job. It wasn't a combination that made Elissa comfy.

"Walker Buchanan. I live upstairs."

Alone. No visitors and he didn't go out much. Oh, yeah. Good times. Still, she'd been raised to be polite, so she smiled and said, "Hi. I'm Elissa Towers."

Under any other circumstances, she would have found another way out of her dilemma, but there was no way she could loosen the lug nuts herself and she couldn't just sit here praying to the tire gods.

She pointed. "If you could be burly for a second, that would be fabulous."

"Burly?" The corner of his mouth twitched.

"You're a guy, this is a guy thing. It's a natural fit."

He folded his impressive arms over a rather impressive chest. "What happened to women wanting to be independent and equal in the world?"

Hmm, so there was a brain behind those dark eyes and maybe the potential for humor. That was good. Neighbors of serial killers always said the guy was so *nice*. Elissa wasn't sure Walker qualified as nice, which was, in a twisted way, a bit of a relief.

"We should have worked on our upper body strength first. Besides, you offered."

"Yes, I did."

He picked up the wrench, squatted down and in one quick movement that left her feeling both inadequate and bitter, loosened the first nut. The other three followed just as fast.

"Thanks," she said with a smile. "I'll take it from here."

"I'm already involved," he told her. "I can put on the spare in a couple of seconds."

Or so he thought. "Yes, well, that's a funny story,"

she said. "I don't have a spare. It's big and bulky and really weighs down the car."

He straightened. "You need a spare."

His statement of the obvious irritated her. "Thanks for the advice, but as I don't have one, it's not very helpful."

"So what do you do now?"

"I say thank you." She glanced pointedly at the stairs leading to his apartment. When he didn't move, she added, "I don't want to keep you."

His gaze dipped from her face to the large nylon bag on wheels, lying next to her on the driveway. His mouth tightened in disapproval.

"There is no way you're going to carry that tire somewhere yourself," he said flatly.

Definitely not nice, she thought. "I don't carry, I drag. I've done it before. The tire place I go to is less than a mile from here. I walk there, Randy patches it for me and I walk back. It's easy. Good exercise, even. So thank you for your help and have a nice day."

She reached for the tire in question. He stepped between her and it.

"I'll take it," he told her.

"No, thank you. I'm *fine.*"

He topped her by at least seven or eight inches and he had to outweigh her by a good sixty pounds… every ounce of them muscle. As he narrowed his gaze and glared at her, she had the feeling he was trying to intimidate her. He was doing a good job of it, too, but she couldn't let him know that. She was tough. She was determined. She was…

"Mommy, can I have toast?"

Why was life always about timing?

She turned to her daughter standing at the entrance to their apartment. "Sure, Zoe. But let me help. I'll be right in."

Zoe smiled. "Okay, Mommy." The screen door slammed shut.

Elissa glanced back at Walker, only to find that stealth guy had used her moment of inattention to pick up her tire and walk toward his very expensive, very out-of-place-for-this-neighborhood SUV.

"You can't take that tire," she said as she hurried after him. "It's mine."

"I'm not stealing it," he said in a bored tone. "I'm taking it to be fixed. Where do you usually go?"

"I'm not going to tell you." Ha! That should stop him.

"Fine. I'll go where I want." He tossed the tire into the SUV and slammed the back shut.

"Wait! Stop." When, exactly, had she lost control?

He turned to her. "Are you really worried I'm going to disappear with your tire?"

"No. Of course not. It's just… I don't…"

He waited patiently.

"I don't know you," she snapped. "I keep to myself. I don't want to owe you."

He surprised her by nodding. "I can respect that. Where do you want me to take the tire?"

So he wasn't giving up. "Randy's Brake and Tire Center." She gave him directions. "But you have to wait a second. I need to get a pair of earrings."

"For Randy?" He raised his eyebrows.

"For Randy's sister. It's her birthday." She drew in a breath, hating to explain. "It's how I pay for the work."

She waited for the judgment, or at the very least, a smart-ass comment. Instead Walker shrugged.

"Go get them."

THE TRIP TO RANDY'S Brake and Tire Center took three minutes and when Walker parked, he found a short, beer-bellied older man waiting for him.

Randy himself, Walker would guess as he opened the car door.

"You got Elissa's tire?" the man asked.

"In back."

Randy eyed Walker's BMW X5. "Bet you take that to the dealer," he said.

"I haven't had to yet, but I will."

"Nice wheels." Randy walked around to the rear of the SUV and opened the back. When he saw the tire in question, he groaned. "What is it with Elissa? They're doing construction across from where she works. I swear, she finds every loose nail hanging around on the road. Always in this tire, too. There's more patch on it than rubber."

More patch than tread, Walker thought as he stared at the worn tire. "She should replace it."

Randy looked at him. "You think? Thing is, you can't get blood from a rock. Hey, times are tight with everyone, right? Got my earrings?"

Walker took the small envelope out of his shirt pocket and handed it over. Randy looked inside and whistled. "Very nice. Janice is gonna love them. Okay, give me ten minutes and I'll have this ready to go."

Walker hadn't wanted to help his neighbor in the first place. He'd taken a short-term lease on the apartment to give himself time to figure out what to do with the rest of his life in quiet and solitude. He didn't know anyone in the neighborhood and he didn't want anyone to know him.

Except for a brief but surprisingly effective interrogation from the old lady living downstairs, he'd kept to himself for nearly six weeks. Until he'd seen Elissa struggling with the lug nuts.

He'd wanted to ignore her. That had been his plan. But he couldn't—which was a character flaw he needed to work on. Now, faced with a crappy tire that was likely to blow the second she hit sixty on the 405, he found himself unable to walk away again.

"Give me a new one," he muttered.

Randy raised his bushy eyebrows. "You're buying Elissa a tire?"

Walker nodded. Best-case scenario, he would replace both rear tires. But he only had the one wheel with him.

The older man puffed out his chest. "How, exactly, do you know Elissa and Zoe?"

Zoe? Walker blanked for a second, then remembered the kid he'd seen around. Elissa's daughter.

He owed this guy nothing in the way of explanations. Still, he found himself saying, "I live upstairs."

Randy narrowed his gaze. "Elissa's a friend of mine. Don't you go messing with her."

Walker knew that even after an all-night bender, he could take the old guy and have enough left over to run a four-minute mile. Randy's posturing would have been almost funny—except it was sincere. He cared about Elissa.

"I'm just doing her a favor," Walker said easily. "We're neighbors, nothing more."

"Okay, then. Because Elissa's been through a lot and she doesn't deserve to be messed with."

"I agree."

Walker had no idea what they were talking about, but anything to move the conversation along. Randy picked up the flat and carried it toward the garage.

"I've got a couple of good tires that'll be a whole lot safer than this one. Because it's for Elissa, I'll give you a good deal."

"I appreciate it."

Randy glanced at him. "I'll even throw a little dirt on it so maybe she won't notice what you did."

Walker remembered her defensiveness about not having a spare. "Probably a good idea," he told the other man.

"YOU'RE POUNDING, DEAR," Mrs. Ford said calmly as she sipped coffee. "It's not good for the crust."

Elissa slapped the rolling pin onto the dough and knew her neighbor was right. "I can't help it. I'm annoyed. Does he really think I'm so stupid I wouldn't notice he replaced my old tire with a new one? Is it a guy thing? Do all men think women are stupid about tires? Is it specific? Does he just think *I'm* stupid?"

"I'm sure he thought he was helping."

"Who is he to help me? I don't know him from a rock. He's lived here, what, a month? We've never even spoken. Now suddenly he's buying me tires? I don't like it."

"I think it's romantic."

Elissa did her best not to roll her eyes. She loved the old woman but jeez, Mrs. Ford would think grass growing was romantic.

"He took control. He made decisions without speaking to me. God knows what he's going to expect for it." Whatever he was expecting, he wasn't going to get it, Elissa told herself.

Mrs. Ford shook her head. "It's not like that, Elissa. Walker is a very nice man. An ex-Marine. He saw you were in need and helped out."

That's what got Elissa most of all. The "being in need" part. Just once she'd like a little extra put by for a rainy day or a flat tire.

"I don't like owing him."

"Or anybody. You're very independent. But he's a man, dear. Men like to do things for women."

Mrs. Ford was nearly ninety, tiny and the kind of woman who still used lace-edged handkerchiefs. She'd been born in a time when men took care of life's hardships and the most important job for a woman was to cook well and look pretty while doing it. The fact that living like that drove many women to alcohol or madness was just an unhappy by-product not to be discussed in polite society.

"I called Randy," Elissa said as she slid the

piecrust into the pan and pressed it into place. "He told me the tire cost forty dollars, but he'd lie in a heartbeat if he thought it would protect me, so I'm thinking it had to be closer to fifty."

She had exactly sixty-two dollars in her wallet and she needed most of them for grocery shopping that afternoon. Her checking account balance hovered right around zero, but she got paid in two days, so that was something.

"If I could afford a new tire, I would have bought it myself," she muttered.

"It's more practical than flowers," Mrs. Ford offered. "Or chocolates."

Elissa smiled. "Trust me, Walker isn't courting me."

"You don't know that."

She was fairly confident. He'd helped because… Because… She frowned. Actually, she didn't know why he'd come to her aid. Probably because she'd looked pathetic as she'd wrestled with uncooperative lug nuts.

She rolled out the second crust. Flats of blueberries had been ridiculously cheap at the Yakima Fruit Stand. She'd pulled in after dropping Zoe off at her party. She had just enough time to make three piecrusts before she had to be back to pick up her daughter.

"I'll finish up the pies after I come back from the grocery store," Elissa said, more to herself than her neighbor. "Maybe if I take him one…"

Mrs. Ford smiled. "An excellent idea. Imagine what he'll think when he gets a taste of your cooking."

Elissa groaned. "You're matchmaking, aren't you?"

"A woman of your age all alone? It's just not natural."

"I like being a freak. It keeps me grounded."

Mrs. Ford shook her head as she finished her coffee. She set down the mug, then slowly pushed to her feet. "I need to get back. There's a *Beauty by Tova* hour starting on QVC. I'm nearly out of her perfume."

"You go, girl," Elissa said.

Mrs. Ford walked to the door that connected their two apartments, then paused. "I left you my list, didn't I?"

Elissa nodded. "Yes. I have it in my purse. I'll bring everything by when I get back."

The older woman smiled. "You're a good girl, Elissa. I'd be lost without you."

"I feel the same way."

Mrs. Ford stepped into her own kitchen and closed the door behind her.

Elissa had been a little disconcerted to discover that her neighbor had access to her house when she'd first moved into her apartment, but that had quickly changed. Mrs. Ford might be elderly and old-fashioned, but she was sharp and caring and adored Zoe. The three of them had quickly become friends, with Elissa and Mrs. Ford working out a system that benefited them both.

Mrs. Ford got Zoe ready for preschool in the morning and fed her breakfast. Elissa handled her neighbor's grocery shopping, got her to doctor's appointments and checked in on her regularly. Not that Mrs. Ford was home all that much. She was very active in the senior center and one of her many friends was always ready to pick her up for bridge or scrapbooking or a quick trip to an Indian casino.

"I want to be just like her when I grow up," Elissa said as she carried the three piecrusts over to the oven.

But until then she had to figure out where she would find the money to pay for a new tire and what to say to her neighbor to make sure he understood that she would never, ever, under any circumstances be interested in him.

Not even on a bet. Not even if he showed up naked. Although, to be honest, if he showed up naked, she would probably look because she hadn't seen a naked man in years. And he was more spectacular than most.

"I don't need a man," Elissa murmured as she set the timer. "I'm fine. Empowered. Only thirteen more years until Zoe is grown and in college. Then I can have sex again. Until then, I will think pure thoughts and be a good mother."

And, very possibly, think about her new neighbor naked. Because if she had to be tempted, she wouldn't mind him doing the job.

ZOE WAS IN BED BY EIGHT and sound asleep by eight-thirty. Elissa collected one of the blueberry pies and her last five dollars and headed up the stairs to Walker's apartment.

Despite the absolute silence from overhead, his SUV was parked in front, so she knew he had to be there. She hadn't seen anyone arrive to pick him up.

Not that she'd been watching. She hadn't! She *might* have been observing the comings and goings in her community as a way to stay alert for trouble and be a good citizen. The fact that she was fairly confident Walker was alone was only a side benefit of her altruistic civic activity.

Not that she cared if he was dating—she didn't. But showing up with a pie and five bucks was weird enough to explain to him, without having to deal with a significant other hovering. Not that any woman Walker dated was likely to consider her much of a threat. Elissa knew exactly what she looked like—the wholesome girl next door. She didn't mind. Her appearance meant her customers were far more likely to be protective than to come on to her, which made life a whole lot easier.

"Procrastinate much?" she asked herself as she forced her brain back to the task at hand. Namely, standing at the top of Walker's stairs, inches from his front door. If he'd heard her climbing, he could be watching her right now, wondering why she'd come this far without knocking.

So she knocked, then waited until the door opened and he stood there, right in front of her.

He looked good. His T-shirt stretched across broad shoulders and a muscular chest. No doubt those muscles were the reason he'd been able to twist her lug nuts into submission without breaking a sweat. His jeans were worn, loose and faded. His dark eyes seemed expressionless, but not in a scary ax-murderer way. More like he kept the world at bay.

"Hi," she said, when he remained silent. "I, ah, made pie." She thrust it toward him and added, "It's blueberry," in case his confusion about the type of fruit was the reason he didn't take it from her.

"You made me a pie?" he asked, his voice low. There was a hint of a question in the rumble, and more than a hint that he thought she was crazy, which she resented. She wasn't the one breaking the rules here.

"Yes, a pie." She thrust it forward until he took it, then held out a worn five-dollar bill.

"You're paying me to eat your pie?"

"Of course not. I'm paying you—" She stopped and drew in a breath. She'd gone from grateful to annoyed in two seconds flat. "You bought me a tire. Did you really think I wouldn't notice that bright, shiny bit of rubber? Is it me in particular or all women in general? Because I know this is a guy thing. You wouldn't have done this if I were a man."

"You wouldn't have needed my help if you were a man."

"Maybe." Probably. But that wasn't the point. "You slunk back here and put on the tire while I wasn't looking. You even rubbed dirt on it so it wouldn't look so new. And let me tell you, that's just strange."

He actually smiled. It was slight—no teeth, but somehow the action made him look open and approachable. "That was Randy's idea."

"It sounds like him."

He took a step back. "Want to come in and talk about this or do you prefer my porch?"

"The porch is fine. This isn't a social call."

The smile faded. "Elissa, I get it. You don't like that I bought you a tire. Yours had so many patches, it was dangerous. I should have let it go, but I couldn't. I'm not going to apologize for what I did. I didn't mean anything by it. I don't want anything." He held up the pie. "Except this. It smells good."

She liked that he wasn't using her tire against her. Gee, how many times had she been able to say that before in her life?

"I know you thought you were doing a good thing," she said slowly. "But you don't have the right to meddle in my life. I called Randy to find out what it cost. I think he lowballed me by about ten bucks, so I'll be paying you back fifty dollars. It's going to take me some time, but the pie is to show I'm sincere about it and here's the first payment."

He looked at the tattered bill. "I don't want your money."

"I don't want to owe you." She might not have much cash on hand, but she paid her bills on time and she never used credit except in emergencies where there was a risk of death or dismemberment.

"You're stubborn," he said.

"Thank you. I've worked hard to get this way."

"What if I told you the money didn't mean anything to me?" he asked.

Meaning what? He had plenty? She sighed at the thought. In her next life she was going to be rich for sure. It was right at the top of her wish list. But in this one…

"It matters to me," she told him.

"Fine. But you don't have to pay me in cash. We could work out a trade."

White-hot anger blew up inside of her. Here it was—the truth. Behind that pretty face was a disgusting, evil, heartless bastard. Just like nearly every other guy on the planet.

Of course. Why was she even surprised? She'd been momentarily attracted to Walker, and based on her stellar track record, that meant there *had* to be something wrong with him. She'd expected a massive flaw. But she hadn't thought it would be this.

"Not even if you were the last man alive after nuclear winter," she said between gritted teeth. "I can't believe you'd suggest that I would be willing…" She wanted to slap him. "It was a *tire*. It's not like you gave me a kidney."

He had the nerve to actually smile at her. "You'd sleep with me if I gave you a kidney?"

"You know what I mean. I'm done here. I'll mail the rest of the money."

She turned to leave, but suddenly he was somehow between her and the steps. How on earth had he moved so quickly?

His dark gaze claimed hers and all the humor fled from his face.

"Dinner," he said quietly. "I was talking about a few meals. You cook every night and I can smell it. I've been existing on frozen dinners and bumming meals off my sister-in-law. When I said a trade, that's what I meant. That's *all* I meant."

He wasn't touching her, yet she felt his nearness.

He was so much bigger than she was—she should have been afraid. She was nervous, but that was different.

Dinner, huh? It, ah, made sense. The more she thought about it, the more sense it made. Because, honestly, who would expect sex after replacing a cheap tire?

"Sorry," she said, dropping her gaze to the center of his chest. "I thought you were…"

"I got that. I wasn't. I wouldn't."

Wouldn't what? Want sex with her? Not that she was doing that sort of thing these days, or for many days to come, but why was he so able to dismiss her? She might be wholesome, but she was kind of pretty. And smart. Smart counted, didn't it?

Maybe he had a girlfriend. Maybe he was engaged. Maybe he was gay.

That last thought made her smile. Somehow she didn't think Walker was gay.

"Let's start over," he said. "I bought the tire because I didn't think yours could take one more patch. Randy charged me forty-five dollars for it. I'll accept the pie and money. You can continue to pay me back as slowly as you'd like. Forget what I said about dinner, okay? The money is fine."

He was doing everything right. So why did she want to argue with him?

"That works for me," she said.

"Then we have a deal."

He shifted the pie to his left hand and held out his right so they could shake on it.

She pressed her palm against his and nodded. “Good.”

His fingers were warm and strong. She felt a little quiver low in her belly. The unexpected reaction made her pull away and take a step back.

Danger came in all shapes and sizes. This particular form was big, powerful and far too sexy for her peace of mind. She still had thirteen years of celibacy ahead of her. Hanging around with Walker wasn’t going to make it easy.

Not that they were hanging. Nope. Not a single hang here.

“I should, ah, go,” she murmured as she edged around him and started down the stairs. “Enjoy the pie.”

“I will. Thank you, Elissa.”

She raced into her house and quickly closed the door behind her. Once there, she leaned against the wood until her heart rate returned to normal.

It was only then she noticed she was still holding the five dollars she’d tried to give him. There was no way she was going back up there tonight. She would leave it in his mailbox or something.

It was painfully obvious she should avoid Walker at all costs. He might be nice on the surface, but her original premise was still true. If she was attracted to him, then there was something seriously wrong with him. Right now, she couldn’t afford another male disaster in her life. She was still paying for the last one.

Literally.

CHAPTER TWO

WALKER DIDN'T HAVE a chance to knock on his brother's front door. He was barely halfway up the walk when the door was flung open and a very pregnant Penny raced—well, waddled—out to greet him.

"You have a toolbox," she said as she hugged him as tightly as her large stomach would allow. "Tell me there are tools inside. Real tools with handles and metal ends and unknown purposes?"

He wrapped one arm around her while he hoisted the metal toolbox with the other. "I left my pretend tools at home. When you asked me to bring tools, I thought you meant the real ones."

"Thank you," she breathed. "I did. I love Cal. He's brilliant and charming and other things I won't mention out of respect for the two of you being brothers, but he's not so handy."

"I heard that," Cal grumbled from the doorway. "I'm very handy."

"Of course, dear," Penny said as she pushed past him. "Are you sure this is okay?" she asked Walker. "Helping out?"

He bent down and kissed her cheek, then closed his hand into a fist and bumped it against his brother's closed fingers. "Happy to be here. You're pregnant, you're still working and Cal's busy running an empire. I've got time."

He followed them through a living room piled with boxes. Penny had moved into Cal's house shortly after the wedding in early July. Even though that was nearly six weeks ago, she hadn't done much in the way of unpacking.

"You're judging me," Penny called over her shoulder. "I can feel it. I know this mess violates your military code of honor or whatever, but just go with it."

"Did I say anything?" Walker asked with a grin.

"You didn't have to."

She tucked her long auburn curls behind her ear and paused in front of the kitchen. "The rest of the place may be a mess, but the kitchen is perfect."

"Why am I not surprised?" Walker glanced at his brother. "How many boxes did you have to find room for?"

"I lost count," Cal said easily. "When I hit twenty-five, I figured there was no point in knowing."

Penny was the executive chef at The Waterfront, one of four restaurants owned by Buchanan Enterprises. It was, in theory, a family-owned business, but only one of the Buchanan siblings worked there.

"I need the right equipment," Penny said as she stepped aside and motioned for Walker to enter the kitchen. "You can't create magic from crap."

"You should put that on your business card," he

said as he took in the pale, buttery walls and the large pot rack hanging above the island. Without the dark red paint, the kitchen looked bigger. Windows let in light and brought out the colors in the new tile backsplash.

"You put in a backsplash but you haven't unpacked or gotten the baby's furniture ready?" he asked before he could stop himself.

Cal looked at him pityingly. "You had to go there, didn't you?"

Penny's gaze sharpened. "I'm sorry. Were you being critical just then? Did you *plan* for me to cook for you today?"

"He didn't mean it," Cal said, stepping between them. "Not everyone understands how your incredible mind works." He lowered his voice. "Walker brought tools, remember?"

Penny laughed. "I know. It's okay. Just don't make me feel guilty. My back hurts."

"Sorry," Walker told her, enjoying their banter. He'd always liked Cal and Penny as a couple and had been happy to see them get back together. "Now about the baby's room."

"It's through here," Penny said, leading the way. "We finished painting last week. Well, Cal did. I supervised."

"From a distance," Cal reminded her.

She sighed. "Right. I wasn't allowed to breathe the fumes. We have the curtains up, too. Now all we need is furniture. We physically own everything—the dresser, changing table, crib—but it's in boxes."

"Very nice boxes," Cal reminded her.

"Oh, yeah. They're stunning. But imagine if we had actual places to put things."

The baby's room was at the back of the house, with a view of the garden. Several large boxes stood in the center of the room. The walls were a soft green, the trim had been painted white. Sheer curtains covered open miniblinds.

"The rocking chair is in the office," Penny said. "Until we get this cleaned up, there's no space for it. I have a big area rug, too, but Cal said we should wait to put it down."

"After we put everything together, we'll clean up, then put down the rug," Cal said.

Walker nodded and set his toolbox on the hardwood floor. "Let's see what you bought."

Penny stepped into the hallway. "I'll get started on lunch. We're having seafood crepes with a light cream sauce, some kind of pasta, I haven't decided yet, and chocolate mousse torte with fresh berries for dessert."

Walker's stomach growled. "Sounds great." He waited until Penny left, then looked at his brother. "You eat like this all the time?"

Cal groaned. "I had to join a gym."

"Worth the price of admission."

"For Penny's cooking? You bet."

They moved the boxes out of the center of the floor and decided to start with the dresser.

"Thanks for doing this," Cal told him as he ripped open the cardboard.

"I don't mind."

"Aren't you still settling in?"

Walker shook his head. "It took me exactly two hours to move in to my apartment and unpack."

"You had stuff in storage, didn't you?"

"Not much." No furniture. Just a few personal things he hadn't wanted to lose. He'd had to buy a sofa, TV and bed.

"Do you like the place?" Cal asked.

"It works for now."

His brother pulled out the sheet of directions and tossed them into the closet. "Why an apartment? You could have bought a house."

"I don't know where I want to live yet," Walker admitted. Or what he wanted to do with the rest of his life. He'd thought he would stay in the Marines until he retired. Then one day he'd realized it was time for him to leave. "No point in getting something permanent until I decide on a location."

"You're staying in Seattle, aren't you?"

"That's the plan." As much as he had one.

"Want to come work for me?" Cal asked. "As a major stockholder, you'd be welcome."

"No thanks. Coffee's your thing."

Several years ago, Cal and his partners had started The Daily Grind. Their initial three locations had grown into a popular West Coast chain that was rapidly expanding across the country. Walker had invested his savings in the start-up and the risk had paid off with a large chunk of shares that had steadily grown in value. He'd never bothered to calculate their exact worth, but he wasn't thinking about getting a job because he needed the money.

"Still looking for Ashley?" Cal asked.

Walker shrugged. "Regularly. I went through another three and haven't found her. But I will."

"I don't doubt it. Oh, Penny said the new general manager at The Waterfront quit."

"Figures." The family restaurants were successful businesses, but keeping executive staff was impossible. Gloria Buchanan, matriarch of the family and all-around bitch, drove the most talented away. "Gloria's not getting in Penny's face, is she?"

"No way." Cal grinned. "I wrote the contract myself. Gloria isn't allowed to step foot in the kitchen without permission."

Walker set out the pieces of the dresser, then opened his toolbox. "Being married agrees with you."

"We got it right the second time around. Six months ago, I wouldn't have thought it possible. What about you?"

"I'm not interested in a second chance with Penny. Or a first one. She's your girl."

His brother punched him in the arm. "You know what I mean. You can't be alone forever."

"Why not? I don't need anyone."

"We all need someone. The difference is some of us are willing to admit it sooner than others."

"I RESENT THIS," Elissa said as she stirred the chili simmering on the stove. "I resent being manipulated, even by my own guilt. It's wrong on so many levels."

All of this was Walker's fault, she thought as she crossed to the mixing bowl and poured the corn bread batter into a greased glass pan. She hadn't been able to shake feeling stupid about her assumption when he'd offered to let her "pay in trade." His comment about smelling her cooking had taken root in her brain and now she was making chili for the express purpose of apologizing. Plus, she still had to give him the five dollars he'd so artfully avoided when she'd given him the pie.

Twenty minutes later, she knocked on the door between her place and Mrs. Ford's.

"I can smell the chili," the older lady said happily. "I took my Prevacid earlier and I'm ready for second helpings."

"Good. Everything is ready. Have a seat. I'm going to run upstairs and tell Walker dinner is ready."

Mrs. Ford raised her eyebrows. Elissa sighed.

"It's not what you think. I still have to give him my first down payment and I'm making up for…well, you know."

She'd told her neighbor all about the unfortunate misunderstanding. Mrs. Ford had taken great pains to point out that a lady did not sleep with a gentleman for any reason other than love or really powerful sexual attraction. Even being given a kidney wasn't good enough. As if Elissa didn't already know that.

"Chili is an excellent choice," Mrs. Ford said. "A very manly dish. No froufrou vegetables or tofu surprise. An excellent move."

"It's not a move."

"It should be. Elissa, darling, he's a very handsome man."

Elissa opened her mouth, then closed it. What was the point of trying?

"I'll be right back," she said, then yelled into the living room. "Zoe, dinner's ready. Please go wash your hands."

"Okay, Mommy."

Once again Elissa climbed the stairs. She walked briskly across the small landing and knocked firmly on the door. No way she was going to let *him* know she felt embarrassed by their previous conversation. Nope, except for the fact that she was cooking for him, she was going to pretend it never happened.

He opened the door. "Hello, Elissa."

Sometime in the past three or four days, she'd forgotten what he looked like. Oh, sure, she could have picked him out of a lineup and been confident he was her neighbor, but she'd lost track of the specifics.

She hadn't remembered how his dark eyes seemed to observe everything without giving anything away. How his strong features made her want to trust him instantly or that his mouth was both stern and intriguing.

He looked solid, steady…dependable. All very appealing traits, given her history with men.

"Hi. You never took the money." She thrust the five dollars at him and held her arm steady until he took it from her.

"Thanks. You didn't have to—"

She cut him off with a flick of her wrist. "I did have to. It helps me sleep at night. I also wanted to apologize for the misunderstanding. I jumped to not very flattering conclusions and I shouldn't have."

"I realize how that could have happened."

She wondered if that was true or if he was just being polite. And then she wondered how his skin would feel if she touched his arms. Was it rough or soft? Did the muscles yield at all or were they—

She mentally put on the brakes and smiled brightly so he wouldn't guess what she was thinking. Dear God, what was wrong with her? She'd seen plenty of good-looking men before. Some even in person. But she'd never reacted like this. It was worse than feeling guilty. Which meant she should get to the point.

"I made chili," she said. "You mentioned smelling my cooking and wanting to trade what I owe you for that. I'm all right with that. So I made chili and corn bread. There's pie left, but you probably still have some of your own, so I don't know how interesting blueberry pie would be. Although I have ice cream. It was on sale. Chocolate chip. Zoe and I do the chocolate thing."

When she realized she was babbling, she pressed her lips firmly together, then cleared her throat.

"My point is, you're welcome to join us." Hmm, that didn't sound right. "Mrs. Ford is already downstairs. This isn't anything but payback. I'm not asking you out or anything. I don't date. Anyone. I don't do anything else, either. I'm not issuing a challenge. I know some guys assume if a woman's alone, it's a challenge. I'm not. I'm not interested in getting involved or having a fling or anything like that. This isn't a good time for me. Zoe's really young and there are other complications."

Big ones, she thought, thinking that Neil was at least six feet and was never going to go away.

"You're saying you don't want to date or have sex with me," he clarified.

"Right," she agreed, before actually processing what he'd said.

"Good to know."

His gaze never wavered and nothing about his expression changed. She wished she could say the same about herself, but no. Even as she stood there, she felt heat climbing her cheeks. No doubt she'd turned bright red. Perhaps because the poor man had never indicated he was interested in her at all. He'd asked for a meal, not a night of hot monkey sex.

"Oh, God," she breathed. "Not that you asked or anything. I'm just—"

He held up one hand to stop her. "Elissa. Quit while you're ahead."

"Good idea."

"I get the message."

"Yippee."

"I understand why you said it. I respect your honesty. Sleep easy. I won't make a pass at you."

Which should have made her happy, but she wasn't sure if he was being agreeable or making fun of her. If only she could slink away and start this day over.

She cleared her throat. "Did you want some chili and corn bread?"

"Yes, but I'll come down and get a plate. I don't want to disturb your dinner plans."

"You mean you want the food but you won't be joining us?"

"Is that a problem?"

A surprise maybe, but not a problem. "Whatever you'd prefer."

"Okay. Let me grab a bowl and a plate and I'll meet you downstairs."

"You don't have to do that. I have plates."

"This way I don't have to return them."

She winced. Definitely mocking her, she thought glumly. Truth be told, she'd earned it. She turned and walked down to her apartment.

Easy solution, she thought. She'd stop talking to the man. That would increase her odds of not making a fool out of herself. She would also add to her "next life" list. In addition to money, she seriously needed to explore the possibility of being slightly less outspoken.

THE ALARM RANG at 4:00 a.m., as it did every weekday morning. Elissa got up immediately—she'd learned her body cooperated better while it was still in shock over the predawn hour. If she hit the snooze button, she was at risk of never getting out of bed.

She showered, then wrapped her hair in a towel while she applied the barest touch of makeup. Tinted moisturizer, mascara, lip gloss. After dressing in her Eggs 'n' Stuff uniform, she ran the blow-dryer until she'd passed from wet to damp, then combed her hair and put it in a quick ponytail. At four-thirty, she walked into the kitchen and inhaled the scent of brewing coffee.

Whoever had invented timers on coffee machines deserved an award, or, at the very least, a star named in his or her honor. As Elissa reached for a mug, she heard a very distinct *thump* from overhead.

The sound was loud and out of place. The moan that followed made her shiver.

Something was going on upstairs. Something she should ignore. Except there was a second thump and a louder moan.

What if Walker had fallen and hurt himself? He looked to be in too good a shape for that, but he could have slipped or fallen while drunk.

She hesitated between not wanting to get involved and knowing she couldn't leave Zoe until she knew everything was all right. After quickly checking on her daughter, who was still sleeping soundly, Elissa grabbed her trusty baseball bat from the hall closet and hurried upstairs.

She knocked briskly, then announced herself in case he was in the throes of some war-induced hallucination. She didn't want him to shoot or maim her in his confusion.

When he didn't answer right away, she knocked again, louder this time, then winced as the sharp sound cut through the quiet of the night.

Finally the door opened. Walker stood there wearing nothing but rumpled pj bottoms. His chest was bare, he needed a shave, and for once his eyes weren't hiding his feelings. He was amused as hell.

"So much for not wanting to get into my bed," he said.

She glared at him. "You were thunking and moaning. It's four-thirty in the morning. What was I supposed to think?"

The humor faded. "Seriously?" he asked.

"I do not make this stuff up."

He looked at the baseball bat. "Was that to take me out or to protect me from whatever was happening?"

"I hadn't decided."

"It's been a long time since someone came to my rescue." His lips twitched as if he were fighting the need to grin.

Ha-ha. Yeah, this was a laughfest. She couldn't believe he was fine.

"So you're all right," she muttered. "Great. I won't bother you again."

She turned to leave, but he grabbed her arm. When she glanced at him, the humor had faded.

"I'm sorry," he said, looking as if he meant it. "I was having a bad dream. I woke up on the floor. I guess I thrashed around until I fell. It was good of you to worry about me."

She sighed. "But unnecessary."

"I could pretty much take anyone."

"Whatever."

"I appreciate you coming to my rescue."

She pulled free of his touch. "Now you're mocking me."

"A little."

At that moment, her entire hormonal system stirred to life and noticed there was a half-naked man standing very, very close. Elissa felt the chemicals pouring through her body. Wanting exploded as her girl parts got hard or melty, depending on their placement. All this and she hadn't even had her coffee.

"I need caffeine," she muttered.

"Me, too."

"I have a pot on and—" she glanced at her watch "—twenty minutes until I have to leave. You're welcome to a cup."

She expected him to refuse. Instead he surprised her by saying, "That would be great," then following her downstairs.

She wanted to point out he had bare feet and wasn't wearing a shirt. Then she told herself that if he didn't care, she should just smile and enjoy the show.

Once in her kitchen, she put down the baseball bat, grabbed a second mug and held it out to him. He waited for her to pour her own coffee before taking the carafe for himself.

"I assume you take it black," she murmured, aware of Zoe sleeping just down the hall.

"I used to be a Marine," he said. "What else?"

She smiled, then leaned against the counter. "Have a lot of bad dreams?"

"They come and go." He shrugged, then took a drink. "Some things can't be forgotten."

"Is that why you left?" she asked. "Too much bad stuff?"

"Maybe."

She had the feeling she was prying. "We don't have to talk about it."

"It's okay. I spent a lot of time looking for

snipers and listening for bombs. Sometimes they come back to me."

She had her own nightmares, but they weren't nearly that violent.

"I hope I didn't wake Zoe," he said.

"You didn't. I checked on her before I went up to your place. She could sleep through a tornado. I vacuumed a lot during her naps when she was a baby. I read somewhere it works for kids who sleep soundly. In her case, it worked."

This was the strangest conversation she'd had all week, she thought. She would never in a million years have imagined a half-dressed, barefoot Walker in her kitchen at four forty-five in the morning, drinking coffee and talking about her daughter and being a Marine.

"She's a good kid," he said.

"I like to think so." She hesitated. "Is it strange to be back in civilian life, having a child living nearby, that sort of thing?"

"There are kids everywhere. At least here, Zoe can grow up safe. I didn't always see that."

There was a lot of regret in his voice. She wondered what he *had* seen, then realized she probably didn't want to know.

She noticed that even that early, his posture was perfect. She tried to subtly square her own shoulders and slump a little less.

"Great chicken," he said.

It took her a second to realize he meant her uniform. She glanced down and laughed at the large hen on her apron. "I work at Eggs 'n' Stuff. It's a breakfast and lunch diner."

"I know it."

"Then you recognized the uniform. Frank, my boss, is a great guy, but we can't talk him out of the chicken. Apparently it dates back to the 1950s. At least the shoes are comfy." She held up one foot, showing her white orthopedic lace-ups. "I'm just waiting for these bad boys to come in style."

"You're on your feet all day."

"Still, a little pretty wouldn't hurt. But they, and the chicken, are a small price to pay. I get fabulous tips, really good benefits and once Zoe starts school, I'll be home before her."

"Who gets her ready in the morning?"

"Mrs. Ford."

"I thought maybe your ex-husband came over to take care of things."

For a full two seconds she thought he was fishing to find out about her marital status. Then she remembered the unfortunate babbling incident a few days before, where she'd flat out told him she wasn't interested in dating or sex, only to realize the poor man hadn't even asked.

"No ex," she said easily.

"Then if I see a strange man lurking in the bushes, I'll beat the crap out of him."

"Absolutely."

She took a last drink of coffee and looked at the clock.

"You have to go," Walker said, putting down his

mug. "Sorry about bothering you. I'll try to have my nightmares more quietly. Thanks for the coffee." He picked up the baseball bat. "And for coming to my rescue."

She sighed. "I hate starting my day feeling foolish."

"Don't. You did a good thing."

He put the bat down and left.

Elissa rinsed out both mugs, slipped the bat back in the hall closet, did a last check on Zoe, opened the door between her place and Mrs. Ford's, then walked to her car.

As it was August, the sun was already up and birds all over the neighborhood were announcing the fact. She drove down the quiet streets and thought about Walker. He was an interesting man. Not a serial killer. She was willing to let that worry go. But he did have his secrets. Of course, so did she.

CHAPTER THREE

DANI BUCHANAN LOVED everything about her job. As assistant to the executive chef, she was in charge of reviewing food orders, making sure the kitchen staff showed up when they should, acting as liaison between the front of the house—the dining room—and the back of the house—the kitchen. During the dinner rush, she expedited plates and made sure the right orders got to the right table at the right time.

With Penny approaching zero hour on her pregnancy, she was spending less and less time at the restaurant, which meant more responsibility for Dani. Instead of feeling the pressure, Dani felt energized. She loved the challenges, how no two days were the same. She enjoyed the foul-mouthed cooks who had made her prove she wouldn't blush at the raunchy jokes. Here in the kitchen of The Waterfront, she was just staff. Not Penny's sister-in-law, not one of "the" Buchanans. She was judged on the job she did, nothing more.

She finished checking the produce delivery and signed the receipt. As the delivery truck rumbled away, Edouard, Penny's sous-chef and the man now temporarily in charge of the cooks, walked in.

Dani eyed his scowl. "Someone not getting any?" she asked sweetly.

"This job is cutting into my social life," Edouard told her with a sniff. "I am forced to leave the clubs before I am ready. Sometimes I am forced to leave alone. I do not like that."

Edouard was French, moody, brilliant and recovering from a breakup. He could have made a reputation for himself, but he didn't want the responsibility. Instead he was happy to be highly paid by Penny and have a life outside of work. Except while she was on semimaternity leave.

He walked into the kitchen and looked at the list of specials.

"You change them every day," he complained. "Why is that?"

"Partly tradition and partly to annoy you."

"We do not have the same people dining here night after night. They would not know if the specials remained the same for a week or so."

"Suck it up, big guy."

Edouard spread out his knives and checked the blades. He reached for a particularly nasty-looking cleaver. "I do not like it when you call me that."

Dani held up both hands and smiled. "Point taken."

"Good. Now I will cook your specials because I am a professional, but I will not be happy about it."

"Duly noted."

He sighed. "When will Penny be back?"

"She hasn't left yet."

"She is not here all the time. I miss her doing the hard work."

He continued complaining, but Dani slipped out of the kitchen and headed to Penny's office. There was more paperwork to be done before things got busy. She settled in front of the computer and entered the information for the produce order. Thirty minutes later, that was complete and she went to get another cup of coffee.

Several of the cooks had arrived. Stocks were already simmering as vegetables were chopped in preparation for that night's dinner. A far cry from Burger Heaven, Dani thought as she filled her mug. Their setup was no more complicated than prepping burger toppings and picking the milkshake flavor of the month.

She'd stayed there too long, hoping her grandmother would notice the great job she'd been doing and move her to this place or Buchanan's, the family steak house. But Gloria never had. A combination of family loyalty and the need for the great insurance had kept Dani in place until a few months ago, when she'd discovered nothing was as it seemed.

The insurance for her husband had become unnecessary when the lowlife cheater had asked *her* for a divorce. As for family loyalty, that was no longer an issue, either. When Dani had pushed to find out why she wasn't getting promoted, her supposed grandmother had gleefully informed her that she, Dani, wasn't actually a Buchanan. Dani had quit that instant.

The momentary act of thumbing her nose at a woman who had obviously always hated her had sustained her for all of forty-five minutes. Then Dani had been left with no job, no home and no idea what to do with her future.

A job offer from Penny to be her assistant had solved all of Dani's problems and had given her time to figure out what she wanted to do while getting fabulous experience for her resume. In addition, Penny's marriage to Cal meant Dani could take over the lease on Penny's house. Plus there was the added bonus of knowing her presence at The Waterfront made Gloria furious. As Penny's employment contract stated she was allowed to hire whomever she liked for her assistant, the old cow couldn't touch Dani.

That was the upside of her life. The downside was finding out she wasn't who she thought. And then there was the small mystery of her father.

Apparently her mother had had an affair that resulted in a pregnancy—Dani. But who was the guy? Did he know he had a daughter? Did he care? If Gloria knew, she wasn't telling. But Dani was going to have to decide what to do.

Someone knocked on the open door, interrupting her musings. She turned and nearly passed out as all the air flew out of her lungs.

A man stood in the doorway. But not just any man. This one was tall, blond and oh so good-looking. Greek-god-like, even. His dark blue eyes and square jaw were male perfection and exactly

Dani's personal fantasy. Was it her birthday? Had someone wonderful sent her a present?

"Hi. I'm Ryan Jennings. I'm looking for Dani or Edouard?"

"I'm Dani." She stood and brushed the front of her tailored blouse, wishing there was a way to subtly unbutton it a little more. She might be on the short side, but she had curves and she was suddenly in the mood to flaunt them.

He smiled. "Hey. Good to meet you. I'm really happy to be here. This is a great store and I'm looking forward to being on the team."

Team? So he would be working here. Hmm, maybe her luck was changing. After the past few months, she was due for something wonderful to happen.

"Gloria Buchanan doesn't exactly keep me in the loop on new hires," Dani said easily, able to forgive the oversight when Ryan was so yummy. "And I haven't talked to Penny yet today. You are going to be…?"

"The new general manager. Gloria didn't tell you?"

"Don't take it personally. She likes to spring things on people."

"Interesting management style."

"You don't know the half of it." She walked around her desk until she was next to Ryan. "Welcome aboard."

They shook hands. She felt definite heat. Until that moment, she hadn't given a thought to her love life. She was in the middle of a lot of personal upheaval and getting involved hadn't seemed important. But suddenly, she saw possibilities.

"I'm a little overwhelmed by all of this," he said. "I only interviewed a couple of days ago. I wasn't sure I'd done that good a job, but she called this morning and made me a great offer."

"Which you took."

His eyes locked with hers. "Lucky me."

Her thoughts exactly.

There were actual sparks, which she hadn't felt in a really long time. Sparks, heat and a lot of potential. She suddenly felt like bursting into song.

"Okay then," she said, telling herself it was important not to act like an idiot in front of Ryan. "Let me show you around the place. Are you from the Seattle area?"

"No. San Diego. I moved up here to help a buddy open a restaurant. Unfortunately the funding fell through and I found myself looking for a job in a strange city."

"Seattle is great," she said.

"I like what I've seen so far."

He smiled at her as he spoke, as if implying he wasn't just talking about Seattle.

She wondered how inappropriate it was to drag him back to her desk and have her way with him. *Or not,* she thought. Maybe she should take things more slowly. Show him the restaurant, let him meet the staff and drag him to her desk in the morning.

She smiled. It was always nice to have a plan.

"ELISSA, PHONE CALL." Mindy held out the phone and smiled. "It's a guy," she mouthed.

Elissa put down the sugar container she'd been refilling in the lull between breakfast and lunch and told herself there was no reason to panic. Only she couldn't seem to stop her heart from thumping wildly or her breath from disappearing.

She almost never got calls at work. The only one she could remember in the past year had been to tell her that Zoe had woken up with a fever and wouldn't be going to preschool that day.

Could Neil have found her again? He always seemed to. It was the Internet. With fifty bucks, you could find anyone. Or maybe someone he knew had come in and recognized her. Or was it worse? A doctor at an emergency room, phoning about a horrible accident that had hurt her daughter?

"Hello?" she said into the phone.

"Elissa, it's Walker. I'm sorry to bother you at work."

Walker? She hadn't talked to him in nearly a week. Not since their predawn coffee moment. "Is everything all right? Did something happen to Zoe?"

"What? No. As far as I know, she's fine. This is about something else. Do you have a minute?"

"Sure. But let me call you back from the employee phone in the break room." She scribbled down his number, then hung up and announced she was taking a break.

Mindy smiled knowingly as Elissa walked past her. She was going to have some explaining to do later.

She settled in one of the plastic chairs and picked up the phone. Seconds later she heard Walker's low voice.

"What's up?" she asked.

"I need to come by the restaurant and I wanted to explain why."

There was an explanation? "It's a public place," she said. "Anyone is allowed."

"I know, but this is different." He paused, then said, "Before I left the Marines, a buddy of mine died. His name was Ben. He was a good kid. Determined. We were friends. He took a bullet and I wrote a letter for his family."

"I'm sorry," she murmured, wishing there were other words, more meaningful words, she could speak.

"He lost his folks when he was pretty young and grew up in foster care. He didn't have any family, so there's no one to send the letter to. But he told me about this girl. Ashley. He was crazy about her and wanted to marry her when he got out. All I know is that they went to high school together and her first name."

"You want her to have the letter," Elissa said, knowing moments like this put *her* life in perspective. Honestly, what did she have to complain about?

"Yeah. Ben went to four high schools in four years. I've made a list of all the Ashleys and I'm visiting them one by one."

Suddenly the call made sense. "Ashley Bledsoe works here."

"She's on the list. I want to come by and talk to her, but I didn't want to freak you out."

She smiled. "I wouldn't have thought of you as a guy who said words like freak."

"I have many sides."

She liked the ones she'd seen.

"Ashley works until two. If you come about one-thirty, we're pretty slow. You can ask your questions and have lunch."

"Sounds like a plan."

She tightened her grip on the phone. "I won't say anything to her," she told him. She sensed it was important for him to have the conversation himself.

"I appreciate that. I'll see you at one-thirty."

She hung up, then stared out the window at the parking lot. Ben must have meant a lot to Walker for him to go to all this trouble. It made sense that living through dangerous situations together would forge strong bonds of friendship. Whoever Ben's Ashley was, she was going to be getting some sad news.

Elissa tried to remember if her friend had ever mentioned a guy named Ben, but the way Ashley dated, it was tough to keep track of all the guys.

She stood and walked out of the break room. Both Mindy and Ashley were waiting for her in the short hallway.

"What?" she asked, knowing they were about to start grilling her.

"It was a man," Mindy said with a grin. "A guy called you. And don't try to pretend it was your dentist or something. He didn't sound like a dentist."

"It was Walker, my neighbor. He had a question."

Ashley and Mindy exchanged glances.

"Uh-huh," Ashley said. "A question that couldn't wait until tonight? I can't believe you're involved and you didn't tell us."

"I'm not," Elissa said firmly. "I swear. Walker is my new neighbor. We've talked a few times, but that's it. There's nothing going on."

Neither of her friends looked convinced. She almost told them he would be stopping by later, but then decided to keep that tidbit to herself. One way or the other, they were going to jump to conclusions. She might as well enjoy their reactions to Walker first, as a small payment for what they would put her through.

WALKER ARRIVED right on time. Elissa didn't see him walk in, but Mindy breathed a quiet, "Oh my," which made Elissa look up.

She had to admit the man was a show all by himself. Even in worn jeans and a polo shirt, he looked both powerful and incredibly sexy.

Mindy glanced at her. "If that's your lunch date, I'm going to be very, very bitter."

Elissa grinned, passed over a package of sugar and went to seat him.

"Hi," she said as she approached. "Are you going to be having lunch with us?"

"Sure. Can you seat me in your section and send Ashley over?"

"Of course."

She gave him a booth by the window. Most of their lunch customers had left. There were only a half-dozen tables still in use.

"The burgers are great," she said. "So are the salads, but you don't strike me as a salad guy. All the omelets are amazing and you can either get hash browns or fries with them. Oh, and don't tip me. You can apply the money to the tire."

"I'll take a bacon burger, fries and a Coke, and I will tip you. You can pay me back with it or not."

"You're a stubborn man."

He grinned as he passed over the menu. "You're not so bad yourself."

"I work at it. Okay, I'll put in your order and send over Ashley."

She walked to the computer terminal and typed in his lunch, then told her friend that the hunk at table fifteen would very much like a word with her.

Ashley's eyes widened. "Elissa, no. He's yours."

"He's not and this isn't about asking you out."

Ashley pouted. "Then why do I want to bother talking to him?"

"Just go."

Mindy watched the exchange. "That's interesting. Want to tell me what it's all about?"

Elissa quickly filled her in. Mindy sighed.

"So he's really not here for you. Bummer."

"I'm okay with it," Elissa said.

"You shouldn't be," her friend told her. "Dammit, Elissa, he's good-looking, nice and someone doing the right thing. Why aren't you interested?"

"I have my plan."

Mindy rolled her eyes. "Going another thirteen years without sex isn't a plan, it's a death sentence. I know you love your daughter and we all admire that, but you're taking yourself a little too seriously."

Elissa appreciated the concern. "You don't understand. I have really, *really* lousy taste in men. If I'm attracted to Walker—and I'm not saying I am—but if I were, there would be something hugely wrong with him."

"That's crazy."

"Not for me."

Elissa watched as Walker held out a picture. Ashley took it, then shook her head.

Elissa poured his drink and carried it to his table.

"She's not the one," he said.

"How many Ashleys have you talked to?"

"Fifteen so far. I found the easy ones first. I had to travel to Oregon and Montana for two of them."

"You're not going to give up, are you?"

"Ben was a good kid. He had a lot of heart. Someone out there has to have cared about him, missed him. I'm going to find her."

"I know you will." Walker wasn't the kind to give up. He had a lot of heart, too, although she would guess he wouldn't want to admit it.

"Your friends are watching us."

She didn't have to turn around to know who he meant. "They're intrigued by you."

"Sorry to bring this into your work."

"It's okay. We haven't had that many things to talk about in the past few days. Now we have you."

"I'm not that interesting."

"You'd be surprised."

THE SPORTS BAR CROWD groaned as the Mariners left two men on base. Walker ignored the game and walked toward the bar. His brother Reid leaned against the polished wood of the bar and smiled at the herd of women surrounding him.

When Reid spotted Walker, he slipped away from his adoring fans and promised he would be back later.

"You haven't been in for a while," Reid said as the two brothers claimed an empty corner table. "Getting lucky?"

Walker ignored that and ordered a beer from the busty, blond waitress who paused by their table.

"I'm good," Reid told her and then turned his attention back to Walker. "Well?"

"I'm busy."

"So you're not getting any." He motioned to the many women in the bar. "See anything you like here?"

"What do they see in you?" he asked.

"They think I'm charming."

Walker wasn't so sure about that, but Reid's many years as a major league pitcher certainly helped his score quotient.

"But enough about me," Reid said. "You've been back, what? Three months? All I know about is one short fling that lasted maybe two nights. It's just not natural for a man to be alone, especially when he doesn't have to be. You've got the soldier thing going for you. Plus, hey, you're a Buchanan."

"You don't have anyone special in your life," Walker pointed out.

Reid held up both hands. "I'm not talking about special. Who needs that? Just a little something to take your mind off things. It might help you adjust to life in the real world."

"What makes you think I'm having any trouble adjusting?"

Reid shrugged. "I did. It's a bitch to go from the roaring crowd chanting my name to this."

"You're doing okay."

Reid's stark expression said okay wasn't good enough.

"It's your first season out," Walker said. "It'll get easier."

The waitress appeared with the beer. Walker took it and thanked her.

"You think it's going to get easier for you?" Reid asked. "You want to tell me you don't still dream about the bombs and the fear and the waiting for the next sniper shot?"

Walker never talked about his time in the military, but he wasn't surprised to hear Reid's accurate assessment of his life. He'd been in several hot spots. How hard was it to guess the big picture?

"It's different," he said.

"Agreed, but it's still an adjustment."

Around them the crowd cheered a home run. Reid didn't bother to look at the giant TV screens.

"Are you sorry you left?" Reid asked.

Walker could read between the lines. He'd had a choice. Reid hadn't. Once he blew out his shoulder, it was all over.

"I made the right decision," Walker said slowly. "There are things I miss about the Marines, but not the killing. Every man has a line. If he crosses it, he becomes a psychopath. I was getting too damn close."

"So what do you do now?" Reid asked. "After you find Ashley?"

Walker shrugged.

"Penny did twenty minutes on how you put the baby furniture together," Reid told him. "You're good at that kind of stuff. Maybe you should buy an old house and fix it up."

"I've thought about it."

He wasn't ready to move just yet. He liked where he lived.

Damn—he was in big trouble if he was lying to himself. It wasn't the place he liked, it was Elissa. Her and that stupid chicken on her uniform. How she'd looked so fierce, standing on his porch with her baseball bat. He wasn't anyone who needed protecting, but she hadn't thought of that. She'd just decided he was in trouble and had come to the rescue.

He hadn't met anyone like her in a long time—maybe ever. Determined and independent with a heart as hard as a marshmallow. She was sexy as hell, too. Especially when she earnestly explained why she wasn't interested in dating or having sex with him.

But he wasn't going to act on it. He knew better than to get involved. Things would only end badly for her and he didn't want that.

"I know some twins," Reid said into the silence. "Interested?"

Walker rolled his eyes. "Not all problems can be solved with sex."

Reid grinned. "Most of them can."

"I'M READY FOR MORE vegetables, dear," Mrs. Ford said from her place at Elissa's kitchen table.

Elissa glanced over at the nearly full salad bowl. "You made quick work of everything."

"It's all in the right tools." The older woman held up a unique little gadget that looked like a cross between garden shears and kitchen scissors. "I saw this Toss and Chop on QVC and knew I had to have it."

Elissa stirred the pasta, making sure it cooked evenly. There was a nice marinara sauce with a whisper of meat—a scant quarter pound she hadn't put in the chili.

"I felt kind of guilty at the mall today," she admitted. "Like a fashion spy or something."

"Why? You went into the store, you saw what was popular and you left. Hardly a crime."

"I know. If I could afford to buy Zoe's clothes, I would. But one of the dresses I looked at cost forty-five dollars. It's not even two yards of fabric."

Instead, she'd gone into the popular stores and checked out the various hot styles. Once home, she'd sketched out a few things to make herself. She wanted to make sure her daughter felt good about her clothes when she started kindergarten. Elissa still remembered the year she'd turned eleven and had shot up a couple of inches practically overnight. She'd gone to school with jeans that were too short and had been teased mercilessly. To this day, she still remembered crying all the way home.

Growing up was challenging enough. She was going to do her best to make sure Zoe avoided all possible pitfalls.

"Jeans and T-shirts are easy," Elissa said. "Thank goodness for Wal-Mart. But the rest of it…"

"You'll do fine. Have you seen Walker recently?"

Elissa stirred the sauce. "Not your smoothest transition."

"I'm old and therefore allowances are made. Have you?"

"Not really." Not if one didn't count his recent visit to the restaurant. She didn't want to get into the reason why he'd been there and if she left that out, Mrs. Ford was likely to assume things were heating up, which they weren't.

"You should consider him," Mrs. Ford said. "You've often mentioned that Zoe needs a father figure in her life."

If Elissa had been swallowing, she would have choked. "You're suggesting Walker for the job?"

"Why not? He's an honorable man."

Elissa could imagine him doing a lot of things, but being a surrogate father to a five-year-old little girl? "There's more to it than just being honorable. He's not exactly emotionally accessible."

"Neither are you, dear."

"Ouch."

Mrs. Ford shook her head. "I'm sorry if that sounded harsh, and I apologize in advance for speaking my mind. Elissa, you're living like a nun. It's not natural for a woman your age. You have a perfectly attractive, healthy man living less than ten feet over your head. You should do something about that. Use it or lose it, I always say."

Elissa didn't know what to think. Parts of her brain actually froze. Was her ninety-something neighbor suggesting she have *sex* with Walker? Sex?

"Actually, you don't say that," Elissa managed at last. "You said I had to be in love first. While I appreciate the advice…" *Sort of.* "The thing is, I don't want Zoe hurt. I don't want her to get attached only to have the guy leave."

"Not all men leave."

True. Sometimes you had to kick them out yourself.

Mrs. Ford's dark eyes narrowed. "It's important for Zoe to know what a healthy romantic relationship looks like. She needs to understand how a man and woman relate to each other."

"That's why we watch television," Elissa said cheerfully. "There are plenty of perfect families there."

CHAPTER FOUR

SATURDAY ELISSA ARRIVED home with Zoe only to find Mrs. Ford standing on the front porch. It was warm and the old lady shouldn't be out in the sun. The fact that she was gave Elissa a bad feeling.

"What's wrong?" Elissa asked as she got out of the car.

"It's the plumbing, dear," Mrs. Ford said with a sigh. "It's all backed up. I spoke to the answering service. Our landlord is on a cruise and the usual plumber isn't answering his page. The service is trying to get someone here on an emergency basis, but they keep pointing out that it's Saturday and it's very expensive for that kind of call."

Elissa groaned. Was that their way of only *pretending* to make the call?

"Let me call them," she said. "Zoe, honey, stay out here with Mrs. Ford."

"Why?" her daughter asked.

"Because when the plumbing backs up, it gets really stinky."

Mrs. Ford smiled. "Stinky is a very good word."

Seattle's other name—the Emerald City—came

from the abundance of trees and lots of rain. But the rain mostly fell in winter. Summer could be hot and sunny for weeks at a time, like now. Unfortunately, most apartments weren't air-conditioned—no one thought it was worth the expense for only a few weeks out of the year.

Which meant Elissa's apartment was not only stinky, it was stifling when she went inside.

The smell was thick and disgusting. She had the feeling it would never wash out of her hair. She quickly went around the apartment and opened all the windows, then did the same in Mrs. Ford's place. On her tour, she noted that every sink and both tubs were backed up.

The same thing had happened right after she'd moved in. Tree roots caused the problem. A quick visit by the plumber with some nifty tool had cleared things up, leaving only the mess to contend with. She had an unfortunate feeling this time wasn't going to be so easy.

"Elissa?"

She heard Walker calling her name and walked toward the sound. She found him in her kitchen.

"Hi," she said. "Welcome to the neighborhood. Any chance I can convince you not to flush or run water?"

Being the upstairs apartment, Walker wouldn't have the backup, although anything he did up there would spill into her place.

"Mrs. Ford said she didn't think the service was trying that hard to find a plumber," he said by way of answering.

"Apparently our usual guy isn't answering his

page. I was just going to call them and give them a stern talking-to. I'm guessing this is caused by tree roots. Our main line runs across the driveway and then into the grove of trees on the east side of the property. At least that's what it was last time."

Walker checked out her kitchen sink, then asked, "Do you know where the trap is?"

"Sure."

She led the way outside. Zoe danced over to stare at Walker. "Can you fix the stinky plumbing?"

Elissa held in a smile. Later she would explain that the plumbing itself wasn't the culprit.

"I'm going to try," he said.

Zoe's eyes widened. "You can *do* that?"

"We'll see."

Elissa showed him the trap.

"I'll go rent a snake," he said. "Let's see if that fixes the problem."

"You don't have to do that," she told him, even as she thought she should keep her mouth shut. After all, Walker would get the job done a lot faster than a long argument with the service, then sitting around and waiting on a plumber.

"What's a snake going to do?" Zoe asked. "Do you have a cage for it? I don't like snakes."

"It's not a real snake," Elissa told her daughter. "It's the name of a special tool."

Walker smiled. "I'll show you when I get back."

"Okay." Zoe looked doubtful.

"I should have this fixed in an hour," Walker told Elissa. "Why don't you ladies go get lunch or something? It's too hot to be standing outside and you don't want to go inside with that smell."

He had a point. Mrs. Ford already looked a little flushed.

"I'll leave the back door open in case you need to get in the house," Elissa said.

"Thanks."

Five minutes later they were in a blissfully cool fast-food restaurant. As Zoe stared at the kids' menu and tried to decide on lunch, Mrs. Ford nudged Elissa in the ribs.

"Father figure," she mouthed.

Elissa grinned. "I know. Who can resist a man with a snake?"

THREE HOURS LATER the pipes were clear and the last of the mess had been cleaned up. Elissa had insisted that Mrs. Ford keep her afternoon movie date with her friends.

After scrubbing out the tub three times, Elissa doused the whole thing in bleach. Still, she was going to have Zoe shower for a few days, until the pipe backup cooties were all gone.

She wandered over to Mrs. Ford's apartment where Walker stood at the sink, rinsing the old porcelain.

"You didn't have to do the cleanup," she said. "We're so grateful to have drainage again. That was enough."

"I didn't mind," he told her as he turned off the water. "Mrs. Ford is too old to get down on her knees and scrub out a tub and there was no reason for you to do two."

There was no reason for him to do one. "But Walker..."

He shrugged. "I've cleaned worse, believe me. I've dug trenches for latrines. This is easy."

"If you say so. You're going to submit a bill for the snake to the landlord, right?"

"Oh, yeah, I'll be sure to get reimbursed for that."

She had a feeling he wasn't going to bother, which made her crazy. "You shouldn't have to pay."

"It doesn't matter, Elissa. I promise."

It was the principle of the thing. But she had a feeling it was an argument she wasn't going to win.

"Come for dinner," she said impulsively. "It's my small way of saying thank you. I'll be grilling chicken and I've already made potato salad. There's even strawberry shortcake for dessert."

He raised his eyebrows. "You have rules."

"You're mocking me," she said. "Zoe will be there and Mrs. Ford, which you very well know. This isn't a date."

"Or even sex," he added.

She felt herself blushing. "Right. Not sex. Come on, Walker. I know you like my cooking. I don't think you hate the company. What's the problem?"

He didn't speak for so long that she thought he wasn't going to answer. Then he said, "I don't want to be around Zoe."

Anger and protective instinct battled for primary emotion. She narrowed her gaze. "You don't like my daughter?" she asked in an icy tone.

"I think she's great," he said. "I like her a lot. I'm not the right guy to hang out with her."

Elissa thought about how patient he'd been earlier when he'd shown Zoe the snake and explained how it worked. He'd been careful to keep her from touching the sharp blades, even as he'd let her turn on the engine.

"That doesn't make sense," she murmured. "Is this a soldier thing? You're too emotionally scarred by what you've seen and done to deal with a child?"

"You don't have to make it sound so movie-of-the-week." He shrugged. "I'm not comfortable around her. I don't want to hurt her."

His words and his actions didn't match. Was there something else, something he wasn't telling her? What was it? Had he lost a child of his own? Fallen for a woman with kids only to have things go badly? There had to be an answer, but she wasn't sure she had the right to pursue the question.

"I'll respect your position," she said. "If you don't want to eat with us, will you at least come get a plate?"

"Sure. Thanks."

He nodded at her and left. She returned to her own apartment and thought about all the guys who had tried to use Zoe to get to her. They'd failed, while Walker's reticence made her trust him more.

For a guy who wasn't trying to get her into bed, he was doing a damn fine job of seducing her.

WALKER STROLLED into The Waterfront about ten in the evening. The dinner crowd had thinned to just a few guests. At a round table in the back he saw Dani, Penny, Cal and Reid. They waved him over.

"Family meeting?" he asked as he approached.

Reid pulled out a chair for him. "Just a friendly gathering. I told you attendance wasn't mandatory."

"Hey, kid," he said and kissed Dani on the cheek. He did the same with Penny, then took his seat. "Who's minding the store?" he asked Reid.

His brother grinned. "I had many volunteers."

Penny threw a napkin at Reid. "Your life is shallow."

"But fun."

"It's time to settle down," Penny told him.

"Not interested. Besides, Walker's home now. Go find him a wife."

Walker reached for an empty glass and the open bottle of wine on the table. "I'm good, thanks."

"Reid, I'm serious," Penny said. "You've been playing the field long enough. It's time to pick one nice girl and make a life with her."

"I don't like nice girls."

Everyone chuckled. Walker listened as the banter continued. Reid and Penny had been friends for years, even after Penny and Cal split up. He'd once confessed to Walker that he'd suspected they would get back together and he'd been right.

"How's the restaurant business?" Walker asked his sister.

Dani jumped, as if she hadn't been paying attention. "What? Oh. Good. I'm keeping busy. Nothing new."

Penny smiled. "There is something new. Or some-*one.*"

"A guy?" Walker asked.

"There's no new guy," Dani told him. "Just stuff."

"Rebound guy," Reid said. "Good for you. Hugh was an asshole. You need to be distracted."

Dani shook her head. "You're the last person I would take dating advice from. Your idea of a committed relationship is sticking around long enough for dessert."

"You looking to get involved?" Cal asked, a hint of worry in his voice.

"Of course not," Dani told him. "My divorce isn't even final. It's not a rebound thing, it's just…nice."

"Leave her alone," Penny said.

"Why are you protecting her?" Reid asked. "You're the one who mentioned the other guy."

"I've remembered that we girls are supposed to stick together."

"I'll change the subject," Reid said. "Walker's buying a boat."

Everyone turned to him. Cal grinned. "Really? How big? When can we go fishing?"

Walker glared at Reid. "I'm not buying a boat."

His brother chuckled. "I know, but I distracted everyone."

"A boat would be nice," Dani said. "We could take day trips."

"There's no boat," Walker told her firmly.

Just then a guy in a tie walked up to the table. "Sorry to interrupt," he said. "Penny, here are the numbers on the menu changes. Everything looks good. Also, I have a couple of suggestions for the tasting dinner."

Penny looked at him, her eyebrows raised. "I'm sorry, Ryan. Did I hear you correctly? You want to change my tasting dinner?"

"You're trying to scare me and it's not working."

"Have you heard about the time I threw a meat cleaver at my husband's head?" she asked sweetly. "Do you really want to mess with me?"

He put another piece of paper in her hands. "I found the perfect wine for the corn cakes."

"We had the perfect wine."

"We had one that was close. This is better."

Penny studied the sheet. "I'll be in tomorrow and make the corn cakes, then we'll talk. If you're wrong, you're in big trouble."

"I can handle it."

Dani shifted in her chair. "Walker, this is Ryan Jennings, the new general manager. Ryan, this is my brother Walker."

Ryan walked around the table and shook hands. "Pleased to meet you."

Walker nodded. "How are you settling in?"

"Great. This is a terrific restaurant. I have a great staff, which makes all the difference. Dani is being very patient with me."

Dani dismissed his comment with a flick of her hand. "There's nothing to be patient about."

Ryan excused himself.

Walker waited until he was gone before turning to his sister. "So that's the new guy."

She blinked several times and did her best to look innocent. "I have no idea what you're talking about."

Cal and Reid both looked at him.

"Ryan?" Cal asked.

"That's my guess," Walker said.

Dani glared at him. "How did you know? We barely looked at each other."

"Impressive," Reid said.

Cal turned to his sister. "Dani, workplace romances can be difficult. Have you thought about what happens if things don't work out?"

"There's no *thing*," she told him. "We're flirting. That's it. Besides, you and Penny got back together at work. In fact, it was in this restaurant. So maybe you should get off of me."

"I'm just saying –"

"Cal, let it go," Penny said. "Dani's a grown-up. She knows what she's doing."

"State the rules up-front," Reid said. "That's what I do. If one of the servers wants to go out with me, I say fine, but you have to be able to handle it when it's over."

"'Go out' being a euphemism for 'have sex with'?" Penny asked.

"I want them to know the score."

Dani pushed away her wine. "I love you like a brother, Reid, but you're a real pig when it comes to women."

"I *am* your brother and why am I a pig? Why do all women object to the fact that I don't want to settle down and be with one person for the rest of my life? Is it the challenge? Do you each want to be the one to change my mind?"

"Not me," Dani said quickly. "That's gross."

"Not me, either," Penny told him.

Cal and Walker grinned. "We're not interested, either," Cal said.

Reid shrugged. "You know what I mean. Why are you getting on me? Walker doesn't want to settle down, either."

"But he's not quite so icky about the volume thing," Penny said. "Besides, there's hope for him. I think secretly, Walker wants to bond."

Walker groaned. "Let's get back to talking about Reid."

"I agree," Dani said. "Walker will find the right woman and fall head over heels. Reid, when you find the right woman, I'm going to guess you'll screw it up completely." She paused, then added. "I don't mean that in a cruel way. It's just you've never had to work for anything in your life. What happens when that changes? Are you up to the challenge?"

"I'm touched by your faith in me," Reid grumbled.

"Don't sweat it," Walker told him. "We'll be single together. The favorite uncles."

They both made fists and banged their knuckles together.

Conversation shifted to how Penny was feeling. Walker listened but didn't participate. Dani had some interesting theories, but she was wrong about him. He wasn't looking to get involved in any way.

Not that he would turn Elissa down if she showed up in his bed one night. She was great. Sexy. Funny. But only in the short term. Despite being a single mother, she had "marry me" written all over her. No way he was going there. He knew better.

Cal leaned close. "Any luck on the Ashley front?" he asked in a low voice.

"None of it good. I'm more than halfway through the list."

"You'll find her."

"I don't have a choice."

Walker was on a mission and he wouldn't rest until it was done. Without meaning to, he thought of Ben. The kid had always been ready with a joke. No matter how bad things got, Ben found something good to talk about. Walker missed him.

He remembered the time the kid had—

The memory shifted and bent until he saw them all standing in the snow. There were no tracks into the cave. There shouldn't have been anyone inside.

But before Walker could check, there was a yell and the sound of a bullet being chambered. Ben had plowed into him with all his strength. Walker had staggered, but hadn't gone down. Still, it had been enough. Ben had taken the bullet....

He shook the memory away and deliberately focused on the immediate conversation. He didn't want to think about Ben—going into the past always made him feel weak. Helpless. He'd been supposed to look out for the kid. Instead, he was the reason Ben was dead.

ELISSA GOT HOME AFTER DARK Saturday night, and considering how long it was light in the summer, that was saying something. She was exhausted but wired from her successful jewelry party.

As she climbed out of her car, she considered leaving her supplies in the trunk and unpacking them in the morning. Except tomorrow was a usual jam-packed Sunday with a million things to do. Better to drag the boxes in now.

She walked around to the rear of the car and opened the trunk. As she reached for the first box a voice spoke out of the darkness.

"Need some help?"

She was so startled, she shrieked, then spun toward the speaker.

"Stop doing that," she said, giving Walker a shove. The man didn't move an inch. "You scared me! Were you the stealth expert in the Marines? Don't you know how to walk and make noise at the same time?"

"I made a lot of noise. You didn't hear it. Do you want me to help you carry your stuff inside?"

She thought about saying no, just on general principle, but then she realized that was stupid.

"Help yourself," she said as she stepped back. "It all goes inside."

"What is it?" he asked as he scooped up everything in her trunk.

"Jewelry. Supplies. Remember the earrings for Randy's sister?"

He nodded as she closed the trunk and led the way to her apartment.

"I make that sort of stuff. Earrings, necklaces, bracelets. I use semiprecious gems mostly. I can't afford the good stuff. But I keep costs down and pay attention to trends. I used to just sell to friends or through referrals, but over this summer, I've started having jewelry parties. This is my third one and they've been really successful."

"Good for you."

She unlocked the front door and led the way inside. As always, Mrs. Ford had left a light on in the living room. Elissa motioned for Walker to dump everything on the kitchen table and went to check on her daughter.

Zoe was sleeping soundly. Elissa kissed her cheek and stepped back into the hall. She returned to the kitchen and closed the door between her apartment and Mrs. Ford's.

"I do individual pieces," she said, pulling out a bracelet. "Or sets." She opened a box that had matching earrings, a necklace and a bracelet.

"Very nice," he said.

She laughed. "You couldn't be less interested. Don't worry. I'm not offended." She crossed to the refrigerator and pulled out a bottle of white wine. "The good news is after I cash all the checks, I'll have enough to pay you for the tire."

"You don't have to. Why don't you keep the money and buy yourself a new rear tire for the other side?"

She appreciated his concern and the suggestion. "I'd like to do that, if you don't mind keeping to our payment schedule."

"You know I don't."

He was right. She suspected he wouldn't care if she never paid him back.

She grabbed two wineglasses and led the way into the living room. As she set everything on the coffee table, she suddenly realized what she'd done. It was late, she'd gotten out wine and had assumed he would stay.

Oops.

"I, ah, just thought we'd talk," she said. "I didn't mean to imply or suggest that we'd…"

He raised his eyebrows. "We'd what?"

"Don't be difficult. Do you want a glass of wine or not?"

"Are you going to make a pass at me?" he teased.

She groaned. "No."

"Then I'll stay."

He took a seat while she poured them each a glass. She settled at the far end of the sofa and faced him.

"To a good day," she said, holding out her drink.

"A good day."

They each took a sip. She doubted he was used to drinking anything this cheap, but she refused to apologize for her choice. It fit her budget and it wasn't too bad.

"You like color," he said, glancing around at the living room.

"I do," she said. "The landlord doesn't care if I paint the walls or put up drapes."

"Sure. You're taking on all the costs and the labor. What's not to like?"

"You should see Zoe's room. It's princess central.

I painted a mural that looks like a castle. Everything is either lavender or pink. Very girly. You probably had an all blue room."

"I think there were some green accents. But yeah, it was all boy."

"Why did you go into the military?" she asked. "Lifelong dream?"

"I'd thought about it," he told her. "I didn't know if I wanted to go to college. My parents died when I was young, so my grandmother raised me. She's a tough old bird."

"Like Mrs. Ford."

He looked at her. "Aside from being female and over seventy, they have nothing in common. Gloria is determined and manipulative. She wants everyone to do what she wants and she does what it takes to get that to happen. The harder she pushed me, the harder I pushed back. Some of it was her, some of it was me being a teenager. Finally I got so mad, I joined up the day after I graduated from high school."

"To spite her?"

"Yeah. It was worth it, just to see the look on her face."

She couldn't imagine having that kind of relationship with her grandmother. Not that the woman was still alive, but she and Elissa had been close before she died.

"That doesn't sound very familial," she said, trying not to be judgmental.

"Gloria isn't a family person. I try sometimes with her. I can't figure out why she won't bend. I'm close to my two brothers and my sister, though."

Elissa had a feeling Walker wanted a better relationship with his grandmother. Now that he was out of the Marines and living nearby, maybe that would happen.

He looked at her. "What about you? Have you lived in Seattle all your life?"

"Except for a brief time in Los Angeles, yes." She hesitated, then shrugged. "I was a typical middle-class kid. When I was a senior in high school, I fell for a guy in a band. Mitch. He was sexy and dangerous—at least in my seventeen-year-old eyes. When he left to go back to L.A., I went with him."

"Zoe's dad?" he asked.

"No. That would be too simple. Once I got to L.A., I realized Mitch wasn't a rock star. He wasn't very good. Or faithful. We split up. I was upset and humiliated and determined not to go crawling back home until I'd made something of myself. And I liked dealing with the music business. I ended up getting a job as a roadie of sorts. I arranged travel, food, that sort of thing. I was good at it."

He smiled. "A rock star roadie. I would never have guessed. So what happened?"

She grimaced. "I met Neil. I'm still not sure why we hooked up. He's seriously into the drug scene and I never was. I couldn't see the point." She sighed. "Don't get me wrong. I partied plenty, but I'm a cheap date. Two margaritas and I'm on my butt. Anyway, Neil's emotionally tortured, self-absorbed, and borderline abusive. Perfect for a displaced nineteen-year-old pretending to be an adult. I fell hard and he let me. When I found out I was pregnant with Zoe, I came home."

The family-friendly version of the story, Elissa thought, but she didn't know Walker well enough to tell him the truth. More to the point, there was no reason for him to know every last sordid detail of her past.

"What about you?" she asked quickly. "Any exotic ex-wives lurking in the background?"

"Never married," he said. "I don't do serious relationships. It was too difficult with my job. I was gone six to nine months a year, every year. I saw a lot of guys get left. I didn't see the point."

"And now?"

"Now I'm still not looking."

"So we're both determined to stay single," she said.

"And not have sex."

She smiled. "Is that your rule, too?"

"It is with you. I intend to respect your wishes."

Damn. Just her luck to be attracted to the one man on the planet who planned to actually do as she requested.

Any other guy would have just gone for it. Honestly, what was he waiting for? It was late, they were alone, alcohol had been imbibed. She wouldn't say no.

That was the killer, Elissa thought glumly. Walker tempted her in a way no man had. Ever. She shouldn't be attracted to him, but she was. Despite her rules and the foolishness of getting involved with the guy living upstairs, if he suggested getting naked right that second, she would have stripped in three seconds flat. The need to feel his mouth on hers, his hands on her body, was almost painful in its intensity.

"I should go," he said as he set down his glass and stood.

Obviously not a mind reader. "Thanks for helping me with my boxes. Let me know if you change your mind about wanting any jewelry. As a gift or something. Or if you get your ear pierced."

She followed him to the door where he paused and smiled at her.

"Do I look like the ear-piercing type?" he asked, his voice low and sexy enough to make her shiver.

"No, but I've been wrong before."

"Not about that. 'Night, Elissa."

CHAPTER FIVE

WALKER LOOKED OVER the list of Ashleys he'd made shortly after moving into the apartment. "Damn popular name," he muttered as he looked at those yet to be crossed off. Ben had gone to four different high schools in four years. Walker had looked ahead two grades and back three to make sure he covered as many of the women as possible.

Several of them had moved out of state. He'd gone to see a couple and had been forced to speak with two by phone. Not his first choice. He had a feeling that whomever Ben had been dating already knew he'd died, but in case she didn't, Walker wasn't comfortable passing that information on over the phone. Plus, he had his letter to deliver.

He needed to…

He paused and listened. There was something

"Hello? Walker?"

He stood and walked to the front of the apartment. After opening the front door, he saw Mrs. Ford standing at the foot of his stairs. She had a dish towel wrapped around her left hand and seemed a little shaky on her feet.

"Sorry to bother you," she said. "I can't climb that many stairs. I seem to have cut my hand. It's silly really. The knife just slipped and—"

He ducked back inside, grabbed his first aid kit and ran downstairs.

"Let's get you inside," he said, ushering the old lady into her apartment and out of the sun.

"I wouldn't normally bother you with something like this," she said as he took her to the sink and peeled back the towel. "But the bleeding doesn't seem to want to stop."

She'd gone deep, slicing the top of her hand and the base of her thumb. Through the pulsing blood, he was pretty sure he saw bone, which was never a good sign.

"You're going to need stitches," he said flatly and reached for the first aid kit. "Let me patch you up temporarily and then we'll drive to the hospital."

"I'm sorry to be a bother," she said, barely wincing as he applied a pressure bandage. "I was watching *Buffy*. You know, *Buffy the Vampire Slayer*? Anyway, it was the episode where Buffy and Angel kiss for the first time and she finds out he's really a vampire. So of course you understand why I wasn't really paying attention to what I was doing."

"Right." He guided her to a chair and urged her to sit. "I'm going to run upstairs and grab my keys. You stay here."

He debated calling for an ambulance, but by the time they arrived, he could be at the hospital. He wasn't sure how much blood Mrs. Ford had lost, but she was lucid and in decent health for her age. If he kept her calm and hydrated, she should be fine.

In addition to his keys, he took a bottle of water from his refrigerator, then ran back downstairs. He found Mrs. Ford waiting by the front door, her handbag over her arm.

"You don't believe in following directions," he said as he helped her outside and locked her door behind them.

"Directions are for sissies." She stared at his car. "I've never been in one of these before."

He looked at her short legs and sensible shoes, then opened the passenger door, scooped her up in his arms and carefully put her on the passenger seat.

She giggled. "It's been a long time since a man did that to me. I'd quite forgotten how much I like it."

Great.

He loosened the top on the bottle, then lowered her seat all the way back. He clicked the seat belt in place.

"Keep your arm up on the armrest," he told her. "It needs to stay elevated. Sip the water, but only a little at a time and stop if you feel nauseated."

"You're very take-charge," she told him. "Elissa needs that in her life."

"No thanks."

She smiled. "I'm an old woman, Walker. How exactly do you plan to stop me from matchmaking?"

Good question.

He closed her door and hurried around to his own. Minutes later, they were on the main street and heading toward the hospital.

"Do you have a cell phone?" Mrs. Walker asked.

"Sure." He pushed the activation number on his steering wheel. "Who do you want me to call?"

He expected her to say a relative, or her doctor. Instead she said, "My reading group. They'll be expecting me. Oh, dear. It was my turn to bring wine."

He held in a groan, then asked for the number. "I'll put you on speakerphone," he said.

The sound of a phone ringing filled the vehicle.

"Very impressive," Mrs. Ford said.

A woman answered. "Hello?"

"Phyllis?"

"Betty? Is that you? Your voice sounds strange."

"I'm calling from a car. You're on speakerphone. Isn't this exciting? So high-tech." Mrs. Ford giggled. "I'm afraid I won't make it to book club today. I've cut my hand."

"Betty, no. Are you all right?"

"Walker said I need stitches, so we're off to the hospital."

"Hospital?"

"I'll be fine," Mrs. Ford assured her.

"I hope so. Is that Walker person there with you?"

"He's driving the car."

"I'm here, ma'am," Walker said, holding in a sigh.

"Are you taking good care of… Betty, did you say Walker?"

Mrs. Ford smiled. "Yes. My new upstairs neighbor."

"The one as good-looking as Angel?"

"That's him."

"Just kill me now," Walker muttered under his breath.

THREE HOURS, several stitches and some fairly strong pain medication later, Mrs. Ford was released from the emergency room. Walker drove home slowly, trying not to jar the old woman's swollen hand. Then he wondered if he should bother. In her current condition, he doubted she would notice.

"The doctor was very nice," she said with a sigh. "And a woman. Pretty. Did you notice?"

"Not really."

"Is that because of Elissa? I think it's very sweet. She's a good girl. So caring and hardworking. She needs a man, you know. Not just to take care of her, but in her bed. A woman can only go without for so long. It's fine at my age. I don't expect to get lucky. But Elissa is so young."

He couldn't believe they were having this conversation. He'd thought the comment about him looking like some damn TV character was the real low point of the day, but he'd been wrong.

"We're here," he said, perhaps with more relief than necessary as he pulled into the driveway of the apartment building.

Elissa rushed out and opened the passenger door. "Are you all right?" she asked Mrs. Ford, then looked at him. "Is she all right?"

He'd phoned her from the hospital to let her know what was going on. Ironic how he'd moved to this apartment in this neighborhood where he didn't know anyone so he could live quietly and anonymously. So far that wasn't happening.

"She's good," he said. "Loopy from the pain medication, but otherwise fine."

"I have stitches," the old woman announced. "And the doctor was very pretty, but Walker didn't even look at her. He only has eyes for you."

"How thrilling," Elissa said. "Let me help you inside."

"I'll carry her," Walker said. "Take her purse and open the door."

She did as he asked. He picked up Mrs. Ford and started toward the apartment.

"At least you don't have to lug me upstairs," she cackled.

"That wouldn't be a problem," he said. He doubted she weighed eighty pounds.

Elissa hovered by the door. "I've already turned back her bed. She'll need to rest. Just put her there. We can get her changed later."

He was going to assume the "we" on the table was her and Zoe, because he had lines he wasn't willing to cross.

Once Mrs. Ford was in bed, Elissa sat on the edge of the mattress and smoothed back her white hair. "You scared me."

"I'm fine, dear. It was all my fault. I wasn't paying attention." She yawned. "Oh, goodness. It must be that pain medication. I so rarely nap."

But her eyes were already closing.

"Want me to put on the television?" Elissa asked.

"That would be nice. Maybe QVC. There's a jewelry showcase this week."

Elissa found the channel, then eased out of the room.

"What happened?" she asked Walker when they were back in her kitchen. He could hear the sound of a video in the background and guessed it was on to entertain Zoe.

"She said she was watching TV and cut herself. The cut was deep so I took her in for stitches." He pulled out the prescription bottle from his shirt pocket. "These are painkillers. She'll need to eat when she takes them so she doesn't get sick to her stomach. And she'll need to make an appointment with her regular doctor to get the stitches out in about ten days. The good news is the cut is on her left hand and she's right-handed. She'll still be able to do things."

Elissa leaned against the counter. "I'm grateful you were here. If you hadn't been…"

"She would have called 911."

"I'd like to think so, but she's so independent." Elissa touched his arm. "I don't know how to thank you."

"Thanking me isn't your job."

"Not many people would have bothered."

"I don't know many who would have let an old woman bleed to death."

"You know what I mean. You've been great and you didn't have to be." She smiled. "I still think it's a surprise you're not married. There had to have been women."

"Why are we talking about this?"

"We don't have to if you don't want to. Is it a commitment issue?"

He groaned. "Elissa, let it go. You told me you didn't want to have sex with me and I believed you. So you should believe me. I'm very content being alone. Don't try to save me. I'm not worth it."

"Of course you are, but it's interesting that you don't believe it. Besides, no one really wants to be alone."

"Using your argument I could say no one really wants to go without sex."

"I'm trying to make smart choices."

Too bad she wasn't trying to drive him crazy because then this conversation would be a big win for her.

"So am I," he said.

"Fine. Dinner is in two hours. I'll be taking care of Mrs. Ford, so you'll have to come get your meal instead of me delivering it. Want me to pound on the floor when it's ready?" she asked with a grin.

"Sure. Or you could just call."

"Far less interesting, but okay."

He started to leave, then paused. "I didn't know who else to phone," he said. "For Mrs. Ford. Family. When she didn't suggest anyone, I didn't want to pry."

"There isn't anyone else," Elissa said with a sigh. "She lost both her sons in the Korean War. Her only grandson died in Vietnam. All her brothers and sisters are already gone. She's all alone in the world."

"No. She has you and Zoe."

"You're right. We're each other's family."

He nodded and left. But as he climbed the stairs, he wondered about Elissa's family. She'd mentioned growing up in the area. Where were her parents, siblings, aunts and uncles? Was she as alone as Mrs. Ford or did she have people who cared about her? And if she did, why weren't they the ones watching out for her?

ELISSA KNEW IT WAS TACKY and even borderline embarrassing. Only someone really desperate would let her five-year-old daughter manipulate the situation. But here she was, being that person.

"I put out the napkins with flowers, Mommy," Zoe said as she stood back and admired the table. "They're pretty."

"I agree."

Elissa took in the three place settings. Three because when Elissa had explained that Mrs. Ford wouldn't be joining them that night, Zoe had said Walker could have her place. Now if he wanted to explain to Zoe why he couldn't make it, that was fine. But Elissa was willing to bet he couldn't.

She'd already delivered a light dinner of soup and toast to her elderly neighbor. Mrs. Ford had eaten a few bites, then gone back to sleep. Elissa made a mental note to check on her in a couple of hours. In the meantime, she had another neighbor to deal with.

There was a knock at the door. "I'll get it," Zoe called as she ran to the front of the house. "Hi, Walker. Mommy made spaghetti, 'cause it's my favorite. There's a really big salad, too. But not with onions. I don't like onions. Are you hungry? We have brownies for dessert. I frosted them all by myself and I made a design. It's supposed to be bows, but it kinda doesn't look like bows. That's why I'm telling you what it is, so you'll know."

They walked into the kitchen with Zoe dragging an obviously reluctant Walker behind her.

"You'll sit here," Zoe said, pointing to a chair. "Mrs. Ford is still sleeping, but that's okay 'cause now we have you."

She smiled winningly. He shot Elissa a trapped look, which she ignored.

"Did you wash your hands?" she asked her daughter. "Dinner is ready."

"Okay." Zoe raced toward the bathroom. "Walker, come on. You have to wash your hands."

He chose not to follow her to the bathroom. Instead he moved close to Elissa and said in a quiet voice, "Pretty low, Towers, using your kid against me."

She held in a smile. "'Using' is such a strong word. Zoe's been curious about you. I know you're concerned about her bonding or whatever, but she sees you practically every day. One dinner isn't going to scar her for life. I'm trying to say thank you, here."

"It doesn't occur to you to thank me by adhering to my wishes?" he asked.

"Not really."

"What if I ignored yours?"

His dark eyes claimed hers as she recalled vehemently stating she did *not* want to have sex with him. What if he ignored her wishes and made a pass at her?

She should be so lucky.

"I'm ready, Mommy," Zoe said as she bounced back in the room.

The next few minutes were a scramble of getting food to the table, drinks poured and seats taken. Once everyone had been served, Zoe leaned toward Walker and smiled.

"Do you have any kids?" she asked.

"No."

"Do you like kids? Some grown-ups don't. Do you?"

"They're fine."

"Do you like *The Lion King*? I love Simba and Pumba the best. Mommy took to me to see the play." Her hazel eyes widened. "It was in a theater and I'd never been to a theater before. There were people playing the animals. It wasn't like the cartoon. It was magic and there was singing."

Elissa stepped in to give their guest a break. "It was Zoe's birthday present. She'd talked about wanting to see the play and when the touring company came here, it seemed like the perfect opportunity."

"Have you seen the play?" Zoe asked.

"No," Walker told her.

"You should go. It's magic."

"So you said."

"Eat, honey," Elissa urged, feeling a little guilty for trapping Walker into dinner.

"Okay." Zoe took a bite of her spaghetti. She chewed, then looked at Walker again. "Do you have any pets? We want to get a dog, but we're not home very much. Mommy says a dog needs a lot of attention. We could get a cat…." Her voice trailed off.

"We're not really cat people," Elissa told him. "I know their independence is supposed to be noble and all that, but if I'm buying the food, I want a little gratitude from my animals."

"I'm scared of the claws," Zoe whispered.

"A girl in her class got scratched up pretty badly. She'd been teasing the cat, so it was sort of her fault," Elissa said. "But it looked awful and it had to hurt. How's dinner?"

He paused in the act of tearing off a piece of garlic bread. "Good."

He seemed to be inhaling his food. She wanted to tease him about going for the land speed record in eating, but knew that wasn't fair. She'd put him in an uncomfortable situation. Not a great way to thank him, despite what she'd said earlier.

Why had she messed with the status quo? Why him? Why now?

"I'm sorry," she said, aware of Zoe listening. "For, well, you know. I shouldn't have done it."

"Why did you?"

"I don't know. I thought it would be nice. I thought we could be friends."

Zoe stared at him. "Don't you like Mommy?"

What had been charming a few seconds ago suddenly became uncomfortable. She regretted allowing Zoe to guilt him into staying for dinner. "Zoe, don't ask questions like that. Walker has been very good to us and to Mrs. Ford. We're grateful for that, but we don't want to keep him too long."

Walker felt like shit. He'd been surprised by the manipulated circumstances, but not offended or angry. He hadn't meant to make Elissa feel bad.

"It's okay," he said, putting down his fork. "Everything is really good." He glanced at Zoe, who watched him warily. "Yes, Zoe, I do like your mother. She's a very caring person and she knows how to cook. I'm looking forward to the brownies you frosted."

Elissa shook her head. "You don't have to—"

"I want to."

"No, you don't."

"Now you're reading my mind?"

"Walker."

He wasn't sure why he was doing this. The easiest thing in the world would be to walk away. To take the escape she offered and go back upstairs. Only he hated the darkness he saw in her eyes and he wanted to listen to Zoe chatter about *The Lion King* or her friends or dogs. He didn't have much normality in his life and he appreciated the chance to experience it, even from a distance.

"Let it go," he told Elissa. "Eat your dinner."

She hesitated, then nodded. "All right. Thank you."

Walker turned to Zoe. "Tell me more about the play. What did the people wear?"

TWO HOURS LATER WALKER stood and stretched. "It was a good story," he said.

Elissa smiled at him. "I can't believe you were willing to sit through *The Lion King.*"

He glanced at the sleeping child curled up on the sofa. "I'm sorry she didn't get to see the end."

"This was only her four billionth time," Elissa said, aware of the quiet of the evening and the closeness of the man.

"Want me to carry her to bed?" he asked.

"You've done enough of that for one day," she told him. "I can manage."

"Okay."

She followed him to the door. Once there, she drew in a breath. "I'm sorry about what happened. I shouldn't have used Zoe to coerce you like that."

"Do you really think I'm not strong enough to resist a five-year-old?"

"She's pretty adorable."

"I agree, but I'm a big, bad Marine. At least I was."

He might be big, but there was nothing bad about him. As far as she could tell, he was one of the good guys.

And she wanted him. Oh, sure, there were a lot of reasons why that was a mistake, but they didn't erase the truth. Her knees trembled at the thought of his body against hers and she knew that if he didn't at least kiss her, she wouldn't be able to sleep for hours. Of course if he *did* kiss her, she wouldn't be getting much sleep, either.

She could feel her body swelling, readying and nothing had happened. What would happen if he ever did touch her?

Apparently, she wasn't going to find out anytime soon.

He smiled, thanked her for dinner and stepped out into the night. She stood by the open door and listened to him climb the stairs.

"Be careful what you wish for," she told herself as she closed the door. "You just might get it."

THE BEST PART of Elissa's day was seeing her daughter when she got home from work. A very close second to that was taking off her very sensible shoes and wiggling her bare toes on the area rug in her bedroom.

It was still warm, so she didn't bother with shoes. Instead she tossed her uniform into the dirty clothes basket and pulled on shorts and a T-shirt. An especially generous table of eight had given her an extra fifteen dollars for the day. A sensible person would put it into an emergency fund, but Elissa was seriously considering a special splurge on takeout.

Maybe she and Zoe could go to the mall and wander around for a while. She could get ideas for fall fashions for herself and her daughter and they could eat at the food court. It was Friday. Maybe they could even take in a movie.

She glanced at her small clock radio. It was nearly three. Zoe was playing at a friend's house until four, when Elissa was supposed to pick her up. They would go to the mall, she decided. It would be a fun treat.

That decided, she walked into the kitchen and got a glass of water. Between now and four she could start on her next—

Someone knocked on the door.

Elissa's heart did a little "let it be Walker" shimmy, which was very annoying. He'd made it more than clear he wasn't interested in her in that way. Maybe he was and he was only doing what she'd asked, which meant she only had herself to blame. Not that there was any way to really find out.

She crossed to the door and opened it. But instead of Walker, there was a well-dressed older woman standing on her small porch.

"Elissa Towers?" the woman asked.

"Yes."

"Good. Invite me in, please."

Elissa blinked. "I don't know you."

"I'm Gloria Buchanan and you know my grandson. Invite me in."

The combination of the woman's imperious tone and her relationship with Walker caused Elissa to do as she'd ordered. She stepped back and allowed the other woman to enter.

Gloria Buchanan was about Elissa's height, very thin and erect. Her tailored dress screamed *designer* and the cost of her shoes would not only replace all of Elissa's tires, but probably the transmission, as well.

Gloria stepped into the living room and slowly looked the place over. Elissa refused to flinch as her gaze lingered on the worn sofa or the mess on the craft table in the alcove. This was Elissa's home and if the old woman didn't like it, she could leave.

"You live here?" Gloria asked, her voice indicating her disbelief that such a thing was possible.

Right up until that moment, Elissa had been planning to offer her a seat and something to drink, but now she wasn't so sure.

"You already know the answer to that question," she said instead.

"You're right. I do. I know many things, but I'm wondering if I can say the same about you. Say, for instance, about my grandson. He is a wealthy and important man. He is going to be taking over the family business very soon."

The wealthy and important didn't surprise her, but the business part did. "He hasn't mentioned it."

"Why would he discuss such a thing with you?" Gloria asked.

She ignored that. "What's your point?"

"You are in over your head, Ms. Towers. Far over your head. Do you know who I am?"

Elissa suspected she meant more than just being Walker's grandmother. "You're dying to tell me, so go ahead. I don't mind listening."

"I am the reason our family is as successful as it is. I have single-handedly grown our four restaurants into—"

"Restaurants?" Buchanan? Buchanan's the steak place? She'd heard of it, but never eaten there. She would need the cash value of the old bag's shoes for that.

"We have four establishments," Gloria said smugly. "Walker was born to money. Something you were not."

"You're stating the obvious," Elissa said, both

confused and annoyed. "Would you get to the point of your visit?"

"I want you out of his life."

Elissa hadn't known what to expect, but it wasn't that. "Are you crazy? You want me out of his life? This isn't 1890. You don't get to dictate who your grandson is friends with. Besides, how did you even know I'm friends with Walker?"

"That is not important. What does matter is who and what you are. Do you think I *want* a former drug-using groupie in my family? Does he know, Ms. Towers? Have you told him how you slept around? How you slept with men to get jobs?"

Elissa held in a gasp of shock. How the hell had Gloria found all that out? "I never used drugs. As for the rest of it, no one cares."

"A lot of people care. A lot of people would be interested in knowing your daughter's father isn't dead. He's alive and as addicted as ever. I understand he gets in touch with you from time to time, asking for money. Wouldn't your life be awful if he wanted custody of his daughter? The child you stole from him?"

How had Walker's grandmother found out Elissa had told everyone, including Zoe, that Neil was dead? How did the old woman know about the money?

Elissa took a step back. She could handle her past coming back to haunt her, but no one threatened Zoe's safety. "Get out."

"Not yet. I have more to say. You will avoid my grandson at all costs. You will refuse to have contact with him. Do you understand me?"

This wasn't happening, Elissa thought grimly. It couldn't be. Her life was normal, boring even.

"I have a lot of friends in the community," Gloria continued. "Good friends. Mr. Frank Church, for example. A very charitable man. He and I serve on several committees together. I believe he owns the restaurant where you work."

Elissa felt hollow and more frightened than she'd ever been before. Frank was a big supporter of several local charities. He was on the board of two. He could easily know Gloria.

"If you don't get out of Walker's life, I'll have Frank fire you," the old woman said calmly. "I'll enjoy doing it, as well." She paused and looked at the craft table. "Tell me, Elissa. Does your landlord know you're running a business out of your apartment? I'm sure you're aware it's a violation of your lease."

This wasn't happening, Elissa told herself. There was no way this woman was threatening her livelihood and where she lived.

"I don't believe you," she said. "Not any of it."

Gloria's gaze turned icy. "Do not stand against me. I will crush you like the bug you are. Walker will be moving soon. Until he does, stay away from him. If you don't, I will destroy you and I will destroy your child. Do I make myself clear?"

CHAPTER SIX

WALKER ARRIVED HOME shortly after five. He saw that Elissa's car wasn't parked in the driveway, then cursed himself for noticing.

He knew better than to get involved with her. He knew it wasn't right. He'd picked this place because he didn't know anyone in the neighborhood, but that hadn't been enough. He'd gone and gotten involved—which still surprised the hell out of him.

As he climbed the stairs, he found himself wishing she were home, that she would stick her head out and think up an excuse to have him in for dinner. He wanted it to be good enough that he couldn't say no, even though he knew he was playing a dangerous game.

He saw something on his front door. An envelope. He didn't recognize the writing, but he had a feeling he knew who had left it.

Anticipation in the form of wanting filled him. A need to touch and be touched, to claim, to give and take. He already knew her scent and the way she moved. Now he wanted to know her taste, her sound, her uniqueness.

He stepped into his apartment, then opened the

envelope. Three ten-dollar bills fluttered to the floor. He unfolded the note.

Thanks for all your help, Walker. Here's the rest of what I owe you. You've been great and I appreciate that, but we both know this isn't going anywhere. You're right to worry about Zoe—she's very impressionable. So let's part as friends and get back to our lives. Best, Elissa.

He read the words twice, confident he'd misunderstood. But the message was clear. She wanted him out of her life.

He accepted her decision. It was the right one—he'd known there would never be anything between them. Somehow she'd figured it out, too. It was better this way—better for everyone.

And yet… There was a nagging knot of worry in his gut. Something that told him Elissa wasn't all right. Something that made him want to find her and talk to her.

Two nights ago, she'd been female temptation incarnate and he'd come damn close to giving in. What had changed?

He looked out his front window at the empty driveway. Elissa and Zoe were usually home in the late afternoon. Why weren't they today? And if he couldn't find her, how could he make things right?

"I CAN'T BELIEVE the old bitch threatened you," Mindy said as she poured them both more wine.

"Me, either." Elissa curled up in a corner of her friend's sofa and willed the fear to go away. "I hate how she frightened me. I hate how I believe her."

Mindy looked worried. "I think you have to. You saw it," she said, nodding at the computer where Zoe was currently entranced by a children's interactive Web site.

Elissa had seen it. All of it. A quick Google of Gloria Buchanan had given her more information than she'd ever wanted. The old cow had a reputation for being ruthless and determined. There had been dozens of articles about her and very few of them had been flattering. She was a rich, powerful woman who generally got her way. Just as scary, she really *was* on some big committee with Frank. There had even been a picture of the two of them together.

"I don't want to lose my job," Elissa said, careful to keep her voice low. "I need the money and the benefits. I love the hours."

"Frank isn't going to fire you. Even if Gloria asked him to, he's not that kind of guy."

Elissa wanted to believe that, but she just wasn't sure. Her once relatively stable little world had tilted off its axis.

"Thanks for taking us in," she told her friend. "I need some time to think."

Mindy smiled. "Stay as long as you like. You know I love you guys."

"We love you, too."

Zoe thought this was all a great adventure. Mindy had a second bedroom with a daybed and a trundle.

Zoe loved the roll-out bed so close to the ground, and Elissa liked them being in the same room. Right now she wanted to keep her daughter nearby.

"I have to go home eventually," she murmured.

"You could stay here," Mindy suggested. "Just for a couple of months. Save your rent money until you have enough to get another place."

"A generous and tempting offer," Elissa replied, almost wishing she could take her up on it. "But I have a lease. And who is Gloria Buchanan to scare me out of my home? She doesn't have the right. I haven't done anything wrong. It's not like I've been trying to trap her precious grandson. I haven't even..." She glanced at Zoe and lowered her voice. "You know."

Mindy grinned. "But not doing 'you know' doesn't mean you haven't been thinking about it."

She sighed. "I'll admit it. I was getting to the point where I would have broken all my rules for one night of 'you know.'"

"I met the man. I'm not surprised."

"I am. I know better. Getting involved isn't an option."

"It isn't now," Mindy said.

Elissa sipped her wine. "I hate being afraid. I hate it. I thought I was done with that."

"You'll feel better in time," her friend told her. "You have to look at the bright side. Who'd want to get involved with a guy with such a crazy grandmother?"

"Tell me about it. I found out, it's over and no one is hurt."

Elissa said the words as if she meant them and she

was reasonably confident that in time they would be true. But right now, she missed Walker. She wanted to talk to him about what had happened and hear him tell her it would be all right.

He was gone, she told herself firmly. Gone for good. She'd gotten off cheap and had been taught, yet again, that men were only bad news for her.

"I'M SORRY," the woman said as she handed back the picture. "I'm sure your friend was a very nice man, but I didn't know him."

"Thanks for taking the time," Walker responded as yet another Ashley closed the door in his face.

He was running out of names. He had never considered that he might not find her, that he might not have someone to deliver the letter to.

He climbed into his SUV and reminded himself that failure was not an option. Ben deserved to have someone mourn him. He deserved to be a part of a family. He wasn't going to give up.

He had a few more names, a few more chances. She had to be out there. She had to....

He leaned back in the leather seat and closed his eyes. He missed Elissa. He wasn't supposed to. He wasn't going to get involved, but he missed her. Somehow over the past few weeks, she'd found her way inside of him. He was used to hearing her laughter through the open windows, discussing various options for dinner, thinking up ways to make her life easier without her finding out it was him doing it. And now she was gone.

She hadn't been back at her apartment in nearly five days. He'd driven to Eggs 'n' Stuff to check on her. He hadn't gone in, because if she wanted to talk to him, she knew where to find him. So he'd parked where he could see inside and she'd been at work. On the surface, everything had looked fine. So why was she avoiding both him and her home?

He was torn between demanding an answer and adhering to her wishes. Wishes that he knew made sense for both of them. Still, he couldn't shake the feeling that something was wrong.

If she wasn't home tonight, he would call and leave a message. Ask her to get in touch with him, just so he could know that she was all right. He would make it clear that he respected her stance and wasn't trying to change her mind.

Which was all bullshit, he thought. The longer she was gone, the more he missed her. When had he allowed himself to get so damn soft?

He pulled into the driveway. His gut tightened when he saw her car still missing, then the tension eased as Zoe opened the front door of her apartment and ran outside.

"Walker, Walker, we're back. Did you miss us? We stayed with Mindy, who has this bed on the floor and I got to sleep there."

Zoe's blond ponytail flopped as she ran toward him. He stepped out of his SUV and smiled at her. "You've been gone, huh?"

She put her tiny hands on her skinny hips and pursed her lips. "You know you missed us."

Her words hit home.

"We missed you, too," she said, before he could think up a reply. "I didn't have preschool today, so Mommy left me with Mrs. Ford. She's still at work. And last night at Mindy's she made me jeans. Come see."

She grabbed his hand and pulled him toward the apartment. Or at least she tried. Walker stayed put.

"Your mom wouldn't be comfortable having me in her house while she's gone," he said. She'd made that clear in her note.

Zoe continued to tug. "Mommy likes you. She cooks you dinner and she makes pie. Come see! Come see!"

Her hand is so small, he thought. She gripped him with a combination of determination and trust. He knew going inside was wrong, but he couldn't figure out a way to explain the situation to a five-year-old. Especially one as determined as Zoe.

"Just for a minute," he said, allowing her to drag him into the apartment.

Everything was as he remembered. The bright colors on the walls, the comfy, worn furniture, the library books scattered on the coffee table. The lingering scent of cooking was gone, replaced by musty disuse. The house had been closed up for nearly a week.

"Over here," Zoe said, pulling him along to the simple worktable in the tiny alcove by the living room.

Next to a sewing machine were a tiny folded pair of jeans. Zoe let go of him long enough to hold them up for him to see. He looked closely.

A fabric butterfly had been sewn just above the

knee on one side. There was a sewn trail leading down the leg to the hem. She turned the jeans over and there was another butterfly on one pocket.

"Look!" Zoe said, pointing to a small white T-shirt hanging on a hook. A matching butterfly decorated the bottom and one sleeve.

"Very nice," he said, not sure what he was looking for.

"They're so pretty." Zoe's voice was reverent. "I have all new clothes for school. Mommy made a lot of them, or she bought stuff at Wal-Mart. I even have new shoes. Want to see?"

"Sure."

Zoe ran toward her bedroom. She returned seconds later with pink athletic shoes.

"Pretty," he told her. "Just like you."

She beamed. "I have a backpack, too. And pencils and paper. I'm learning to write my letters. I know most of 'em from Mommy helping me read, but now I'm writing them. And…" She paused to add the right drama to the announcement. "Mommy said we're asking Santa for a computer for Christmas."

He wondered how many hours of jewelry making and selling a computer would cost Elissa. She'd only just gotten a new rear tire to match the one he'd bought. He knew prices had come down, but she would have to save for months. It was already late August.

He knew buying one for her was out of the question. She'd already made it clear she didn't want anything to do with him. She'd had a fit over a fifty-dollar tire. She'd kill him in his sleep if he bought her a computer.

But he wanted to. He wanted to step in and make her life easier. The money meant nothing to him.

"Are you a handsome prince?" Zoe asked.

Walker stared at her. "What?"

"There's always a handsome prince," she told him. "In the stories. I asked Mommy when we're getting ours, but she says they're not real." She glanced around, then lowered her voice. "I think she's wrong. I think they are real. You're nice and you used to be a soldier. That's almost a prince."

Without meaning to, he could suddenly see through Zoe. Behind her were his men and behind them, a tank. He'd seen this before, the overlaid images, and he'd learned to ignore them until they went away.

The need to run nearly overwhelmed him. Damn, he had to stay away from this kid. Elissa was right to break things off. A prince? Him?

"I'm not a prince," he said.

"I think maybe you're selling yourself a little short."

He turned and saw Mrs. Ford standing in the entrance to the kitchen.

"Hello, Walker," she said.

"Ma'am. How are you feeling?"

She held up her left hand. There was a small bandage covering the cut. "Better than the last time you saw me."

"Buffy and Angel work things out?"

She laughed. "They're trying. Thank you for asking."

He shifted uncomfortably. "I didn't mean to come in. Zoe wanted to show me her new clothes."

Zoe nodded vigorously.

"I'm sure she did," the older woman said. "You, of course, wouldn't want to refuse her."

He shrugged. "I know Elissa would have preferred..." He hesitated, not sure what to say in front of the kid.

"Things have gotten complicated," Mrs. Ford said. "She told you?"

"She left me a note saying we were..." He looked at Zoe again. "I understand. She's busy and has her own life."

"Ah, so that was the explanation."

He didn't like the sound of that. "Meaning?"

"You're a resourceful man, Walker. You figure it out."

What? "Figure what out? Did something happen?"

"I don't know." Mrs. Ford touched Zoe's head. "Why don't you put your new shoes away, dear? You want them to be perfect for your first day of school."

"Okay. Then do you want to have mac and cheese for lunch?"

"I would love that."

Zoe took off down the hallway. Mrs. Ford turned back to him. "Elissa is scared. I've seen her worried, tired, concerned, but never afraid, and I don't like it."

He didn't like it either.

"Who or what scared her?" Mrs. Ford asked. "She won't tell me. But about a week ago, a stranger came calling. An older woman." She paused. "I loathe that term, *older.* However, she was. A few years younger than me. Very beautifully dressed, and her car—it was lovely."

Walker went cold, then he got mad. "Silver? A Jag?"

"I'm not familiar with car types, but yes, it was silver." Her gaze narrowed. "You know her?"

"I have a good idea who she is."

Zoe ran back into the living room. "I put them away."

"Good for you," Mrs. Ford said. She looked at Walker. "Can you fix this?"

"Absolutely."

ELISSA PACED the length of her kitchen. The living room was bigger and therefore more satisfying in the pacing department, but Zoe was playing and Elissa didn't want to upset her by appearing agitated.

Still, she couldn't help wanting to scream her frustration. She'd only moved back that morning, taking a quick break between breakfast and lunch to move her stuff back from Mindy's house. Zoe had been in the house less than five hours before she'd invited Walker in.

Her daughter had told her all about his visit. How he'd admired her new clothes and shoes and had told her she was pretty. Even if Elissa managed to inoculate herself against his casual charm, Zoe was falling hard and fast.

Under normal circumstances, that would have been enough reason for worry, but with the threat of job loss or eviction hanging over her head, the pressure was really on.

Mindy thought Elissa should come clean, just tell him what had happened and get his take on things. It was sound advice, rational even. But what if he didn't believe her? Walker might claim a troubled relationship with his grandmother, but Gloria Buchanan was family. When push came to shove, Elissa knew who he would side with. He hadn't known Elissa long enough to trust her. If Gloria denied everything, then Elissa was totally screwed and right now she didn't need the pressure.

Still, she had to do something. While Mindy's offer of moving in with her had been sweet, it was impossible. She, Elissa, could stay away from Walker, but how did she explain to her daughter not to talk to their nice neighbor anymore?

"I hate this," Elissa muttered. "I hate all of it." The fear, the uncertainty, the pressure of having other people control her life.

The phone rang. Elissa hesitated. Was it Walker? He'd already left a message saying he wanted to talk. What was she supposed to say to him? The truth? Some form of it? Nothing?

She chose to be cowardly and let the machine pick up. But a familiar "Hey, babe" had her lunging for the receiver before Zoe heard any more of the caller's message.

"Hello," she gasped.

"Elissa. You're there."

She clutched the phone as tightly as she could and turned her back to the living room. "How did you get this number, Neil?"

He laughed. "I have my ways, babe. You know that. Long time, no talk. How's it going?"

How was it going? Her life was a disaster. Hearing from him was the last thing she needed. "I don't have any money."

Neil sighed heavily. "You always say that, but you manage to find some anyway. The thing is, Elissa, this is different. I want to get clean."

She rolled her eyes. How many times had she heard that before? "Good for you."

"It's for the music. I can't write anymore. Not with this shit screwing up my head. So I'm going into rehab. I thought I'd come see you first, though."

Fear clutched her chest and dug in sharp, heavy claws. "I don't want to see you. Don't come here."

"You can't stop me, babe. I don't say that to threaten you, but because it's true."

Then why did it feel like a threat?

"How's the kid?" he asked when she didn't respond. "Don't forget, she's mine, too. I've been real good about letting you keep her, but that could all change, Elissa."

She wanted to scream. When she'd found out she was pregnant, Neil had insisted she get an abortion. She'd refused, he'd beaten the crap out of her, then gone out to party. She'd escaped, taking only what she could carry.

"Stop calling, Neil," she said quietly. "There's no money and you'll never get my child. No court would ever allow you to even see her. You've never cared and you don't care now."

She hung up, then quickly put the receiver on the table so he couldn't call back.

They'd played this scenario out countless times before. Sometimes he made good on his threat and showed up in Seattle, and sometimes he didn't. She never knew which it was going to be. All she knew for sure was that he would never get his hands on Zoe. She would do anything to protect her daughter. She would run. She would disappear. She would even kill Neil if she had to.

WALKER STRODE into his grandmother's office. He'd always hated the white-on-white decor. Even as a child, he felt the place was cold and hungry. Like a giant white moth, waiting to swallow the unwary.

"Walker," Gloria Buchanan said as she rose from behind her large gilded desk. "How lovely to see you. I was going to make an appointment for you to stop by and here you are, all on your own."

She smiled welcomingly and held out her arms, as if expecting them to embrace. He kept his distance.

Her smile never wavered. "I wanted to talk about you joining the company. Now that you've finally realized you never belonged in the Marines, you can take your place here. There's so much work to be done. Our most recent president quit. I don't understand what it is about businessmen today. None of them have any staying power." She sighed as she led the way to the sofas in the corner. "I'm getting older, Walker. I won't be able to run things forever."

He continued to stand in the center of the room.

She perched on the edge of the sofa and raised her thin eyebrows.

"You're not going to join me?"

"No," he said flatly. "I'm not here to have a polite conversation."

"If we're going to talk about your future—"

"We're not," he said, interrupting. "I have no future here. I don't give a damn about you or the restaurants. There's nothing you can say or do to get me to work here for thirty seconds."

She looked more bored than intimidated. "You're being dramatic."

He ignored that. "I'm not here because of my future. I'm here because of Elissa."

Gloria didn't pretend not to know what he was talking about. Instead she stood and glared at him. "I don't know what that little bitch has been saying—"

"Nothing," he said, cutting her off. "I haven't spoken to her. I'm here to talk to you."

He walked toward the sofa until he stood in front of his grandmother. "You're going to tell me exactly what you said and how you threatened her. Every single word."

He had to give the old bat points—she didn't flinch. "I will not speak with you looming over me. I am not a new recruit, Walker. You can't frighten me."

Which was a shame, he thought. She could use a good shaking up.

He took a step back and folded his arms across his chest. "What did you say to her?"

Gloria sank back onto the sofa and leaned against the white cushions. Her pale yellow suit provided the only spot of color in the room.

"I agree that she's pretty," Gloria said. "In a common sort of way. I would have thought she'd look harder, what with her background."

Walker knew his grandmother well enough to guess she'd gone digging into Elissa's past. She knew so much about her grandchildren, he'd long ago decided that she had them followed. Which would explain how she found out about Elissa.

He didn't bother telling Gloria that there wasn't anything about his neighbor that could shock him. He'd been to war—what could Elissa have done to come close to his sins?

"She traveled with rock bands," Gloria said with relish. "Apparently she slept with various men to get jobs, or just because. I wasn't clear on that. Her child's father is a known drug addict whom she supports." She stood. "Her own parents have refused to have anything to do with her for years. Is that what you want? A drug-using groupie and her bastard daughter?"

He smiled. "That's the best you could do? I expected a lot more. So she slept around when she was young? I know who she is now."

"You see what you want to see. Do you have any idea what your money would do for her? How it would change her life?"

He did. The problem was Elissa wasn't interested in handouts. He would bet she never had been.

"She's a whore," Gloria insisted. "You've never had to pay for a woman before, Walker. Why start now?"

He felt no anger, only coldness. If she'd been someone else, if she'd shown any human feeling, he might have pitied her. As it was, he could only walk away.

But first…

He shook his head. "You blew it, Gloria. I was never interested in Elissa. Not in any way that was a threat to you. But you've played your hand. You've gotten into her life and screwed around. Now I have to make it right. That means spending more time with her. You should have left well enough alone."

She stiffened. "I forbid you to see that woman."

"You think I care? You haven't been able to order me around for a long time. You forget—you don't scare me."

"You will listen to me. You will…"

She opened her mouth and gave a small gasp. Her hand rose to her throat, then fell away. Without warning she dropped to the ground.

Walker was at her side in an instant. Even as he rolled her onto her back to check her breathing, he pressed his fingers against her neck to feel for a pulse.

There wasn't one.

CHAPTER SEVEN

CAL AND PENNY WERE the last to arrive at the hospital. Cal kept pace with his very slow-moving wife. Walker eyed Penny's belly and had a feeling that she was even bigger than the last time he'd seen her, which he hadn't thought possible. Wasn't there a point beyond which a woman's stomach simply couldn't expand?

Everyone embraced, then Cal helped Penny into one of the chairs in the waiting room.

"What happened?" he asked when she was settled.

"We were arguing and she collapsed," Walker said flatly. He'd already told Reid and Dani the story. "There was nothing dramatic. No chest clutching. She gasped and fell. She wasn't breathing, so I called 911, then started CPR. She was breathing on her own by the time the ambulance arrived. My guess is she had a heart attack."

"Who knew she had a heart?" Dani muttered.

Walker wasn't surprised that no one complained about her comment. Each of them had a complicated relationship with Gloria. On the one hand, she had done nothing to endear herself to her relatives. On the other, she was an old woman who might still die.

Penny reached for Walker's hand. "Are you all right?" she asked.

He shrugged. "I'm not the one who passed out."

"I know, but you were with her. I don't want you to blame yourself for what happened. It could have been any one of us. We've all argued with her."

"Countless times," Cal added.

"I don't feel guilty," Walker said. "Just uncomfortable." He hadn't liked seeing her unconscious. He hadn't liked doing CPR on her. "Our fight wasn't heated enough to bring this on."

"Good." Penny squeezed his fingers, then released them. "I can almost feel sorry for her."

Dani sprawled next to her on the sofa. "Why would you?"

"Because her entire family is gathered here and no one really loves her. We don't wish her ill or want her to die, but no one is worried."

"She brought it on herself," Cal said. "She pushed each of us away, time after time."

"I know. It's just the duty card. I hate that." She looked at her husband. "You really love me, right?"

Cal bent over and kissed Penny on the mouth. "You're not allowed to doubt me."

"I know and I don't. Not really. It's just all this and the hormones and my back hurts."

Just then the doctor walked in. She was tall and thin, in her late forties. "The Buchanan clan?" she asked with a weary smile.

Cal stood and nodded. "That's us. How is she?"

"The good news is your grandmother is very

likely to have a full recovery. Your brother, the one who rode in with her…"

"That was me," Walker said.

"Yes, of course. You were right. It was a heart attack. Not life threatening as such, but there was some damage. Still, with time, rest and medication, she should be able to resume something close to her normal life. However, there is a complication."

The doctor paused and checked the chart she held. "Your grandmother isn't a young woman. Unfortunately, when she fell, she broke her hip."

Walker glanced at Reid, who shifted uncomfortably.

"That can't be good," Penny said.

"It's not. The break is fairly bad. We're going to have to operate to put things back in place. After that, she has a long road of physical therapy ahead of her. She will be here at least ten days. After that, a skilled nursing facility specializing in that sort of thing. Under normal circumstances, she could be there for months. However, if you wanted to provide home nursing care, she could be released in about four weeks."

She tucked the chart under her arm. "I know this is a lot to take in. What's important is that she survived the heart attack and there's every reason for optimism. Let's make an appointment for all of you to come see me in a couple of days and we can sort this all out."

"Thanks, Doctor," Cal said, offering his hand.

When she'd left, no one spoke. What was there to say?

"As the most neutral nonblood relative, I'll go first," Penny said. "There are two problems. Gloria and the company."

"The company can run itself for a while," Cal told her.

"The president just quit," Walker said. "She told me before she passed out. So someone has to be in charge."

Cal swore under his breath.

"There's also the home health care issue," Penny reminded them. "I don't think Gloria is going to last very long in any kind of skilled nursing facility. You know how she is. They're going to throw her out and then what?"

"As she pointed out to me so clearly just a few weeks ago," Dani said, "she's not my grandmother. So I'm not getting involved in her recovery or the company. I'm sorry to be difficult, but there it is."

"No one blames you," Walker told her. Gloria had gone out of her way to make sure Dani understood she would never be a part of the company or Gloria's world. A difficult situation had been handled cruelly.

"I'll take care of the home health care," Reid said.

Everyone looked at him. He shrugged. "I hate her the least. It's a few phone calls, some interviews. No big deal."

"You'll need more than one nurse," Penny said. "She'll need round-the-clock care at first." She smiled. "Please actually *look* at their résumés rather than hiring them based on their bust size."

Reid grinned. "Trust me."

Penny groaned.

"Which leaves the company," Dani said. She turned to Walker. "I love you to pieces, but you're the only one without a job."

He took a step back. "No way. I told her there was nothing she could say or do to get me to work for her."

"Apparently you were wrong," Cal said, sounding far too cheerful. "The good news is you won't be working for her. Not technically." His humor faded. "Seriously, it's just for a few weeks. No one expects you to stay there permanently."

Walker would rather go on an unarmed patrol through downtown Baghdad. "I don't know the business world," he said, trying not to sound desperate.

"Management is universal," Cal told him.

Walker knew he was trapped. Who else was there?

"Just for a few weeks," he said. "Don't get any ideas about me taking over."

"Agreed," Cal said.

ELISSA SMILED at the bright young woman sitting across the desk. "Zoe is very excited to be starting kindergarten."

"We're happy to have her," Julie Beamer said. "It sounds as if she already has a head start on a lot of what we're going to cover this year. You said she knows her letters."

"She recognizes all of them and can write most of them. We're having a little trouble with *G*. She's also reading very simple words."

"Excellent." Julie made a few notes on a pad. "I believe you mentioned Zoe's father is dead?"

"That's right," Elissa said easily. As far as the world was concerned, Neil didn't even exist. Despite his threats, she knew he wanted nothing to do with his child. For him, Zoe was little more than a means of extortion.

"We're very much looking forward to having her in class. If you would tell her I can't wait to meet her."

"I will," Elissa promised.

Elissa left the meeting and headed to her car. Her baby was starting school. She was both excited that Zoe was ready to take the next step in her young life and a little choked up to have her daughter growing up so quickly.

Had it been like this with her mother, she wondered, then wished she hadn't. Thinking about her family only made her sad.

Her parents had never forgiven her for running away. While she tried to understand their anger, she couldn't help wishing they'd loved her enough to let her be a part of their lives. She'd moved back to Seattle partly with the foolish hope they would run into each other. They hadn't.

Sometimes Elissa thought she would try to speak with them again. But fear of another rejection always made her hold back.

When she got home, she found her daughter waiting impatiently on the porch.

"Did you see her?" Zoe asked as she raced toward the car. "Is she nice? Does she want to have me in her class? Are we going to have fun?"

Elissa caught her and swung her in the air. "Yes,

yes and yes. Miss Beamer is very nice and smart and she's very excited about how much you already know. You're going to have a wonderful year."

As she spoke, she found herself glancing up at Walker's apartment. Of course he wasn't there. After leaving her a single phone message, he hadn't tried to get in touch with her. He showed up late and left early.

It shouldn't matter. She'd made it clear she didn't want anything to do with him, and he'd taken her at her word. Wasn't that good news?

She tried to convince herself it was. The thing was, she'd thought he would at least want to know why. She'd thought her sudden disappearance might concern him. Obviously she'd been wrong. She'd read far too much into their conversations. She'd thought he'd been interested and he hadn't been.

"Can we go look at my clothes?" Zoe asked. "Can we pick what I'm going to wear the first day? And the next day? And the next?"

"Of course."

Elissa set her daughter down and took her hand. As they walked into the apartment, she felt an unfamiliar sense of emptiness. It took her a second to realize she was lonely for someone who was more than a friend.

She wasn't looking to get married or for anything permanent, but every once in a while she thought it would be nice to have someone hanging around for a while. Someone to share things with. Someone to care.

SHORTLY BEFORE NINE on Friday evening, there was a knock on Elissa's door. Her first thought was that the horrible old woman had returned. That somehow she'd found out how much Elissa missed Walker and she was back to exact her revenge.

Instead, when she stared out the peephole, she saw Walker standing there.

When she opened the door, her first instinct was to throw herself in his arms and demand to know where he'd been. Her second was to rip off her T-shirt in invitation. Instead she went for something a tiny bit more subtle and simply invited him in.

"You okay?" he asked as he closed the door behind him.

"Fine. And you?"

"Not bad." He held out a bottle of red wine. "I thought we could talk."

Not words she usually expected to hear from a man. "And you need to get me drunk first?" she asked.

He smiled. "I hadn't planned to."

Bummer.

She led the way into the kitchen and handed over the corkscrew. He made quick work of opening the bottle. She put glasses on the counter and he poured.

"So what is the topic of conversation?" she asked, before taking a sip of the very smooth wine. The flavor burst on her tongue without being overpowering. Must be nice to be able to afford something over three dollars a bottle.

"My grandmother."

Determined not to react, Elissa led the way into the living room. "What about her?"

"I know she was here."

"Okay."

He glanced around the empty, quiet room. "Zoe in bed?"

"Yes, fast asleep. I just checked on her a few minutes ago."

"Good."

"Because…"

"Because I might be using some language not appropriate for a five-year-old." He motioned to the sofa and sat across from her in a club chair.

She wasn't sure why he was here. Was he planning to take his grandmother's side or hers? "Walker, I don't know what—"

"Gloria threatened you," he said flatly. "I know the generalities, but not the specifics. Want to fill me in?"

"Not really." When his steady gaze never wavered she added, "She obviously doesn't want us involved. As we're not, I don't see a problem."

"My grandmother isn't a subtle woman. I'm guessing she threatened your job somehow, or even Zoe. Am I close?"

She shrugged.

Walker frowned, then leaned back in his chair. "Sorry," he said. "I don't like her. No one in my family does. She's a manipulative bitch who will do anything to get her way."

She relaxed a little. At least he hadn't assumed she, Elissa, was in the wrong. "Okay, then. Yes. She threatened to get me fired and evicted if I didn't get out of your life."

He swore again. "I'm sorry. One day you were gone. I wish you'd told me what had happened."

"It's not your problem."

"It happened because of me."

"Maybe. I didn't want to…"

"You weren't sure whose side I'd be on," he said. "I'm on yours. Don't worry."

"I wasn't worried, exactly."

"Of course not." He smiled at her. "You don't have to sweat it. She won't bother you again."

"Did she get back on her broom and return to the mother ship?"

"No. She's in the hospital. She had a heart attack, fell and broke her hip."

"Oh, God."

Elissa didn't know what to think, let alone say. Gloria had been horrible, but even so she wouldn't have wished for something like this to happen.

"She'll be all right," he told her. "She'll be in the hospital for a while, then at a place getting physical therapy."

"Okay. I'm at a loss here."

"Me, too. No one in my family expected this. My brother Reid is taking care of finding private duty nurses, while I'm going to be taking over the company." He sipped his wine. "I'm not exactly executive material."

"I'm not so sure about that. All you need is attitude and a suit."

"Why do I think there's more to it than that?" he asked wryly.

"Sure, if you want to make things complicated." She clutched her glass and knew she was going to have to get to it eventually. "She mentioned you're a part of the Buchanan restaurant chain."

"There are four places. Not much of a chain."

"Still. It's a really different world. I'm sure she told you all about me and my past."

"I don't care, Elissa," he said flatly. "You'd told me a lot yourself and I'm in no position to judge."

Ha. As if she believed that. "I want to make it clear I never did drugs. I wasn't interested. I know that's not a huge moral mountain or anything, but it's important to me. The other stuff, well, some of it is true." Especially the part about Zoe's father. How on earth could she have fallen for Neil?

"I meant what I said," he told her. "I don't judge you. Or anyone."

"But I—"

He leaned forward and set his drink on the coffee table between them. "You what? Partied? Slept with some guys? Elissa, I've killed people. Sure, it was in the line of duty and it was my job and it probably saved lives, but they're still dead. Some of them deserved it, but some were just kids pretending to be soldiers. Some weren't supposed to die. Not on either side."

She thought about what he'd told her before. "Are you talking about your friend Ben?"

He shrugged. "He took a bullet for me. It all happened so fast. I don't know how they got in the cave. That shouldn't have happened. But they did and he died to save me. He was a kid. Some skinny kid from Seattle. He wasn't even a good Marine. But damn, did he have heart. He didn't have anyone but me and the Marines and now he's gone."

She felt his pain as if it were her own. She felt his emptiness and knew these ghosts were the ones to cause him to cry out in his sleep.

"Walker, you didn't do anything wrong," she whispered as she put down her drink and moved toward him. She wasn't sure what she was going to do, she only knew he needed comfort.

But as she approached, he rose and suddenly she was in his arms, his hands on her back, his mouth on hers.

Everything happened so quickly, she didn't have time to think. Which was all right because the feel of his lips on hers made it impossible to form thoughts.

His kiss was firm and confident without being demanding. She felt the heat of him, and his strength. He moved his mouth against hers, discovering, arousing, making her strain toward him in an attempt to convince him that more was a really good idea.

She pressed against him, liking how his muscles provided a warm resting place for her body. While he rubbed his fingers against her back, she explored his shoulders and upper arms.

She felt the first brush of his tongue on her lower lip and parted for him. When he slipped inside she felt heat pour through her. Body parts melted. Her thighs and stomach tightened, while her knees nearly gave way. Her breasts swelled.

Wanting swept through her. Need, and hunger. It had been so long, the sensations were almost unfamiliar—but still very, very welcome.

He tasted of wine and sex and promise. When he drew back, she whimpered, but then he kissed her jaw and the side of her neck. His lips traced the line from her ear to her shoulder. He pushed her hair aside and nibbled on the back of her neck.

Liquid desire washed away any lingering resolve she might have mustered. She was more than willing to take things to the next level. Make that the next fifteen levels. She wanted them both naked, clinging, touching, riding each other until they were too exhausted to ever do it again.

She opened her mouth to tell him so when he stepped back.

"Sorry," he said. "This was not in your game plan."

Screw the game plan. Had she been able to speak, she would have told him just that. But she was too stunned by her incredible response to him to do more than breathe.

"Even if you were interested," he continued, "I'm the wrong guy. You and Zoe need someone who's going to stick around. That's not me."

"You're moving?" she managed to ask, her voice thick and unsteady.

"Not this week. I meant in general. I'm not a good bet."

"Why not?"

"I saw too many guys get dumped while overseas. Love is fleeting at best."

"It doesn't have to be like that."

"You seen any different?"

My parents. Except she didn't say that aloud. Were her parents even still together?

"I'm not looking for forever," she said. "I just find it interesting that someone as caring as you isn't looking for more."

"You think I'm caring?"

She managed a smile. "Did I just violate the male code by saying that? Should I take it back?"

"I'm a real bastard, Elissa. You need to understand that."

She almost giggled. Right. A real bastard who took Mrs. Ford to the hospital and spent time with her daughter while Zoe showed off her new school clothes.

"Bad to the bone," she said. "I got it."

He narrowed his gaze. "I'm not kidding."

"I know. You're practically evil."

"Are you making fun of me?"

"Maybe. A little. Gonna get me now?"

"You should respect what I'm telling you. I'm not a good bet."

She sighed. "Actually, I do believe that."

Not because of anything he'd said, but because of her own past. He might not be bad, but she was a walking, breathing disaster when it came to men. Neil was proof of that.

"So we'll just be friends," he said. "Pretend this never happened."

"Of course," she said, knowing she was lying. She planned to relive that kiss every night for the next month. But repeating it in person? Not likely. Fool me once and all that.

He slipped his hand against the back of her neck and drew her to him. "You're a real temptation. You know that?"

She was painfully normal. Average height, average looks, average body, with the added thrill of a couple of stretch marks. A temptation? Who was he kidding?

But there was a heat in his gaze. A fire that thrilled her as much as it made her want him more.

"And how do you feel about temptation?" she asked.

"I walk away."

CHAPTER EIGHT

DANI SIPPED the hot coffee and stared across at the view of Lake Union. She was due at the restaurant in an hour, but until then she planned to enjoy the perfect summer morning.

It was just after ten, when those who had regular jobs had disappeared into their offices and the lunch crowd had yet to fill the sidewalks.

The Waterfront should do lunch, she thought. The location was good. With some minor modifications, a lot of their dinner menu could be cut down or translated into salads and sandwiches. They could…

"*So* not my problem," she said aloud, to remind herself she wasn't technically a Buchanan anymore. She didn't give a damn if the restaurant made a profit or not, just as long as it stayed in business until Penny returned from maternity leave and Dani could find another job.

Or maybe she should do something more, she thought. Like go find her father.

Who was he? She had no idea how to begin the search. Gloria had long ago gotten rid of all Dani's mother's things. Could there be papers of some kind? A diary?

The only person who would know for sure was the one person Dani didn't want to talk to—Gloria.

"What has you looking so serious?"

She turned and saw Ryan standing next to her.

"Hi," she said, both surprised and delighted to see him. "What are you doing here?"

"Getting coffee. It's my morning spot. And you?"

She held up her drink. "Getting a slow start on my day. Do you really come here every morning?"

He glanced at the front of the Daily Grind. "Sure. It's on my way to the restaurant. Why?"

"My brother Cal owns the chain. When he started, he and his partners opened three places at once. This is one of them."

Ryan chuckled. "So I spend my life in service to the Buchanan empire."

"Four restaurants isn't exactly an empire," Dani said. "Although Cal's business would qualify. They're expanding back East." She lowered her voice. "Apparently they're going to have to offer more coffee choices that aren't as strong. I guess we scare them with too much intensity."

"Wimps," he said.

She laughed. "One of the new East Coast reps said we all have our taste in our feet."

Ryan grinned, then his humor faded. He put his hand on her arm. "I was sorry to hear about your grandmother. Are you all right? Is there anything I can do?"

"I'm all right," she said, not seeing any point in

getting into her current maelstrom of feelings. Gloria wasn't her grandmother. The woman had made her life a living hell for years. And all that time, Dani had done her best to make the old woman happy. Until she'd learned the truth, she'd never been able to figure out why she kept failing. But even after all that, she couldn't help feeling bad about what had happened and how Gloria was going to have to face her recovery pretty much on her own.

"How are you liking the restaurant?" she asked, not wanting to talk about Gloria anymore. "All settled in?"

He shook his head. "That's going to take a while. The place is great. Talk about busy. When the orders get going, that kitchen is crazy. How do you keep it straight?"

"Sometimes I don't," she admitted. "If you think it's insane now, wait until Penny gets back. Edouard is a good chef, but he doesn't challenge himself the same way. Penny liked to test herself on the specials."

"Everyone talks about how great she is," Ryan told her. "I'm looking forward to working with her."

His blond hair looked gold in the bright morning sun. It was perfectly cut, maybe a tiny bit too long, which only made her want to touch the layered strands more. He was good-looking without being pretty, funny, smart and possibly interested in her. Did life get any better?

Okay, her divorce wasn't final, but wasn't she entitled to a rebound guy? Someone who would take her mind off her lying, cheating bastard of a husband and show her a good time? Wasn't it the law?

"Penny's the best," Dani said. "I'm glad she's my sister-in-law again."

"Again?"

"She and Cal were married before. Things didn't work out between them for a lot of reasons. But when Cal hired Penny to bring The Waterfront back from the brink, they were thrown together a lot. One thing led to another and now they're married again."

"With a baby on the way," he added.

Dani nodded, not bothering to explain Cal wasn't the father. It was yet another Buchanan complication and she saw no point in scaring off her potential boy toy.

She giggled. *Boy toy?* What would Ryan think of the title?

"Okay, you're always doing that," he said. "You laugh at something and only you know the reason."

"Sorry. I guess I find myself entertaining."

"You make me laugh," he said.

Was it her imagination or had he just moved a little closer?

Before she could decide, he glanced at his watch. "Tell you what—we have a good hour before we have to be at the restaurant. Let's walk around the city some. You can show me your favorite sights and I'll be impressed."

A shiver of pleasure rippled through her. "Sounds like a plan." She glanced around to get her bearings, then pointed. "Let's go that way. I'll take you to the big downtown Nordstrom store. I know what you're thinking. It's just another department store. But you'd be wrong. It's an amazing place."

She held her coffee in one hand while her other hung free. Without warning, Ryan captured it in his.

"You have no idea what I'm thinking, Dani. None at all."

He laced his fingers with hers and squeezed slightly.

Okay then, she thought, barely able to breathe from the shock of a strange man holding her hand after a good ten years of being with Hugh.

He was right—she didn't know what he was thinking. But she had to admit, she kind of liked it.

ELISSA WAITED until her shift was over to knock on Frank's open office door. He looked up and waved her in.

"Hey, Elissa. How's it going? How's Zoe? She excited about starting school?" The man was in his fifties, overweight and genuinely nice. She knew she'd gotten lucky when she'd found this job.

"Very. Every night we discuss what she's going to wear the first week and it constantly changes." She smiled. "I met her teacher and she seems great. So we're happy."

"Good. Good." He waved to the chair in front of his big, paper-covered desk. "What can I do you for? You have plenty of vacation time racked up. Want to use some?"

"Not just yet." Not only couldn't she afford to go anywhere right now, she always liked to keep plenty of vacation time in the bank in case of emergency. One serious bout of the flu for either her or Zoe could use up her sick leave and she liked having a buffer.

"I know you're not here about money," Frank joked. "You've never once asked me for an advance."

She fidgeted, wishing she did want a loan, or something equally easy to discuss. "No, it's not money. I just..." She pleated her apron between her fingers. "You know I like working here, Frank. It's been great, these past three years. The money is terrific, I love the hours and you offer the best benefits in town."

Frank groaned. "Elissa, no. You can't. Come on, honey, don't leave. You're one of my best people. I can depend on you, the customers love you. Who's trying to steal you away?"

"What?" She shook her head, although it was nice to know he wouldn't want to lose her. "No, I'm not quitting. Not at all. I want to stay. I love my job."

He frowned. "Then what's this all about?"

"I, ah..." She cleared her throat. "Do you know Gloria Buchanan?"

Frank sighed heavily and leaned back in his squeaky wooden chair. "Oh, yeah. Old, rich, pain in the ass, if you'll excuse my French."

Elissa felt an instant and overpowering sense of relief. "You don't like her?"

Frank shrugged. "I don't know her. She's on a lot of the same charity committees I'm on, although she's always in charge. Has to be. I hate working with her, because it's her way or a big fight. I swear, she could wear down a rock. I stay quiet and do my bit." He looked at Elissa. "How do you know her?"

"I don't, but I know her grandson. He lives in my

building. We're just friends, but somehow Gloria found out and came to see me."

"I'll bet that wasn't pretty," Frank grumbled. "What did she do?"

"Made some vague threats." They hadn't been vague, but suddenly Elissa didn't feel much like explaining them.

But Frank was a bright guy. "She use my name? Did she threaten you with—" He swore under his breath. "Let me guess. The old bitch doesn't think you're the right type for her precious grandson? She said she could get you fired."

"Something like that."

"Elissa, that would never happen, no matter who came to me. I judge my people on what I see here, every day. You know that, right?"

She nodded, feeling more foolish by the second. "I know. I shouldn't have let her get to me. I just got scared."

"Who wouldn't? Gloria Buchanan is not a nice person. You stay clear of her."

As Gloria was currently in the hospital recovering from a heart attack, that wasn't going to be difficult.

"Thanks, Frank," she said as she stood. "I appreciate you talking to me."

"Anytime. You have a problem, you come to me. Nobody gets to my girls."

She smiled and left. But as she walked into the back room and crossed to her locker, her smile faded. How could she have been so stupid? How could she have let one mean old woman frighten her so much? Why hadn't she thought things through instead of running?

It was her past, she acknowledged. Those first couple of years after she'd had Zoe had been awful. She'd had to work while caring for a baby and paying for day care. She'd always been one step away from disaster. She'd learned to lie low. Apparently the scars from that time hadn't completely faded. And that, combined with Neil's ongoing threats, had a way of making her jump to conclusions.

No more, she told herself. She wasn't going to let anyone run her life. Next time a rich old woman threatened her, she would stand her ground.

A fairly safe promise, she thought as she got her purse and her car keys out of her locker. How many other rich old women were going to bother with her?

Still, she felt better for having made the decision. And for knowing her job was safe. As she headed toward her car, she had the urge to talk to Walker and tell him what had happened. She wanted to share her relief—and, okay, she wanted to hear his voice.

It was the kiss, she was forced to admit. It had changed everything. Not only had she experienced passion for the first time in over five years, she'd done so with a man she trusted.

How long had it been since she'd felt that for any guy? Not that it mattered. Even if she was willing to break her "no sex for thirteen more years" rule, Walker wasn't. He'd made it clear that he wasn't willing to take things to the next level.

Better for them both, she thought, then sighed. Lying to herself was never a good sign.

WALKER ENTERED Gloria's office at seven in the morning. He'd put off going in for three days, but he no longer had a choice. He'd agreed to take responsibility for Buchanan Enterprises and he would. Hating every minute of it didn't count.

He stepped off the executive floor and headed for his grandmother's office. The hallway was quiet and dark, which made him want to look for snipers. He ignored the urge and kept moving.

Apparently he was the first to arrive. Or so he thought until he rounded the corner and saw a small, dark-haired woman putting her purse into the bottom drawer of her desk.

She looked up when she saw him and offered a smile that made her look both uncomfortable and afraid.

"Mr. Buchanan," she said. "Good morning. I'm Vicki, one of your grandmother's assistants. We spoke on the phone a couple of days ago. Let me again say how sorry we all are to hear about what happened. Our prayers are with Mrs. Buchanan through her recovery."

The speech was really nice, but it would have been a whole lot more meaningful if she'd been able to say it without looking as if she would bolt at any second.

"Thank you," he told her. "The family appreciates everyone's concern."

She nodded. "Would you like me to show you around the floor? Or would you prefer to see the office? There's coffee, of course. Kit sets it up on a timer every evening before she leaves."

"Kit is my grandmother's other assistant?"

"Yes, Kit works from two in the afternoon until midnight. We trade off our weekends and there are two other executive assistants who have the training to take over if one of us has to be gone."

She reminded him of a nervous dog. He would swear he could see her trembling as she spoke.

"Let's take things slowly," he said, his voice as calm as he could make it. "I'll need to see my grandmother's calendar for the next couple of weeks. Also, if you could let me know about monthly and quarterly meetings that might be coming up."

"Of course." She pulled a small pad out of her skirt pocket and wrote quickly. "Is ten minutes sufficient? I could work faster."

"How about any time before nine this morning?"

Vicki blinked at him. "But that's a two-hour window."

"I know."

"All right. Let me show you the office, then I'll get your coffee."

Walker had never been an officer, so he'd never been in a position to have someone bring him anything. He could only imagine what would have happened if he'd asked.

"Why don't you show me where the coffee is and I'll get it myself?"

"But you can't," she breathed. "Mr. Buchanan—"

"Walker," he said. "Call me Walker. I don't know

how my grandmother ran things, Vicki. To be honest, I don't know much about the company. I'm here to keep things from falling apart until she gets better. So you're going to have to be patient with me."

"Of course," she said, looking terrified. "I'm sorry. I wasn't being critical."

She was like a wounded wild animal, ready to run for cover. It made him tired just to be here.

"You weren't critical. You offered to get me coffee. There's a difference. Now let's go see where I can get my caffeine fix for the next hour."

She led the way into a small kitchen, then watched as he poured himself a mug of the steaming coffee.

"Help yourself," he said when he was finished.

"Mrs. Buchanan prefers that the staff doesn't use her personal equipment. I'll go down to the lunchroom later. We have a machine there."

He'd known Gloria was a real bitch, but even he was surprised by how she treated her people.

"I'm not going to say anything," he told Vicki. "Just help yourself."

Then, while she watched in obvious amazement, he poured a second mug and handed it to her.

"I, ah, thank you," she whispered.

"You're welcome." He kept his smile easy, while on the inside, all he could think about was getting the hell out of here. Right now snipers didn't sound all that bad.

"THE MANAGERS FROM the various restaurants meet here twice a week," Vicki said an hour later as she walked him through Gloria's calendar. "Except for The Downtown Sports Bar. Reid is supposed to be in charge, but he doesn't come to the meetings."

"Not a surprise," Walker said with a grin. "My brother isn't into following the rules."

Vicki nodded without smiling back. "Mrs. Buchanan sees the chefs once a week, except for the chef at The Waterfront. It's in Chef Jackson's contract that she doesn't have to attend those meetings. That doesn't make Mrs. Buchanan very happy."

Walker wasn't surprised. Lucky Penny, missing out on meetings with his grandmother.

"There are mini staff meetings every afternoon at four and major ones once a week. Then each department meets with Mrs. Buchanan individually once a week."

"That's a lot of meetings," he said. "When do these people get their work done?"

"A lot of them stay nights," she said earnestly. "Mrs. Buchanan has very high standards."

"I knew she was difficult," he muttered. "I didn't know she was insane."

But he wasn't surprised Gloria had to micromanage every aspect of the company. She would never trust anyone to get the job done correctly.

He looked at the printout. "We're going to make some changes here."

"Of course," Vicki said as she stood on the other side of the desk.

Walker hated being in the large white-on-white

room, but the other woman's hovering only made him more uncomfortable.

"You gonna settle somewhere?" he asked.

"Excuse me?"

"Sit down."

Vicki's eyes widened. "Mrs. Buchanan prefers us to stand while we—"

"Mrs. Buchanan isn't here. Sit."

Vicki perched on the very edge of the chair across from his. A muscle twitched in her jaw. He glanced at the clock on the desk and saw it was barely after eight in the morning—too early to start drinking, but damn, was he tempted.

He looked at the jam-packed schedule, including a standing appointment with a Mr. J from a private investigation agency—no doubt how she knew so much about everyone's personal life—and decided it all had to stop.

"Cancel everything," he said.

Vicki's mouth opened, then closed. "Excuse me, sir?"

"Cancel everything. Every meeting, every appointment. I want to start over. Can you send an e-mail to everyone telling them to wait to find out the new schedule?" He would take care of the mysterious Mr. J himself.

She paled. "Of course. I'm happy to do that."

"Good. I'll meet with the different managers and department heads, but later in the week when I've had time to review the quarterly statements. Then go ahead and set up meetings for me at each of the four restaurants. Do them on different days. The Waterfront can be last—I know they're in good shape."

Vicki seemed to fold in on herself. "I'm sorry to have to ask, but are you saying you'll go *there?*"

"Sure. It'll be easier to coordinate a time if I work around their schedules."

She wrote frantically.

When she paused, he said, "Would it be possible to get the recent quarterlies this morning?"

"Of course. They're on my computer."

"Good. When it's convenient."

She wrote some more.

"Does Kit like working nights?" he asked.

Vicki blanched. "I don't know. Is there a problem? Would you like me to —"

He raised his hand to stop her. "Breathe," he said.

"Excuse me?"

"Breathe. Take a deep breath and let it out."

She did as he requested, but didn't look any more relaxed.

"No one is getting fired," he said. "No one is even getting beaten. It is more than possible that I will violate the executive assistant code by asking you to bring me lunch because I don't want to go to a restaurant and despite the fact that we own four, our corporate headquarters has nothing better than a few vending machines."

"I'm happy to get you lunch," she said. "Every day."

"Good. But on company time. Not your own. As for Kit's hours, I won't be working until midnight. So if she would prefer the day shift, that's fine with me. I'm sure there's plenty to keep the two of you busy."

She wrote frantically.

"Vicki," he said, then waited until she looked at him. "You don't have to write everything down."

"I want to get it right the first time. That's very important."

"What happens if you make a mistake?"

Her expression of panic made him feel as if he'd kicked her. "Never mind," he said. "For what it's worth, you don't have to get it right the first time."

She nodded, but he doubted she believed him.

Was the entire staff like this? No wonder the company had run through three presidents a year for the past decade.

How much cleanup would he have to deal with? People working while afraid wasn't efficient. As he'd learned in his previous line of work, some fear allowed a soldier to keep the edge, but too much got him dead.

He thought about how his grandmother had tried to control her grandchildren. When that had failed, had she turned to her employees?

"Things are going to be different while I'm here," he told Vicki. "Feel free to spread the word."

CHAPTER NINE

ELISSA DID HER BEST to concentrate on the dozen or so blue topaz stones sitting on her kitchen table. Her budget didn't usually allow for anything this nice, but one of her regulars at the diner knew someone in the jewelry business, so she'd been able to get the cut stones at a great price. In return Elissa was going to transform a bolt of fabric into bedroom drapes. All in all, a great trade.

She had an idea for six pairs of earrings, assuming she could match up the stones. If not, she would use the leftovers in a coordinating necklace, or maybe a pendant-pin combination. So many ideas.

Normally she would have been lost in her work for hours, but this particular Saturday there was the added distraction of Walker sitting not two feet away on the other side of her kitchen table.

She still wasn't sure how he'd come to be there. One minute she'd been getting out of her car after dropping Zoe off on a play date and the next, they'd been talking and she'd invited him inside.

"Your grandmother has two assistants?" she said, as Walker talked about his first couple of days running the company. "Who needs two?"

"Apparently she does. I won't meet Kit until next week, but Vicki spends her day trembling in fear. She seems convinced if she doesn't do whatever I say perfectly the first time, I'll have her shot at dawn."

"That would almost be funny if it weren't so sad."

"Everyone is like that," he said. "I walked into a few offices yesterday to introduce myself and the people were all terrified. I couldn't get anyone to say anything but how much they love my grandmother and their jobs and how thrilled they are to be working there."

Elissa wrinkled her nose. "No offense, but I find it really hard to believe they're that fond of your grandmother."

"I keep expecting to find a closet full of bamboo canes, or a medieval torture rack behind a closed door. She had meetings scheduled all day. Every department reported to her daily. The restaurant personnel were expected to come to her."

"You'll get it sorted out," she told him, confident it was true. The man had handled troops while under fire—how hard could it be to whip an office staff into shape?

"There's so much to learn," he said. "I never paid attention to the restaurant business before. They don't even call it a restaurant. It's a store."

She grinned. "I know."

He shook his head. "Sorry—you work in a restaurant. Then you know what I'm talking about. Cal, one of my brothers, is giving me a crash course in restaurant management. There are fixed costs, like the building. Food costs and labor costs are broken down by the meal. Penny, Cal's wife, is a chef. I'm meeting with her next week to learn about the back of the store. I don't know anything about how a kitchen works."

"Not even in real life," she murmured.

He narrowed his gaze. "Is that a crack about my cooking?"

"To the best of my knowledge, you *don't* cook."

"What's your point?"

"That it's all information you can learn. If you have good people in place, then the restaurants will take care of themselves."

"They'd better." He leaned back in his chair and grabbed the iced tea she'd made. "I never much thought about the family business as anything real. It was just something I wanted to avoid. Now I feel like I'm rescuing people from the bowels of hell."

"You are. I know she's your grandmother and you probably love her very much—"

"Not really."

She didn't believe that. Family was impossible to ignore forever. Look how long she'd tried, and there were still days she thought about her parents and wondered if she ever crossed their minds.

"I'm just saying," she continued, "she couldn't have been someone easy to work for. You're doing a good thing."

He shrugged uncomfortably.

"Speaking of being foolish..." she said.

"Were we?"

"Sort of. I talked to my boss. He knows your grandmother, but they're not close and there's no way she could have convinced him to fire me. I can't believe I let her intimidate me that way. I just collapsed like a wet tissue. I should have been stronger than that."

"Elissa, I have grown men with MBAs cowering behind their desks. It's not you. Gloria would terrify anyone."

"She doesn't scare you."

"I know her. Don't take it personally. You're plenty tough."

"I'm not, but thank you for saying so."

Even though she wasn't getting any work done, she liked having him around. He was easy to talk to, and easy to look at. A nice combination. While intellectually she knew it was best that he wasn't interested in starting anything with her, the stubborn, emotional side of her brain regretted that they would never get more involved. He would have been a great guy to get to know.

Yeah, right until she found out his pesky, awful flaw. Because if she liked him, he had one. She should be—

Walker stood up and walked toward the living room.

"Am I boring you?" she asked.

"What? No. I thought I saw someone outside."

"Like?"

"I don't know. He looked suspicious."

Her first thought was that Neil had made good on his threat and found her. Then she dismissed the idea. Neil wouldn't lurk. He would simply pound on the door and demand money.

Walker turned back to her. "I want to ask you

something. My sister-in-law is pregnant and there's going to be—"

He turned suddenly and raced out of the apartment. Elissa went after him and was stunned to see him following a guy she'd never seen before.

Her first thought was relief that the man wasn't Neil. He was too short and his hair was too dark. Her second was to wonder who was hanging out in her front yard, looking through her windows.

She caught up with them as Walker tackled the guy and they fell onto a neighbor's lawn. Before she knew it, Walker had the guy's right arm bent behind his back.

"Mr. J, I presume," Walker said.

"Who?" she asked.

"This guy works for my grandmother. I don't know his real name. He's in her calendar as Mr. J." Walker shook the man. "I called your company yesterday and fired your ass."

"I don't know what you're talking about. I don't work for your grandmother."

"Right." Walker tightened his grip on the man's arm. "Then who hired you?"

"I can't—" The man gave a little scream as Walker pushed his wrist higher toward his shoulder.

Elissa winced but didn't stop him. She didn't like the idea of strange guys hovering around her apartment. She asked the next obvious question.

"Was it Neil?"

Both Walker and the man looked at her.

"No. His name is Bobby," the stranger told her. "He says he's your brother."

ELISSA STUDIED THE MAN in the baseball cap. He was so ordinary looking. "I wouldn't have guessed you were a private detective," she said, as the man, who'd introduced himself as Derek, drank a glass of iced tea.

"We're supposed to blend in," Derek told her. He held the glass in his left hand and rotated his right shoulder. "You've got some grip, buddy," he said to Walker.

Walker leaned against the counter, legs braced, arms folded. He looked ready to attack and kill, if necessary. Elissa was glad he was on her side.

She was still having trouble getting her mind around Derek's confession of his client. "Bobby's still a kid," she said, not sure she believed her brother was trying to get in touch with her.

"He turned eighteen on his last birthday. He starts at UW next week."

Her brother going to the University of Washington? The last time she'd seen him, he'd just gotten braces. Of course that had been eight years ago.

Thinking about her brother made her want to ask about her parents, but she knew better. They'd made their position clear.

"He wants to talk to you," Derek said as he reached in his pocket and pulled out a piece of paper. "Here's his cell number. He'd really like you to give him a call."

She supposed it meant something that her brother had spent his money to find her. She took the paper and stuffed it in her own pocket.

"I guess it wouldn't hurt," she said, not sure how

she felt about contact with him after all these years. "Tell him I'll give him a call in the next few days."

"And nothing else," Walker added.

Derek looked at him. "What do you mean?"

"You will not give out any personal information on Elissa. Not her address, or phone number, not the name or location of her place of employment. I don't care what your contract with the kid says. If you put her in any danger, you will answer to me."

It was like watching a rabbit try to face down a tiger. Derek folded instantly. "I won't tell him anything."

"If I find out you have, I will hunt you down. Are we clear?"

Derek put down the iced tea and nodded vigorously. "I, ah, should probably go."

"Excellent idea," Walker said. "I'll see you out."

Elissa stayed in the kitchen and sank into one of the chairs. When Walker returned, he sat next to her.

"You okay?" he asked.

"I don't think so. This is so weird. I haven't talked to Bobby since I found out I was pregnant." She drew in a breath. "I ran away when I was seventeen and I never called my parents to say I was okay. I felt bad about that later. It was selfish and stupid, but that pretty much defined my existence. Then I let myself forget about them. I was busy holding down an exciting job. When I got pregnant and Zoe's father turned out to be an asshole, I left him. I also called home."

His dark eyes hid his thoughts, but she wasn't worried about him judging her. Walker wasn't the type.

"What happened?" he asked quietly.

"I got Bobby. He said the folks were still pretty pissed off, but he'd check with them to see if they were willing to talk to me."

"Did you tell him about Zoe?"

She shook her head. "I figured calling after all this time was enough of a shock. Besides, I still had enough pride not to want their pity. That came later."

"They weren't interested," he said, not asking a question.

"Apparently not. He said they didn't want anything to do with me. That I'd made my decision and now I had to live with it. So I did."

"Are you sure he was telling the truth?"

Elissa nodded. "I thought about that, too, but only for a minute. Bobby was always a great kid and we got along really well. My mom had trouble getting pregnant the second time, which is why there's such a big age gap between us. I could have hated him for being the favorite after he was born, but I loved him too much. We had fun together. I couldn't imagine him lying to me about that."

"You gonna call?"

"Probably. I need a couple of days to get used to the idea of having contact with him again, but then I will. I'd like Zoe to know her uncle."

"Want to come with me to my sister-in-law's baby shower?"

The question wasn't quite as shocking as finding out her brother was trying to get in touch with her, but it was very close.

"What?"

"Penny's shower is tomorrow. I thought about asking you before, but then I wasn't sure you'd want to come. It's just family. You'd like Dani and Penny. The food will be good."

His voice trailed off. For the first time since meeting him, Elissa had the idea that Walker was nervous.

"You're asking me to go with you to your sister-in-law's baby shower?"

"Zoe, too," he said. "It's not a date."

"Good to know."

"I bought a car seat. She registered at a baby store, so that's what I got. They wrapped it. I can put your names on the card."

They weren't dating but he was willing to share the gift?

Elissa didn't know what to think. She believed him when he said he didn't want to get involved, and if he was strong enough to ignore the sexual attraction between them, then she could, too.

She knew they would both face a lot of questions, yet she couldn't resist finding out more about Walker's private world. What was he like with his family and who were the people who knew him best?

"What time?" she asked.

"Four. Penny's cooking. It's her party and she shouldn't, but she's a chef and who else would she trust with the food?"

"Okay," she said slowly. "Sure. We'll go. Oh, and I'll bring my own present."

"Are you sure? I don't mind adding you and Zoe."

"We're good."

"Then I'll pick you up at three-thirty."

"Sure."

She walked him to the door, where they stood awkwardly for several seconds. Then he turned and headed up the stairs.

Not a date, huh? If it looks like a duck and walks like a duck, what else could it be?

WALKER'S CAR still smelled new. Elissa inhaled the rich scent of expensive leather and eyed the complicated-looking console. In the car world, money could really buy happiness.

"So you're one of four," she said, knowing it was more important to learn about his family than wallow in car-envy.

"Right. Cal, Reid, me and Dani. Cal's married to Penny. Reid may or may not bring a date. He tends to go through women quickly. Dani is in the middle of a divorce."

"When's Cal and Penny's baby due?"

Walker hesitated. "Cal's not the father."

"Oh. That's interesting. Will the biological father be there, too?"

"No. Penny used an anonymous sperm donor. She had always wanted a family and the traditional route didn't seem to be working for her."

"I admire a woman with initiative." And one who volunteered to be a single parent. Elissa loved Zoe, but sometimes it was tough being the only grown-up around.

She glanced back at her daughter, who bounced

along with the music from Walker's portable CD player.

"I'm guessing your high-tech CD player has never heard a Disney sing-along CD before," she said as she faced front again.

"Not my style."

"Some of the tunes are catchy. We put that kind of music on when we're cleaning house."

He smiled. "Interesting choice."

Not that she could imagine him singing along as he dusted. Of course she couldn't imagine him dusting. Or doing anything mundane. She could picture him with a rifle or even a hunting knife. Better yet, bare chested with a hunting knife. Yum.

Her personal fantasy carried her through the next couple of miles, right up until Walker turned right at the base of a street and drove what felt like straight up.

"They live here?" she asked as she took in the old, elegant houses and the incredible views of both the city and the water.

"Uh-huh."

"Queen Ann Hill?"

"Uh-huh."

Figures. While she knew in her head that Walker obviously came from some kind of money, his current lifestyle allowed her to forget. "Where do Reid and Dani live? Next to Bill and Melinda Gates?"

"Reid has a houseboat. Dani's currently staying in Penny's old place." He glanced at her. "Why are you upset?"

"I'm not. It's just..." She shrugged. "I'm fine," she

said, not willing to admit the obvious wealth freaked her out. She'd read about the houseboats in Seattle. The crappy ones went for a million, while she'd had to pay off a fifty-dollar tire five bucks at a time.

They pulled in front of a pretty brick-fronted two-story house. While Zoe turned off the CD player and unfastened her seat belt, Elissa followed Walker around to the back where she collected the two boxes she'd brought and he grabbed the wrapped car seat.

"Ready?" he asked.

She was starting to question her judgment in accepting his invitation. What if his siblings were more like Gloria than like him? What if they resented her or looked down on her because she worked in a diner and hadn't finished high school? What if—

The front door opened and a petite, pretty woman with hazel eyes and a fabulous haircut stepped out to greet them.

"Walker," she said with a smile, but her gaze locked on Elissa and Zoe. "You made it."

"Hey, Dani." He paused and urged Zoe in front of him, then put his hand on Elissa's back. "This is Elissa. She lives in my building. And her daughter, Zoe."

Dani's smiled widened. "Wow. Okay. Nice to meet you. Come in. Everyone else is here. Hey, guys, it's Walker. And he brought a friend."

Elissa groaned, then elbowed Walker in the ribs. "You didn't tell them you were bringing me?"

"Penny always makes more than enough food," he said, obviously confused about her dismay.

"It's not about food," she muttered, wondering if

it was good news to realize that in some things, Walker was just as clueless as every other man on earth.

He escorted her and Zoe into a large open living room filled with presents and trays of food. Two men stood by a table. They looked enough like Walker for her to guess their identity.

A very pregnant auburn-haired woman waddled in. "A friend," she said, then stopped when she spotted Elissa and Zoe. "How nice." She smiled. "I'm Penny Buchanan. Oh, goodie. You brought me presents."

Despite her nerves, Elissa found herself laughing. "Congratulations on the baby," she said as she handed over her two boxes.

"Thank you." Penny eyed the box Walker held. "That looks big enough to be a car seat."

"You said it's what you wanted," he said, sounding slightly uncomfortable.

"And it is. Come on," Penny said, taking Elissa's arm. "You met Dani already. This is Reid," she said, pointing to the man on the right. "And Cal, my husband. This is Elissa and Zoe. Walker's friends."

"So we heard," Cal said pleasantly and shook her hand. "Welcome."

"Thank you." Elissa turned her attention to the other man and froze. He looked familiar. Incredibly familiar. The name clicked. "Oh my God. You're Reid Buchanan."

The Reid Buchanan. A Seattle native who had pitched major league baseball for ten years. He'd quit last season because of a blown shoulder. She still remembered—

"Hey, baby," he said smoothly.

Eek! She'd worked at a restaurant long enough to recognize *that* particular tone of voice. It came from a man who assumed a woman was interested. Uh-oh.

She carefully took a step back and leaned against Walker. "I've always been a bit of a baseball fan," she said. "This year I've been too busy to follow the season much, but usually I'm right there on my sofa, cheering."

Cal chuckled. "Nicely done, Elissa. Good deflection, quick recovery." He lightly punched Reid in the arm. "You gotta get over yourself, guy. Not every woman wants to be with you."

Reid shrugged good-naturedly. "Most of them do."

Elissa looked at Zoe, who was listening intently, and held in a groan. Hopefully her five-year-old would miss the nuance of the conversation.

Penny bent down to Zoe. "I've made margaritas for everyone else. They're a grown-up drink I don't think you'd like. But I also made these really cool berry slushies. I thought I was going to have to drink them all by myself, but maybe you could try one and if you like it, you'll have some."

Zoe nodded tentatively.

Penny straightened and held out her hand. "Why don't you and your mom come into the kitchen and you can have a taste?"

"Okay."

Zoe took Penny's hand. Elissa followed them and everyone trailed along behind.

Dozens of delicious smells filled the bright kitchen. While Penny poured a bright red drink from a blender into a glass, she glanced at the stove.

"Dani, give the front two pots a stir, will you? Cal, honey, check the bread in the oven. It should be toasted by now. Pull it out and put in the pastries. Reid, I need fifteen minutes on the timer. Elissa, are you up to zesting? I need one orange and three limes zested. Everything is in that bowl. Walker, there's a couple of big flank steaks on the counter. Could you cube them, please?"

In a matter of seconds, everyone was hard at work. Elissa zested her limes elbow-to-elbow with Walker.

"She really knows her way around a kitchen, huh?" Elissa said in a whisper.

"She could have been an Admiral," Walker murmured back. "Penny knows how to be in charge."

Elissa glanced at the pregnant woman who sat at the small table with Zoe. They were both sipping their bright red drinks. Zoe giggled at something Penny said.

This was nice, Elissa thought. Walker's family might be wealthy, but they were just like everyone else. No one seemed to be in competition with Gloria for an evil witch award, which was comforting. She was having a good time and even more important, Zoe was getting out and seeing a big family in action.

Elissa thought of her own family. They'd been on her mind ever since she'd found out Bobby was trying to get in touch with her. Sometimes she understood why her parents had made the decision they had, and sometimes she wondered why they couldn't love her enough to give her a second chance. They were missing out on their own grandchild. Zoe was growing up and these years could never be recaptured.

It had been their decision, she reminded herself. Their loss. Only now, watching the love and affection in Walker's family, she understood it was her loss, too.

"SHE'S NICE," DANI SAID, coming up to stand behind Walker as they watched Penny open a huge box her friend Naomi had sent.

"I think so."

"I like her daughter, too."

He looked at Zoe, who sat at her mother's feet watching intently as the presents were opened.

"She's a good kid."

"I'm glad you're dating," Dani said.

"I'm not."

His sister leaned close. "You can pretend all you want, big brother, but you have it bad."

"At the risk of sounding like an eight-year-old, do not."

"You can lie to yourself all you want, but don't lie to me. It's all there. The way you watch her, the way she watches you. We can all feel the heat."

He didn't bother to tell her that heat wasn't a relationship. Of course he wanted Elissa—what man wouldn't? She was an irresistible combination of sweetness, intelligence and caring. Plus, he'd kissed her and now he knew how good it could be between them.

"There are complications," he said, hoping to deflect Dani.

"Such as your reluctance to make a commitment? Why is that? If you let this one get away, you're a fool."

There was so much she didn't know, he thought. So much she would never know. They were, as Penny had said, a family of secrets and he certainly had his share.

Penny picked up the two boxes Elissa had brought. "You don't even know me," she said. "You really didn't have to do this."

Elissa grinned. "I've tasted your cooking now. Think of them as gifts of worship."

Penny laughed. "Okay, that kind of praise I can handle."

She opened the smaller box first. Inside were a pair of dangling earrings. Walker recognized them as Elissa's work. Penny gasped. "I love them."

Dani pushed past them and bent over the jewelry. "Me, too. Where did you get them?"

"I made them," Elissa said with a small shrug. "It's sort of a part-time job."

"I want them," Dani said.

Penny snatched them out of reach. "Get your own."

"I'd like to." She looked at Elissa. "Can you make a pair like that?"

"Ah, sure. Or I can do something different. I have a lot of designs."

Dani plopped down next to her. "Good. We'll talk when this one is done with her presents."

Penny reached for the second box. "I would like to point out that Elissa was the only one sensitive enough to bring the expectant mother a gift just for herself."

Cal patted her arm. "The baby is your present."

"Ha." Penny ripped the wrapping paper, then opened the white box. She reached inside and held up a small blanket in shades of yellow. "It's lovely. Did you crochet it yourself?"

"I wish," Elissa said. "My neighbor makes them. Doesn't she do beautiful work? I love how soft the yarn is."

"Mrs. Ford made me a blanket," Zoe said. "It's pink and has gold trim."

Penny leaned forward and touched the girl's nose. "It sounds like the perfect blanket for a princess."

Zoe beamed. "It is."

"We should have brought her," Walker said. Maybe with the old lady along, people would get off of him about dating Elissa.

"She's on one of her day trips to a casino," Elissa told him, then looked back at Penny. "My neighbor is fabulous. She's in her nineties and does exactly what she wants. She's sweet and feisty and I adore her."

"Sounds like everything Gloria isn't," Dani muttered.

"Elissa met her," Walker said.

Dani patted her arm. "You have my sympathy."

CHAPTER TEN

WHILE THE WATERFRONT was all about light and air and the view of the water, Buchanan's was about old-world atmosphere and intimacy.

Walker arrived at the restaurant shortly after lunch for his meeting with the staff and let himself in the front door. As he stepped into the cool, dim interior, he tried to remember the last time he'd been in the place. Two years ago? Three?

High-backed booths lined the perimeter of the main dining room, with more rows of booths in the middle. The only tables were for large parties and they were set up in the two alcoves and the private dining room.

He could hear voices coming from the back. The cooks would be prepping for dinner. Buchanan's had an in-house butcher who was responsible for cutting all the meat, which was responsible for earning Buchanan's its reputation. The regular menu had a token chicken dish along with a couple of pasta choices. The specials always included a single fish choice. But people came to Buchanan's to eat good steaks.

He glanced around at the red leather and dark

wood. The paneling was old, but well kept. The old-fashioned light fixtures had passed from outdated back to trendy.

He noted the folded piles of white tablecloths and other linens. Clean dishes were stacked on a long sideboard, ready to be put in place. By four that afternoon, the store would be vibrating with activity, but now there was only the low rumble of voices and the sounds of trucks in the street.

One side of the double swinging door opened and Ron Alcorn walked into the main dining room. Buchanan's general manager stopped when he saw Walker, then smiled and hurried toward him.

"I thought you'd come in the back door," he said as they shook hands.

"I wanted to look around first," Walker said. "The old place still looks good."

"We think so. Business has been excellent." His smile faded. "We're all very sorry to hear about your grandmother and wish her a speedy recovery."

Based on what Walker had seen at the main office, he doubted that. Gloria was obviously hell to work for. She made some drill sergeants he'd known look like choirboys.

"Thanks for your concern," he said. "She'll be out for several months. In the meantime, I'm going to be making a few changes."

Ron's tension was subtle but visible. Walker had an idea about the other man's concerns, but he decided to deal with them later. First he wanted to talk to the kitchen staff.

"Everyone in back?" Walker asked.

"Yes. You said not to bring in the waitstaff, so I didn't make this a mandatory meeting. A few of them came in on their own time."

"That's fine. You can pass on the message to the others when they show up for their shifts."

He led the way into the kitchen.

The restaurant had been built when real estate was cheap and labor practically free. There was room for nearly two dozen to work in the open space.

The grill dominated one wall, butting up to an old oven. The steaks would be seared on the grill, doused in butter, then finished in the oven so they didn't dry out.

Today there were fewer than ten cooks, including a recent culinary graduate who made the salads.

"Afternoon," Walker said. "Thanks for taking the time to see me."

The men exchanged glances, obviously wondering why he thought there'd been a choice.

"Most of you know my grandmother recently suffered a heart attack. When she collapsed, she broke her hip. While she's laid up, I'll be running the company, including Buchanan's. I've been over the numbers and everyone here is doing a damn good job. Sales are up, customers are happy and that makes my job easier." He turned to Ron. "You have a good staff. You pick good people. They work hard. I was a little concerned about the sick leave policy. It's not what anyone could describe as generous, so I'm increasing it by two days. You're still required to give notice, but otherwise, the change is effective immediately."

There was a moment of silence, followed by stunned applause.

Walker went over a few more minor points, then ended the meeting. After speaking with each person individually, he took Ron aside.

"Anything else?" he asked the manager.

Ron shifted uneasily. "Nothing I can't handle."

Walker had wondered if the other man would come clean or if he, Walker, would have to mention it first. He would bet Ron's reluctance was more about his fear of Gloria than his character.

"Someone's stealing liquor," Walker said flatly. "I went over how much you're buying versus how much you're selling and the numbers don't add up. Even spilling a bottle a day, you're still coming up short."

Ron swallowed. "I know," he admitted. "I'm trying to figure out who's doing it. I have a good idea, but I'm waiting to catch him. I didn't mention it before because…" He shrugged. "I wanted to present the problem and the solution."

He wanted to save his job, Walker thought, not really able to blame him. Hearing the news of liquor theft, Gloria would have fired Ron immediately.

"I'll give you a week," Walker told him. "If you haven't fixed things by then, I'll come in and fix them for you." He was willing to give Ron a little more time, but not to be taken advantage of.

"That's fair," Ron said. "So, how long have you been in the restaurant business?"

"About ten days."

Ron looked surprised. "You're good at it."

"I was in the Marines before that. I led men into fights I knew we might lose, in which a lot of them were going to end up dead. Compared to that, this is easy."

"JUST A LITTLE LOWER," Penny said with a moan as she lay back, eyes closed, body supported by several sofa cushions. "Oh, yes. Just like that."

Reid dug his thumbs into the ball of her foot and wondered what it was about women and foot rubs.

"Shouldn't Cal be doing this?" he asked.

"He should and he will when he gets home. In the meantime, you're here and I'm taking shameless advantage of you." She opened one eye. "Does this make you uncomfortable? Is it too intimate?"

"We're talking about your feet, Penny," he said.

"But it's something guys do to get women into bed." She opened the other eye. "You do realize I've never had a sexual thought about you? Even once. And now I can't imagine having sex ever again. I'm so huge and swollen. It's disgusting."

Penny was his friend, so he accepted her words in the spirit he knew she meant them. It wasn't as if he'd ever seen Penny as anything but another sister. As for Cal, well, his brother had his sympathy.

"Remind me never to have kids," he muttered.

"You're careful, you should be fine." She closed her eyes again and moaned as he pulled on her toes. "You're really good at this."

"Practice."

"When I feel human again, I must remember to ask one of your women what you're like in bed. I mean, you have numbers that would impress a rock star, but what's the style like?"

He thought of the screams and moans, not to mention the nail marks on his back. "I do okay," he said modestly.

"If your foot rubs are anything to go by, then you do better than okay." She placed her hands on her stomach. "Come out, come out, wherever you are. Mommy is more than ready to have you in this world."

"Just a couple more weeks."

"Easy for you to say. You can still sleep at night. I just lie there, hating how I feel. On the plus side, he or she is very active."

"Still don't know the gender, huh?"

"We want it to be a surprise." She thrust her other foot at him. "Have you been to see Gloria?"

"A couple of times."

Penny raised her eyebrows. "Really?"

"She's old and frail."

"Since when?"

He smiled. "Don't worry. I still know she's a snake, but I kinda feel sorry for her."

"Then you're the best one to handle her nursing care. How's that going?"

"I spoke with her doctor, along with a physical therapist. I have some names. We'll work three nurses in rotating eight-hour shifts, with a fourth to cover days off. Whoever Gloria hates the least will get the prized day shift."

"I'm impressed."

He scowled. "I'm not useless. I can do more than throw a baseball."

Not that he wanted to, but he didn't have a choice anymore. He swore silently, knowing better than to go down that road.

"Still, it's nice of you to look after this," Penny said.

"Cal and Dani are too emotionally tied up with Gloria to deal with it and Walker's running the business. Oh, Gloria said to bring the baby to her as soon as he's born."

"I assume that was an order," she said mildly.

"You bet."

She opened her eyes again. "I feel sorry for her, too. She had so much—a great business, a large family, and now there's nothing. You and Walker are neutral about her. Cal and Dani obviously dislike her. No one wants anything to do with her."

"It's not like you to be so kind," he said.

"I know. It's because I don't have to deal with her. When we're both back at work and she's bugging me about my menus and making snide comments about the food I cook, then I'll hate her, too. But until then, I can afford to be generous."

"Maybe Walker will stay in charge of things. He might find he likes running the company."

"I wish," she said, "but my luck's not that good. Besides, being in charge would mean sticking around. Walker doesn't like to do that. It means risking getting involved."

Reid stared at her. "What are you talking about? Walker left because it was his job."

"And why did he go into the Marines in the first place?"

"To screw with Gloria."

"I know that's what everyone says, but I don't believe it. I think there's way more to the story. Walker has always held himself a little apart from everyone. Maybe this time will be good for him. Maybe Elissa will be good for him. I really liked her and Zoe."

"They were all right." Elissa had been pretty and easy to talk to, which he liked in women he wasn't going to sleep with. Otherwise, conversation was a waste. "You're wrong about Walker. He doesn't hold back."

"What do you know about him?" Penny asked. "What do you know about his dreams? His fears? His deepest, darkest desires?"

"We're guys. We don't talk about that stuff."

"Exactly. You have me to talk to. Cal has me and Dani. Who does Walker have?"

"I don't know. His buddies from the Marines?"

"Have you met any of them? Does he bring anyone around?"

He felt uncomfortable with the questioning. What was it about women and feelings? "Leave Walker alone. He's fine."

"He's not, but I'm hoping he will be eventually."

"THERE ARE MESSAGES!" Zoe said excitedly as Elissa climbed out of her car after work. "Me and Mrs.

Ford listened to two of them when they called and there are even more."

"That's great," she said as she closed the car door and bent down toward her daughter. "Don't I get a hug?"

"Oh, Mommy." Zoe hugged her quickly, then pulled on her hand. "Come on and listen."

Elissa allowed herself to be dragged into the house. Sure enough, her normally quiet answering machine blinked excitedly. There were six messages and when Elissa played them back, they were all about ordering jewelry from her.

Apparently Dani and Penny had done more than just wear her creations, they'd talked about them. In the past ten days, Elissa had sold more than a dozen pieces and booked three at-home jewelry shows. If this kept up, she could actually start buying more expensive materials *and* open a savings account.

"You're famous, Mommy!" Zoe said with delight. "Everyone knows your pretty work."

"I guess so."

The phone rang.

"Hello?"

"Elissa Towers, please," said an unfamiliar female voice.

"This is Elissa."

"Oh, hi. I'm Marcia Bentley and I'm in charge of booking people into the Labor Day Crafts Fair we have every year. Are you familiar with it?"

Was Marcia kidding? It was the biggest craft show in the state. Elissa had gone several times, mostly to get ideas, and she'd been overwhelmed by the variety and quality.

"Of course," she said quickly. "It's wonderful."

"I'm glad you think so. One of my regulars has a family emergency and won't be able to make it. I've heard so much about your work that I wanted to offer you her spot. It's on one of the main aisles, very close to several food and drink vendors. Are you interested?"

Elissa sank onto a kitchen chair. Talk about a once-in-a-lifetime opportunity. "Of course," she said, barely able to speak from the shock of it all. "I'd love to be a part of the fair."

"Good. If you'll give me your address, I'll get the contracts to you right away. You can sign them and send me back a check."

Marcia filled in a few more details, then hung up with a promise to get the paperwork out that day.

When Elissa hung up, Zoe danced impatiently. "Who was that, Mommy?"

"A lady about the big Labor Day Craft Fair. She said I can have a booth."

Zoe grinned. "That's good, right?"

"It's the best."

Her daughter yelled with excitement, then ran through the open door in the kitchen to share the news with Mrs. Ford.

Elissa stayed in her seat and waited for her brain to stop spinning. This was incredible. Okay, yeah, the cost of the booth would set her back some, but she would more than make it up the first morning. Her biggest problem was inventory.

She got up and crossed to her workbench. Her finished jewelry was in boxes on an upper shelf. She would need several hundred pieces for that show—which meant hours and hours of work and using her emergency credit card to buy supplies, but it would be worth it. She could easily clear a couple thousand dollars *and* have enough money to pay off the bill when it arrived.

Talk about a lucky break. Or *was* it luck? Did Penny or Dani have anything to do with the invitation? Or Walker? She wouldn't be surprised if it was him. This was exactly the sort of thing he would do.

She found herself wanting to share her good news with him, only he wasn't home. These days he put in long hours at Buchanan Enterprises. She hadn't seen him in nearly a week. She missed him. Funny, six weeks ago she'd barely known who he was. Now everything seemed to remind her of him.

Ever since she'd run away with Mitch and had ended up in Los Angeles, she'd accepted that her taste in men sucked. But now, with Walker in her life, she wondered if that had changed. Had she at last found a good one? A man she could trust to always be there for her?

Because that's what she wanted—someone she could depend on to stick with her no matter what.

"YOU DON'T HAVE TO DO THIS," Elissa said stubbornly as she locked her front door. "You're busy. Go run your company."

"I'm coming," Walker told her. "You don't know what's going to happen."

She resisted the urge to roll her eyes. "Bobby's a kid."

"He's a guy and he's eighteen. Anything could happen. You haven't seen him in a long time. You don't know anything about him."

Walker had a point, if only a small one. "Fine. Waste your time pretending to be my bodyguard."

"It's my time to waste."

He led the way to his SUV and held open the passenger door. Zoe and Mrs. Ford had gone to the local senior center for an afternoon of scrapbooking. It was Bring Your Grandchild day.

Elissa was silent until they reached the 405 freeway and headed south. She was meeting Bobby in a coffee shop by Southcenter Mall.

"It's been a long time," she said as she looked out the window. "I have no idea what he'll look like. I was seventeen when I left. He was just a kid. He'll be practically grown-up by now."

"You can't change the past," Walker told her. "Regrets are a meaningless waste of time."

"So you never have them?"

"I try not to."

She was pretty sure everyone had regrets, whether about things done or left undone. If she'd known then what she knew now…

"I'm glad you came along," she told him. "I don't think Bobby is dangerous, but it's nice to have company."

He gave her a smile that made her insides quiver. What was it about this man that made her want to rip off her clothes and have at it right here in the front seat?

Sure he was good-looking, but that had never moved her before. So why Walker? Was it his strength, both physical and emotional? The way he always seemed to know when she needed a good rescuing? And speaking of that, when, exactly, had she lost the ability to get by on her own?

He mentioned something about one of the restaurants and they talked about work until he pulled up in the parking lot. Suddenly her stomach hurt and she wasn't sure she could catch her breath.

"I've done my best not to think about my family for over five years," she whispered. "Now that's not possible. Do you think he'll recognize me?"

"Have you changed much?"

She shook her head. "My hair is shorter. I used to wear it nearly to my waist. But that's the only real difference. Well, I'm older, but let's not talk about that."

She opened the passenger door and stepped into the parking lot. No strange young men lurked there, so she followed Walker inside.

There was a tall, nice-looking teenager in the foyer. Elissa smiled absently at him, then turned away. It was only his gasp of surprise that had her looking back at him.

"Bobby?" she asked, unable to believe this tall, broad-shouldered kid was her skinny little brother.

"Hey, Elissa." He tried to smile, but couldn't quite make it happen. "How are you?"

"Shocked. Wow—you're so grown-up."

His eyes were the same, she thought in amazement. So was his mouth. But his hair was darker and longer, and he was so big. Suddenly she was grateful to have Walker along.

She didn't know if she should hug him or shake hands. Neither seemed right so she settled for introducing Walker.

Bobby's eyes widened. "I never thought you'd get married."

"What? No. We're just friends. Walker's here for moral support."

Just then the hostess walked up and asked if they would like a table. Elissa asked for a quiet one and they were led to a booth in the back. She slid in first, then Walker sat next to her. Bobby was across from them.

The waitress appeared promptly. Bobby got a soda, while she and Walker asked for coffee. When they were alone, Elissa leaned toward her baby brother and studied his face.

"You look so different," she said.

"You don't," he told her. "Just prettier."

"Very smooth."

He shrugged. "I mean it. I've wondered about you. Ever since you called, I couldn't stop thinking about you and wondering how you are. I c-couldn't…"

Elissa was stunned when his voice cracked and tears filled his eyes.

"I'm sorry," he whispered. "Elissa, I'm so sorry. I never meant to hurt you. I was just so mad. When you left…"

"You didn't hurt me," she said, not sure why he was so upset. "I'm the one who ran away."

"I know… It's just…" He gulped the glass of water the waitress had left. "You know how they always were. With me, I mean."

She nodded, feeling more confused than anything else. "They loved both of us, Bobby. You had the added advantages of being the boy and being hard-won, but I know they cared about me."

At least, they had. Before she'd run off and they'd turned their backs on her.

Once again she wondered—would it have made a difference if they'd known she was pregnant? Would they have reconsidered? She was torn between wanting to understand their position and her anger at parents who would leave a child alone on the streets.

"They *did* care," he said earnestly. "I swear, Elissa. When you ran off, they went crazy. Mom cried for weeks. We put up flyers and offered a reward."

She winced. This shouldn't surprise her, yet it did and she felt more than a little guilty for what she'd put them through.

"I didn't know."

"It was bad," he said. "Dad wouldn't talk and Mom kind of lost it. She went away for a rest. I don't know what really happened. When she came back, everything was different."

Went away? Meaning what? A breakdown? Elissa didn't know what to think.

"If they were that upset, why didn't they want to talk to me when I called?"

"It wasn't like that. Oh, God..." Bobby brushed his hands over his eyes and stared at her. "Elissa, I'm the one. It's my fault. I never told them you called. When I said I'd talk to them, I lied. I didn't say anything. I'm sorry," he added quickly. "I was mad because it was like I didn't exist anymore. I hated you for what you'd done. But later, I kept thinking about you, all alone, and how you'd wanted to come home and I was the reason you hadn't."

Tears poured down his cheeks now. Elissa didn't know what to think. He hadn't ever spoken to her parents? They hadn't known she called? Maybe, just maybe, they hadn't rejected her.

She felt as if the world had shifted on its axis. All these years she'd alternated between hating her parents and vowing she would show them that she was more than capable, that she had never needed them for anything. All the struggling. Living in the halfway house while getting bigger and bigger with Zoe. Barely making it year after year.

Rage filled her, chilling her body and making it impossible to accept or forgive.

"I was pregnant," she said flatly. "When I called about coming home, I was pregnant, alone, broke and terrified."

Bobby dropped his head and began to sob. "Elissa, I'm s-sorry."

Sorry? He'd changed her life forever and he was sorry? She wanted him punished. She wanted him thrown out and forced to survive the way she had. She wanted blood and...

Walker took her hand in his and squeezed her fingers. “How old was he?” he asked.

Four words. Four simple words that put her world back in place and allowed reason to filter into her brain.

“Thirteen,” she said quietly. “Just thirteen.”

Thirteen and angry and stupid, she thought as Bobby continued to cry. An angry, stupid boy who had also had massive changes in his life.

She didn’t want to understand. She hated that she could see his side of things, but she did. Which meant she couldn’t hate *him.*

Oh, but she hurt inside.

“Do they know now?” she asked.

He shook his head. “I c-couldn’t say anything. I felt so bad about what I did, plus I thought it would hurt them more. They would know they’d missed their chance with you and it was all my fault.”

That sounded a whole lot more like he was covering his own ass than worried about his family.

“I didn’t tell them I’d found you,” he continued. “I didn’t know if you’d want me to.”

Her parents hadn’t rejected her. Her parents didn’t hate her. Maybe they never had. She felt tears in her eyes and a crazy desire to be in her mother’s arms. She wanted to be little again and never grow up.

Nothing was as she thought. All the decisions she’d made were based on something that might not be true.

“I worked all summer so I could hire a detective,” Bobby said, raising his head slightly and looking at her. “I wanted to find you and tell you the truth.”

He looked young and scared—two things she could relate to.

"Are you going to talk to them?" he asked. "They still miss you, Elissa. They don't talk about you much, but your pictures are everywhere and at Christmas, they always fill your stocking."

A couple of tears escaped and ran down her cheeks. Walker's strong hand gave her something to hold on to and she squeezed his fingers as hard as she could.

She remembered her stocking. She'd made one for Zoe that looked just like it.

"My mom's the one who taught me to sew," she told Walker. "She could make anything."

"She would be impressed with what you're doing now," he told her.

Maybe, she thought, considering the possibility for the first time. How odd. Nearly as strange as thinking she might not be alone in the world anymore. That she might have people she could lean on.

Just then the waitress appeared with their drinks. She set them down without saying anything and hurried away. No doubt the display of emotion made her uncomfortable. Elissa knew she wouldn't want to be serving this table.

"What are you going to do?" Bobby asked tentatively. "Do you want me to tell them?"

"No," she said slowly as she wiped away the tears. "I need time to think about all this. I guess I'll go by and see them." Should she do that? Should she call first? Dropping in on them didn't seem right, but she wasn't sure she could figure out what to say on the phone.

"Can you tell me when?" Bobby asked. "I want to be there to tell them what happened. I'm ready for them to know what I did."

There was something in the way he said the words that made her think he meant it. Part of her crowed that it was about time, while another part of her appreciated his willingness to grow up and accept the consequences.

"Sure," she said. "I have your cell number. I'll give you a heads-up when I'm ready to make an appearance."

He nodded, then swallowed. "I know you hate me, Elissa. I deserve that. But I hope, eventually, we can, you know, be close again."

"I don't hate you," she said reluctantly. "I'm not happy about what you did, but I can almost understand it."

Tears filled his eyes again. "Thanks. I, ah, wondered. Did you keep the kid?"

For the first time since walking into the diner, she smiled. "Yes, I did. Her name is Zoe. She's five. Which I guess means you're an uncle."

Bobby brightened at the thought. "Yeah? Cool. Can I meet her sometime?"

"Sure."

Suddenly she felt as if she'd run a marathon. Her body ached and she couldn't seem to catch her breath. She dug ten dollars out of her jeans' front pocket and tossed it on the table.

"We have to go," she told her brother as she released Walker's hand and slid out of the booth. "I'll be in touch."

Bobby scrambled to his feet where he topped her by at least six inches. "You promise?"

She nodded.

He leaned forward and wrapped his arms around her. She resisted the embrace for three heartbeats, then hugged him back.

Walker was silent on the way to the car.

"You have to tell me what you're thinking," Elissa said. "I can't read your mind."

"I want to beat the crap out of him."

"I'd probably have to stop you, but I appreciate the support."

He held open the passenger door. "You really think you could stop me?"

She stared into his dark eyes. "Physically, no. But I could try reason. Or a food bribe."

"Pie might work."

She smiled. "That can't have been pleasant. Thanks for coming with me."

"You're welcome. How are you doing?"

"I don't know. Everything is different. When I woke up this morning, I understood everything about my past and how it made me the person I am. Now that's all changed. I'm angry and I can't figure out why or at whom. Everything is different."

"You're still who you were before."

"Maybe. But for how long? I've gotten used to being alone. Now I have a family again."

"Is that a bad thing? You like being with people. Mrs. Ford, your friends from work."

"That's different. I chose them."

As he walked around to his side of the SUV, she wondered if she'd chosen Walker or if he'd chosen her, and if, in the end, it would matter.

CHAPTER ELEVEN

WALKER MOVED THROUGH the large space. He wasn't sure where he was—maybe a ballroom in a hotel. There were so many lights everywhere—lights and noise and the sound of women's laughter.

He circled the crowd, aware of being out of place. He was thirsty and while there was a glass in his hand, he couldn't lift it to his mouth and drink. Was it too heavy? No, it was his arm. He couldn't move his arm.

The lights faded, then blurred. He couldn't see the edges of the room, only the women. All of them suddenly facing him, staring, pointing. They were angry—he knew that much—but he couldn't say why.

"I don't know Ben," one of them said, and he recognized her from one of his many "Ashley" visits.

"I don't know Ben," another said. He remembered her, as well.

Then he realized he knew all of them. He'd spoken to them and they hadn't been able to help him.

"I don't know Ben."

They repeated the words over and over until he thought his head would explode.

"I don't know Ben. He has no one. No one, not

even you. You let him die. It should have been you. It should have been you."

The voices got louder and louder. He tried to answer, to tell them he already knew it should have been him, but he couldn't speak. He lashed out, but the women only came closer and closer. Finally he took a step back and then he was falling and falling only to wake up on the hard floor, his heart racing, his body aching and his soul dark and battered from the truth.

It *should* have been him.

ELISSA PARKED across the street from the familiar house and looked at the rambling two story where she'd grown up.

There were changes. The once-green siding was now beige. The pine trees flanking the west side of the property had grown even taller and the small Lexus parked in the driveway was nothing like the old Taurus station wagon she remembered.

Maybe she should have called, she thought as she turned off the engine. Maybe it would have been better to give her parents a little warning. The problem was, she hadn't been able to figure out what to say. Just showing up would be shocking, but it would force a conversation.

She'd called Bobby earlier that morning and he'd told her both her parents planned to be home most of the day. So that was something. She wouldn't be left standing alone on the front porch.

Knowing she was only wasting time, she pocketed her keys and walked to the front door where she rang the bell. She heard a faint "I'll get it," then the door opened and, for the first time in eight years, her mother stood in front of her.

Leslie Towers was just shy of fifty, with highlights in her brown hair and hazel eyes that Bobby had inherited. Elissa noticed a few more lines, but otherwise her mother looked exactly as she remembered her. Only more surprised.

"Hi, Mom," Elissa said, wishing she hadn't left her purse locked in her car. Holding it now would give her something to do with her hands. As it was she shoved them in her jeans' pockets and tried to figure out what she should do next.

Tears filled her mother's eyes and her mouth trembled. "Elissa?" she asked, her voice wavering. "Elissa, is that really you?"

Elissa nodded.

"Leslie, who is it?" her father asked as he walked through the living room. "I'm not buying any more magazines. We already get too many as it—"

He stopped next to his wife and stared. "Elissa?"

She nodded. "It's me. A little older—and hopefully wiser."

Her father, a tall man who wore glasses, reached toward her. "Elissa?" he repeated.

"Oh, Kevin," her mother breathed. "She's back."

Suddenly Elissa found herself pulled into the house and into their embrace. She was hugged and squeezed until she couldn't breathe, but breath didn't seem important just then. She closed her eyes and felt as if she'd finally, *finally* come home.

There were tears all around. Elissa hadn't expected to cry, but there she was. Bobby appeared and joined the group hug, then they separated and there was a moment of awkwardness.

"I don't know what to say," her mother admitted, staring at her. "I can't believe you're here."

"In the flesh," Elissa said with a small shrug.

Her parents exchanged a glance as if not sure what to do next. They seemed happy, yet wary, which made Elissa wonder again if she should have phoned ahead and warned them she was coming.

"Let's go in the kitchen," her father said.

Her mother nodded, then led the way.

"Sit, sit," her mother told everyone as she pushed Elissa into a chair at a glass-topped table. "I'm sorry. I'm in shock, I think. I can't seem to figure out what to do next. Are you all right? Are you hungry?"

"I'm fine," Elissa said, glancing around. Gone were the tile countertops and the harvest-gold appliances. Now the kitchen counters were dark granite and the ovens and cooktop a gleaming stainless steel. "You remodeled the kitchen."

"About four years ago. I couldn't stand scrubbing that awful grout or dealing with the stove anymore." As she spoke, she pulled out a pitcher of iced tea and several glasses.

Elissa's father took the seat across from hers and reached for her hands. "How are you really?" he asked.

The contact felt both familiar and strange. She squeezed his fingers. "I'm good, Dad. How are you?"

"Fine. Fine. Still at the bank, of course."

"Your father's been made district manager," her mother said proudly.

"Wow, that's great, Dad."

Her mother carried the iced tea glasses to the table. "Come join us," she told Bobby who hovered in the background.

He reluctantly took the fourth chair.

Elissa accepted a drink, then sipped while everyone stared at her.

There was a surreal combination of old memories and a new situation. She wasn't sitting in her usual chair. The view was wrong, even discounting the remodel. But she couldn't remember where she usually sat.

"You've grown up," her father said.

"You're so pretty," her mother told her. "You're all right? Healthy and everything? Do you have a job?"

"I'm good. I'm a waitress and I make jewelry on the side."

Saying it all aloud made her want to cringe. She'd been raised to believe she would go to college and have a career, not work in a diner and barely get by. Still, she'd survived on her own under difficult circumstances and she refused to apologize for that.

"So you don't need money?" her father asked.

Elissa stiffened. "No, Dad. I didn't come here for money or anything. I wanted to get in touch with you."

"Kevin, don't," her mother said. "Elissa's back. That's a good thing."

"I know that," her father said. "I'm happy. It's just..." He frowned. "You were gone for so long. We didn't know what happened to you. Your mother..."

"I missed you," Leslie said, interrupting him and smiling. "Where do you live now? In Washington?"

Elissa remembered what Bobby had said about her mother having to go away for a rest. Had she had some kind of emotional collapse? Guilt settled in her stomach. If something had happened, Elissa's disappearance was the reason.

"I live here. In Seattle."

"Seattle?" Her mother's mouth trembled. "So close. For how long?"

"A few years now."

"But you n-never..." Leslie pressed her fingers to her mouth. "I see."

Elissa's father released her hand. "You didn't want to call and let us know you were all right? You didn't think that was important?"

Bobby swallowed and stood. "That's my fault." He cleared his throat. "Mom, Dad, I have to tell you something. I'm really sorry. I know you're going to be angry and upset and I can't blame you. What I did was wrong."

Both their parents stared at him. "This isn't a good time, Bobby," Leslie said, her voice shaking. "Not a good time at all."

Kevin put his hand on her shoulder. "Just relax, Leslie. We're fine. Everyone is fine."

Bobby shifted his weight and looked as if he would rather be run over and left for roadkill than speak. "I, ah, I'm the reason Elissa never got in touch with you before."

As Elissa still didn't know how she felt about what Bobby had done, she didn't feel the need to come to his rescue now. She kept quiet while he explained her phoning and what he'd told her.

Her mother turned back to her. "Elissa, no! How could you believe that of us? Of course we wanted to talk to you, have you come home. Do you know what we went through? Do you know how hard it was? How horrible?" She stood and faced her son. "Bobby, why? You saw. How could you have kept this from me?"

She took a step, then gasped and sank back in the chair. Kevin was at her side in an instant.

"Leslie?"

"I'm fine."

Elissa half rose, then sat down. "Mom, are you all right?"

Her mother gave her a shaky smile. "Of course. This brings back so much. Don't worry about me."

The words said all the right things, but the darkness in her eyes told another story. Her leaving had changed everything, Elissa thought unhappily, and not for the better.

"I'm sorry," she said. "I'm so sorry I ran away. I should have called."

"You should have come home," her father snapped.

Elissa stiffened.

"She tried," Bobby said. "Don't blame her, blame me."

His willingness to take all the responsibility surprised her. "It wasn't just that," she told her brother. "I shouldn't have left in the first place."

"I'm better, Kevin. I'm all right," her mother said, then patted her husband's hand. "It was that boy, wasn't it? The one you were dating."

"Mitch," Elissa said. "Yeah, he's the one I ran away with. We ended up in L.A."

"I knew it," her mother said, fighting tears. "I just knew it."

"We looked in Los Angeles," her father said. "There were too many kids down there. On the streets, in shelters."

Elissa hated thinking what they must have gone through. "I wasn't in either place. I lived with Mitch for a few months. Then we broke up and I got a job with another band." She decided to gloss over the more sordid aspects of her earlier life. "It turns out I had a great knack for finding cheap accommodations and making other travel arrangements, so that's what I did. I was paid in cash and usually rented a room in an apartment with a bunch of girls, so there's no way you could have traced me."

There was that look again, between her parents. What were they thinking? That she was nothing but a disappointment? That they'd expected no more of her?

"I can't believe you thought we wouldn't want to talk to you," her mother said. "I loved you, Elissa. You were my daughter."

Elissa did her best not to read too much into the past tense of the words. "I know, Mom. I was young and stupid and…" She almost said *scared,* but quickly changed it. "Confused. I felt a lot of guilt and what Bobby told me actually made sense at the time. Looking back, I know I should have asked more questions."

Her mother pointed to the empty chair. "Sit down, Bobby. What you did was wrong, but we'll talk about it later."

Her brother did as requested, but he looked as if he wished he could disappear. For the first time since hearing his story, Elissa felt compassion for him. What he'd gone through couldn't have been easy.

"I screwed up big-time," she said honestly. "I'm so sorry. If I could change what I did, I would."

Her mother attempted a smile. "It's all right. You're home. That's enough, isn't it, Kevin?"

Her father nodded slowly, as if he would need more convincing.

Elissa's throat tightened. Somehow she'd expected open arms and unconditional acceptance. Not questions and a messy past.

Her mother drew in a breath and squared her shoulders. "So, what brought you back to Seattle?"

Interesting question, Elissa thought, not sure how much she wanted to tell her parents. "I got pregnant," she said, knowing there was no point in hiding that. "That's why I called home. I was scared…anyway, it all worked out."

Her mother paled. "You have a baby? I have a grandchild?"

Elissa nodded. "Her name is Zoe. She's five and

about to start kindergarten. She's wonderful, Mom. Smart and funny and curious about everything."

"A grandchild? Oh, Kevin." The tears started again.

"You named her Zoe?" her father asked, his voice a little warmer now.

"After Grandma Zoe."

"She would have liked that," he said gruffly.

"Who's the father?" her mother asked. "I take it you two aren't together anymore?"

"He's dead," she said, knowing there was no point in trying to explain the Neil portion of her life. Sometimes she still didn't understand it herself.

"But he was a rock singer?" Her father asked the question in the same tone of voice he would use to ask if she recently picked up head lice.

"And a songwriter." She drew in a deep breath. "I know I made a lot of mistakes. Everyone does—mine just had permanent consequences. But I survived. I have a good life. Zoe and I are happy together. I made it and I guess I owe a lot of that to what you taught me when I was growing up."

"If you'd respected what we'd taught you—" her father said, but her mother cut him off with a shake of her head.

"What made you come back now?" her mother asked.

Elissa looked her brother. "Bobby hired a private detective to find me. He wanted me to know what he'd done and try to make things right. Once I knew you hadn't turned your back on me, I wanted to get in touch."

"Of course we wouldn't turn our backs on you," her mother said. "Elissa, you're our daughter and we love you. We'll always love you. No matter what."

Would they? Did they? Then why had the detective who found her been hired by her brother rather than her parents? In L.A. she'd been living off the grid, but in Seattle she had a job, an apartment, credit cards. She wouldn't have been that hard to track down. Neil did it on a regular basis. But they hadn't.

She knew in her heart that if something had happened to Zoe, she would never have stopped looking, no matter what. So what had made that different for her parents?

ELISSA SPENT THE REST of the afternoon working on her jewelry and thinking about the meeting with her family. While they'd said all the right things and had expressed interest in meeting Zoe, she couldn't help feeling that something was off.

Maybe it was her. Maybe her fantasy of the homecoming was so based in perfect television families that she couldn't deal with reality. Maybe she was wishing for the moon.

Needing someone else's counsel, Elissa waited until Zoe was asleep, then walked up to Walker's apartment.

"I understand that we have an undefined relationship and that we both agree that we're not getting involved," she said when he'd opened his door. "But I like to think we're friends, and right now I need someone to talk to, so you're going to have to suck it up and be that person. Do you have a problem with that?"

He stared at her for a couple of seconds, grinned, then asked, "Do you want me to bring liquor?"

"Sure. If you have it."

"I'll be right down."

He appeared at her front door less than a minute later. She sighed in appreciation at the bottles of vodka and tonic he brought nearly as much as the way he looked in worn jeans and a loose T-shirt. There was something to be said for a winning combination of potentially mind-numbing booze and male eye-candy.

"You have ice?" he asked.

"Always. I even have a lime."

She led the way into the kitchen where she got out her ice tray, then collected two glasses. Her lime was a naked little thing, huddling in the fruit basket.

"I used the zest earlier," she said as she sliced it into eighths. "We had Caribbean tacos for dinner. Lots of citrus."

He poured, she squeezed, then they silently toasted each other. She took a drink, then sighed as the cold, tart drink settled in her stomach.

"Perfect."

He led the way into the living room. When they were both settled on the sofa, he asked, "What happened?"

She took another drink. "I went to see my parents today. It was weird. Like being in a time warp. Everything was nearly the same, but it wasn't. I felt uncomfortable and angry and confused. My mom is different. More emotionally frail. My dad was critical. I wanted a big party to celebrate my homecoming and all they had were questions."

"In some ways it's easier not to have to answer to anyone. Now you're back in their lives. There are going to be explanations and misunderstandings. None of you are the same."

"I get that. Time has passed. But I feel like everything is my fault. I'm the one who left and set this all in motion."

"You're only responsible for yourself."

"Am I?" She clutched her drink in both hands. "I think my mom had a breakdown or something. *That's* my fault."

"No, it's not. Her reaction to the situation is her responsibility."

"Isn't that like saying if I hit someone with my car, their injuries are their fault because they weren't fast enough to get out of the way?"

"Not the same at all. Yes, you ran away and there were consequences. But you can only be blamed for some of them. If she lost it because you ran away, then she wasn't strong in the first place."

"That's a little too tidy for me. What I did pushed her over the edge."

"Why do you feel it necessary to take on all the pain?"

Good question. "Habit, maybe. I'm always the one responsible."

"With you and Zoe, sure. But not anywhere else. I'm not saying you were right to run away. It was a dumbass teenage response to whatever was going on. But you made it and without a lot of outside help. That's good. Yes, your parents suffered and you're the reason. But you didn't make your mother have a breakdown. There was something already in her that caused that."

"I hope you're right. My guilt card is pretty full." She sipped her drink. "Family stuff is never easy."

"I know."

"You never talk about your parents. Just Gloria and the siblings."

"Sounds like a rock band," he said. "No parents. They died a long time ago. They weren't very close. I guess they'd been in love once, but by the time I was aware of their relationship, they were just going through the motions. My dad drank a lot. I think it was to escape from his mother. My mom was quiet—sad, I guess. Gloria made her life hell in more ways than we'll ever know."

She hated thinking Walker hadn't had a wonderful childhood. "I'm sorry."

"Don't be. I had my brothers and Dani. We were there for each other."

"That's something. I can picture the four of you banding together against the evil queen."

He smiled. "No one ever called her a queen, but there were plenty of other names."

"I won't ask."

"I stayed away from her as much as I could. So did Reid. Cal and Dani tried to make it work with her. Cal even went into the family business out of college. He lasted longer than I would have. Dani got her master's and came back home, prepared to run the empire. Gloria stuck her in Burger Heaven and never let her out."

"Why? Dani's great. Please don't tell me it's a woman thing. That only men can run the company."

Walker hesitated, then said, "Dani's not a Buchanan. Our mother had an affair with some guy. Dani is the result. We knew, but Dani didn't. Gloria couldn't forgive her for not being a Buchanan. It's the ultimate sin."

"I'd never have guessed," Elissa said, shocked by the revelation. "I won't say anything, of course."

"I appreciate that. The truth is coming out, but Dani's still dealing with it herself."

"Isn't it funny how one moment in time changes everything? If I'd only come home after Mitch and I broke up. If one of my parents had answered the phone instead of Bobby."

"If Ben hadn't pushed me aside and taken that bullet."

She looked at Walker and saw he hadn't meant to say that aloud.

"How much do you think about that?" she asked.

He shrugged. "It should have been me."

"Why? Why do you think it was your time and not his?"

"Ben had something to live for."

"Don't you?"

Is that what caused Walker to hold back? He didn't think he was worthy? She supposed it was possible, but why would he believe that? What had happened to put him on that path?

"I get by," he said at last.

"You do more than that."

He shrugged. "I'm running out of Ashleys. What if I don't find her? I owe him that."

"You're trying. He would understand the effort."

Walker finished his drink, then looked at her. "Ben was like a puppy. He was always sniffing around, wanting to be friends. He wanted to hang out together, do things."

She read the truth in his eyes. "You didn't."

"He was a kid. We had nothing in common."

"You feel guilty."

"Maybe," he admitted.

"Is finding Ashley going to make up for what you didn't do while he was alive?"

"No," he said simply, "but it might let me sleep at night."

His pain called to her. Maybe it was a female thing. Maybe it was a mom thing. Or maybe it was just how she felt when she was around him. Regardless of the cause, she put down her drink and moved closer.

"It's not your fault," she said, cupping his face in her hands and staring into his dark eyes. "You didn't kill him."

"It should have been me."

"You keep saying that. It's not as if the bullet had your name on it. It was circumstances, a quirk of fate. Yes, it's horrible that Ben's dead, but your suffering doesn't bring him back. Based on the little you've told me about him, he wouldn't want you doing it, either."

"I don't know. I think he might get a kick out of it."

"Don't be smart with me, mister."

One corner of his mouth turned up. "Or you'll what?"

In less time that it took for light to travel across the room, the mood shifted. What had been friendly and sharing became charged with emotion and sexual energy.

She was aware of how close they were, how she leaned against him and how her fingers touched his face. She could feel his heat and the stubble on his cheeks. His gaze locked with hers, drawing her in, grabbing her with the erotic threat of never letting her go.

Suddenly she didn't want to be let go. She was tired of being sensible and thinking things through. Yes, he was the wrong man, but so what? She was used to that. She would deal with the consequences later.

She shifted so that she was on her knees, then dropped her hands to his shoulders. At the same time, she leaned in and pressed her mouth against his.

He had to have known what she was going to do and for a second she wondered if he would resist. But the instant her mouth brushed his, he wrapped his arms around her and pulled her onto his lap. Then she was sprawled across him, his tongue in her mouth and his hands everywhere.

He kissed her deeply, sensually, plunging into her as he mimicked the act of lovemaking. At the same time, he ran his palms up and down her legs. His long fingers seemed to touch every inch of her as they moved teasingly close to the apex of her thighs, then drifted away.

She clung to him, needing to hold something solid as her mind darted from sensation to sensation. She hadn't been with a man since she'd left Neil and given birth to Zoe. Long-dead nerve endings exploded to life and begged for the sustenance of Walker's touch.

Her breasts swelled and her nipples got so hard, they hurt. Between her legs she felt a gush of moisture. Her insides were heavy.

He broke the kiss and nibbled his way along her jaw. She tilted her head to give him more access, inviting him to continue. At the same time she longed to rip off her clothes so they could get right to it. She was ready—hell, she'd been ready for years.

He put his hands on her waist and urged her to sit up. Not sure what he was doing, she complied, only to have him shift toward the center of the sofa and then position her so she straddled him.

At first the beauty of the situation escaped her. Then, as she leaned in to kiss him and she felt his hands slide from her waist up her rib cage, it all became clear.

Even as his tongue circled hers, teasing, playing, inviting, he cupped her breasts. His large hands covered her curves. Exquisite pressure had her moaning. Every inch of her was so sensitized, she thought she might pass out from the pleasure of him touching her like that.

When he brushed his thumbs against her nipples, it was all she could do not to scream.

Sensation rocked her. Her skin was on fire, yet she was so hungry, nothing was enough. She deepened their kisses, needing everything he had for her. He met her demands and clamped his lips around her tongue, then sucked hard.

More, she thought frantically. She needed more.

He read her mind, or maybe just the way she writhed against him. While he kept one hand on her breast, he moved the other between her legs.

Even through the layers of panties and jeans, she felt the pressure of his fingers. She pressed down and he pressed up and when he found that one spot of pleasure, she groaned.

A very tiny, sensible part of her brain told her this was not a good idea. That she would regret this later. But the part of her that had done without for so long didn't really give a damn.

So when he unfastened the button on her jeans, she didn't protest. And when he moved her to one side, she helped push them down. And when he slipped to the floor between her legs, turned to face her and bent low to kiss her intimately between her thighs, she could only breathe a prayer of thanksgiving.

The man knew what he was doing, she thought in relief as he pressed his tongue against her swollen center. He moved slowly, leisurely, forcing her to keep pace with him when her choice would have been to run as fast as possible to the finish.

He circled around, then returned to that one spot

and began to lick it over and over. At the same time, he slipped a finger inside of her and rotated it.

One finger. That was all, but it was enough. Her muscles clamped around it and held on. Deep in her belly she felt a pulsing kind of tension. The kind that warned her she wasn't going to hold on for very long.

"No," she moaned. "Not yet." She had to make this last longer than thirty seconds.

But she couldn't. Not when he continued to rub his flat tongue against her sensitive flesh and she could feel his hot breath on her. Not when he thrust in and out of her, teasing her into an arousal that was surely going to make her explode.

She clutched the edge of the sofa and tried to think of something mundane. Laundry. Yeah, laundry. Then she imagined him taking off his clothes so she would do the laundry. She imagined him hard and naked and plunging into her and she was gone.

At the first contraction, she drew her legs apart, exposing all of herself to him. She moaned, she held in a scream, she begged him never to stop.

When she'd wrung every last bit of pleasure from the experience, she put her feet on the floor and wondered what on earth she was supposed to say. Getting naked hadn't been on her to-do list, despite all the fantasies she'd had about him.

He rested a forearm on her bare thigh, kissed her belly and said, "I'd like to take credit for that, but I think it's more a reflection of how long you've been out of the game."

She felt a blush climbing her cheeks. “Yes, well, I’m sure it’s both.”

He rubbed his thumb across her mouth. “It just happened, Elissa. It doesn’t have to mean anything.”

Which meant what? That it didn’t mean anything to him or there was no pressure?

Her gaze dropped to his very obvious erection. “And for our second act,” she said lightly.

“No second act.”

He stood and then pulled her to her feet. She felt very strange, standing there naked from the waist down.

“I wanted to do that,” he said. “I don’t get to do it enough.”

“But…”

“No buts.” He kissed her forehead. “I’m a guy who doesn’t want to get involved. You’re not the fuck-and-run type.”

Okay, but who would be doing the running? Him or her?

“We can’t just leave you like that,” she said.

“I’ve been through worse.”

“But we could…” Her voice trailed off as she wasn’t sure what she was offering.

“No, we couldn’t. Trust me. This is better.”

And then he was gone. The front door closed behind him, leaving her feeling exposed in more ways than just being undressed.

What had just happened? How could he do that to her and just leave?

CHAPTER TWELVE

REID GLANCED at the résumé in front of him. Sandy Larson, age thirty-five. She had a bunch of initials after her name, which he assumed was a good thing for a nurse.

So far he'd had three interviews with women who were qualified, but didn't come close to having personalities that could stand up to Gloria. He was already bored with the process, so he was thinking he'd just hire them and call it a day.

Someone knocked on his office door promptly at ten-thirty. He glanced up and saw a tall, large-breasted blonde with big green eyes and a smile that could light up Chicago.

"It really is you," she said with a laugh. "When I got the information from the service and they said Reid Buchanan, I'd hoped, of course, but I never dreamed I'd actually get a chance to meet you."

She strolled into his office, her hips swaying in obvious invitation. "I'm Sandy and I'm a huge fan."

He stood and walked around his large desk. "Really. Follow the game?"

"Less now that you're not playing." She held out her hand. "This is a real thrill for me."

He took her fingers in his and held them longer than he should have. When the welcome in her eyes didn't fade, he knew he was in.

"So you're a nurse," he said, leading her to the sofa in the corner.

"Uh-huh. About twelve years now. I did ten in a hospital and then I went into private duty nursing. I get to meet the most interesting people…like you."

He sat down next to her on the leather and angled toward her. "My grandmother is a very demanding woman."

"That's okay. I've had crabby patients before. Mostly they're mad about something. I've found if I can figure out what, I can deal with them."

"Intuitive and smart. You're quite a package."

She smiled. "Do all the women fall for your lines?"

"Yes. Are you going to be an exception?"

"Now why would I want to do a stupid thing like that?"

ZOE WAS AS EXCITED as if it were Christmas morning. She'd climbed into Elissa's bed shortly after five in the morning and demanded to know how long until they left.

While Elissa wrestled with a lot of unresolved feelings and questions, her daughter felt only the thrill of suddenly discovered grandparents. Now there was more family, potentially more people to play with and go out with and visit with. So many of her videos and DVDs involved extended families, and now Zoe could be a part of all that. Elissa understood her excitement and tried to respect it, but somehow she couldn't shake the tightness she felt in her chest.

Of course it was hard to know how much of that was about her parents and how much of it was about what had happened with Walker. While she couldn't regret the pleasure he'd given her, the circumstances were a little confusing. He'd been aroused, and she didn't think he was involved with anyone. So why had he walked away like that when she'd made it clear she was interested in making things mutual? Were his reasons about her? Should she start getting a complex or checking out her butt in a mirror?

Considering the ice cream she'd downed after he'd left, the latter wasn't a very good idea. And in an effort to be rational she had to admit his reasons might not be about her at all.

She paused in the act of stroking on mascara. "I need a vacation." She shook her head, finished applying her makeup, then walked into her bedroom to get dressed.

Zoe had been ready since six-fifteen and she hadn't gotten that way quietly, which meant Elissa had been up way too early after a fairly late night. Not that she'd slept. One would think that much pleasure would be mind-numbing, but not in her case. She hadn't been able to stop thinking about what had happened.

"Mommy, hurry," Zoe said from the doorway.

Elissa glanced at the clock. It was barely after eight. "Honey, we can't get there until at least nine, which means we aren't leaving until about eight-forty. Can you keep yourself busy until then?"

"Okay."

Her daughter disappeared. Elissa debated what to wear. Jeans seemed too casual, but she didn't want to put on a dress. Still, it seemed important to make a good second impression. Maybe khakis and a blouse.

Fifteen minutes later she'd chosen her clothes and had even used a round brush to give her hair a little curl. As she put away her blow-dryer, she realized the apartment was very quiet. Too quiet.

A quick search told her Zoe was not inside. Elissa stepped into Mrs. Ford's kitchen, but her place was dark and still. Panic exploded as she debated what to do next, when she heard footsteps overhead. Not unusual, except that this time there were two sets.

As it was unlikely that Walker had left her living room and gone out to find someone to share his bed, she had a good idea who his visitor was.

Seconds later a smiling Zoe opened Walker's door. "I told him about my new grandma and grandpa and he wants to come with us. Then he can meet them and they can meet him. Isn't that great, Mommy?"

Elissa had planned to avoid her sexy neighbor for at least ten days. She didn't know what to say after what had happened. "Thank you" seemed weird, but not acknowledging the subtle but measurable movement of the earth seemed rude.

The object of her musings stepped behind Zoe. "She's pretty excited about all this," he said.

Simple, polite words. Nothing to indicate that the previous night he'd kissed her so intimately, he'd made her see stars.

"She had me up at five," Elissa said, then held out her hand. "Sorry she came up here to wait. Come on, honey, we should go finish getting ready."

"I asked Walker to come with us," Zoe said, ignoring her mother's hand. "He should come with us. Grandma and Grandpa will want to meet him, too."

Walker watched the emotions chase across Elissa's face. She hadn't planned on seeing him again so quickly, not after the previous night. She was embarrassed and confused and he would guess she didn't understand why he'd ended things the way he had.

He wondered if she would feel better if she knew how hellish his night had been and how many times he'd started down the stairs to finish what they'd started.

He hadn't acted and he wouldn't tell her how tempted he'd been. This way was better—this way was safest for all of them. He knew who and what he was, while all she saw was what he let her.

"Zoe, Walker doesn't want to come meet my parents," Elissa said. "I'm sure he has plans and even if he doesn't, he would be a complication."

Right. Someone she would have to explain and with everything going on with her parents right now, not a good idea.

He crouched down and smiled at Zoe. "I'll go another time."

"Now," the little girl said stubbornly. "Mommy always lets me bring a friend. You're my friend, too."

"Zoe, no," Elissa said flatly. "We're going now."

Her daughter took her hand and allowed herself

to be led away. Walker told himself it was better this way. That both he and Elissa needed time.

But five minutes later she was back on his porch.

"I have a flat," she told him, not looking him in the eye as she spoke. "I replaced the second rear tire, but I didn't get a spare. Randy's place won't open for a while and I was wondering if you could give me a ride to my parents'. I don't want to explain a cab and I don't really want them here."

He found it interesting that she was more willing to deal with him than have her family at her house.

"I'm happy to," he said. "I'll drop you off and then come get you when you're finished."

She raised her gaze to his. "No. If you can stand it, you might as well come in." She sighed. "I meant that to come out more graciously than it did."

"I understand."

"Do you? Do you know how confusing all of this is? A month ago I didn't know who you were. Three months ago, you weren't even living here. I don't know what happened last night—I mean I know, but I don't understand why you didn't…"

She shook her head. "Damn. I promised myself I wouldn't get into this with you. It's just hard. I keep going to the typical weenie female response, wanting to know if it was my fault."

"It wasn't," he told her, not sure how she could ever think it was.

"I didn't think so. But it's not… Men don't do that sort of thing and then leave."

"Agreed."

"Are you going to tell me why?"

"Mommy, I'm ready," Zoe called from downstairs.

"Let me get my keys," he said, more than willing to use the distraction.

Before he could turn away, she touched his arm. "You weren't the one who... You didn't do anything to my tire, did you?"

He wasn't surprised by the question. In her position, he would have wondered the same thing.

"If you have to ask," he said slowly, "then isn't it better that things ended when they did?"

"WILL GRANDMA MAKE cookies sometimes?" Zoe asked from the backseat of his SUV. "On TV grandmas always make cookies."

"I'm sure she will," Elissa told her. "My mom makes the best peanut butter cookies."

"Yeah!"

Zoe practically danced with excitement but Walker sensed Elissa wasn't quite so enthused. Her tension grew with each passing mile. When he turned onto her street and headed for the house she'd pointed out as theirs, he half expected her to bolt from the car.

He parked and a middle-aged couple stepped out of the beige house. Elissa released her seatbelt.

"We're here," she said in a bright voice thick with tension.

Walker got out and walked around to the passenger side. He opened the door for both Elissa and Zoe. Elissa grabbed his wrist and dug her nails into his skin.

"You're staying."

He didn't know if she meant it as a request or a statement. Either way, he nodded.

"Hi," Elissa said with a smile. "Mom, Dad, this is my friend Walker. He lives in my building. I had a flat this morning and he gave me a ride. And this is Zoe."

Elissa reached for her daughter, but the five-year-old wasn't standing next to her. Walker glanced down and was shocked to see the child hovering just behind him.

Elissa crouched down. "Honey, it's okay. Don't be scared."

"It's all right," Elissa's mother said, staring at the little girl with a painful mixture of hope and disappointment. "It will take her a while to get used to us."

Elissa's father stepped toward Walker. "I'm Kevin. This is my wife, Leslie."

Walker shook his hand. "Good to meet you, sir."

They were ordinary people who had lived normal lives. No doubt they had loved their daughter as much as they could and hadn't understood why she'd run away. He wanted to tell them it wasn't their fault. When you least expected it, life took a shit on your head. People died or stopped loving you or went away. And it wasn't anyone's fault.

But he knew they wouldn't understand.

Leslie Towers crouched in front of Zoe. "Do you know who I am?" she asked.

Zoe put one hand on the back of Walker's leg. "My grandma."

"Then you know it's my job to love you and spoil you, right?"

Zoe nodded without speaking.

"Do you like cinnamon rolls?" Leslie asked.

Zoe nodded again.

"I just made some. Would you like to help me put on the icing?"

Another nod.

"Good." Leslie stood and held out her hand. Walker found himself in the unfamiliar position of encouraging Zoe to go with her grandmother.

Elissa moved close. "Thank you," she said in a low voice. "I guess the excitement only lasted until reality set in. She'll be okay now."

"What about you?"

"We'll have to see."

AN HOUR AND A HALF LATER, breakfast was over and Walker found himself in Kevin's den, ostensibly to watch a baseball game, but in truth to be grilled by Elissa's father.

Walker wanted to tell him there was no point to this—that he wasn't going to be in Elissa's life very long, that he wasn't someone she was going to settle for, but he knew the other man wouldn't understand.

"What sort of work do you do?" Kevin asked when they were seated in matching recliners.

"I left the Marines a couple of months ago. Right now I'm working in the family business. We own a few restaurants."

Kevin frowned. "Buchanan's?"

"That's one of them."

"Impressive. Good. Elissa needs a steady sort of man in her life."

Walker wished he were back in Afghanistan. "Elissa and I are just friends, sir. As for the type of man she needs, you're going to find she's a very different person than you remember. She has put together a life for herself. With time you'll see—"

Zoe ran into the room and headed directly for him. As she scrambled up onto the seat, he put his hands under her arms to help her.

"They're fighting," she said, her eyes wide. "Mommy and Grandma."

Kevin sighed. "I was afraid of this. I'd better go see what's going on."

Walker nodded, but his attention was on the child. Why had she run to him?

She sat on his lap as if she'd done it a thousand times before. As if he were a part of her life.

"Grandma wanted to know what Mommy was really doing with those rock bands," Zoe said in a low voice. "Mommy got all choky and said she hadn't done anything wrong. Grandma said something about dugs and I ran away."

He suspected the comment had been about drugs rather than dugs, but he didn't correct her. She was five and didn't need to know the difference.

"Why is Grandma mad at Mommy?"

How to answer that? "They didn't talk for a long time," he said slowly. "When people don't talk, they get confused."

"So if they talk now, they'll stop being mad?"

"It may take a little time."

"How long?"

"I don't know."

She sighed, then leaned against him. "I'm never going to stop talking to Mommy."

"Good for you."

He spoke without thinking, intensely aware of her slight weight as she relaxed against him. Just like that—as if she were safe. As if he would never hurt her or abandon her. As if she could trust him.

DANI TYPED on the computer, pulling up previous specials. She agreed with Penny's philosophy of not repeating items on the same menu. Obviously popular specials would be offered again at The Waterfront, but she was determined to make sure there was a different mix of soup, salad and entrée specials every time.

Normally the head chef would handle this, but Edouard refused to take on any more responsibility. He was already complaining about the longer hours while Penny was out on maternity leave. Luckily, Edouard was nearly as good a chef as he was a complainer.

It was late, after midnight, and the only sound came from the front of the store where the cleaning team made their way through the dining room. Dani liked this time of night, when she could feel that she was one of only a handful of people still awake. It was like being part of something special and unique.

She hit a few more keys, then sent the file to the

printer. The menus would be easier to compare when she could lay them side by side. After all, there was a lot on the line for her. She wasn't just filling in to help a friend, she was adding substance to her résumé. Once Penny had the baby and returned to the restaurant, Dani would be moving on. Right now she had the pleasure of knowing how much her presence here made Gloria crazy, but that wasn't a reason to make a career choice. In a couple more months she would be ready to go out and do her own thing.

She rose and crossed to the printer on the far side of the office. As the machine silently spit out paper, she heard someone walking down the hall. She stuck her head out and saw Ryan leaving his office. At the sight of him, her stomach flipped over a couple of times.

"You're working late," she said, hoping her smile said "I'm a friendly colleague" and not "boy, do I have a crush on you."

"I could say the same thing." He walked toward her. "I've been running numbers for the first half of the month. What's your excuse?"

"Specials for the menu. I don't want to duplicate an exact selection we had before. How are the numbers?"

He stood in front of her, close enough that she had to tilt her head slightly to still meet his gaze.

"Excellent. We're still filling up most nights, which makes me wish there was a way to expand the dining room."

Dani winced. "Not without making the kitchen bigger. We're running at capacity back there. You bring in any more customers and the chefs will be cooking in the alley."

"We could barbecue back there," he said with a grin. "People would think it was nouvelle cuisine."

"You underestimate our customers."

"Maybe." He looked up. "What about expanding to a second floor? I'll bet there's room up there. We could put in a second kitchen."

Dani considered the possibility. "It's a huge renovation and speaking from experience, you'll never get Gloria to go for it."

"Gloria isn't in charge right now."

"Unless you can get it done before she's back, I'd suggest you wait." She frowned. "To be honest, I have no idea what Walker would think of the idea. If you're serious, I guess you could run it past him."

"I might."

He tucked a strand of hair behind her ear. The light brush of his finger on her skin made her shiver.

"Why Walker?" Ryan asked quietly. "Why aren't you in charge of Buchanan Enterprises? You have the brains, the education and the experience. You could have done a hell of a job."

His words pleased her even as she knew there was no way she was going to tell him the truth about her family. Not yet. It would only break the mood, plus she'd yet to find a casual way to throw "hey, did I mention I'm not really a Buchanan" into a conversation.

"How do you know all that about me?" she asked instead.

"I checked out your file."

"Really? I'm not sure I approve of that."

He shifted until they were almost touching. "I wanted to know more about you."

Words to get lost in, she thought as her gaze locked with his. Suddenly it was difficult to breathe and she found herself wanting to place her hands on some part of his body. At the moment, pretty much any part would do.

"You could have just asked," she pointed out.

"All right. I will." He bent down and brushed her mouth with his. "Tell me everything."

Which, under other circumstances, would have been an excellent plan. Only right now, she was too busy savoring the feel of his mouth on hers and loving the way he wrapped his arms around her.

He drew her against him. She let herself lean against his hard body. She parted her lips and he teased her tongue with his own.

They were kissing, she thought in amazement. Kissing and everything about the experience was so different from being with Hugh. It had been ten years, she thought hazily since she'd kissed anyone else. Ten long years that had ended in broken promises and too many tears on her part.

"I should have done this ages ago," she murmured.

Ryan raised his head. "Done what?"

"Kissed you."

MONDAY MORNING WALKER woke up in a crappy mood. He wasn't sure of the cause. Maybe the awkwardness yesterday between himself and Elissa was to blame. Maybe it was the need to keep moving that had begun to bother him more than usual. Maybe it was the growing sense that he wasn't going to be able to find Ben's Ashley.

Whatever the cause, he started the day ready to rip someone's head off. As that wasn't possible, he did the next best thing. He visited his grandmother. The way he was feeling, Gloria couldn't do much damage.

He found her on the cardiac care ward, in a large private room. She was sitting up in bed, several pillows behind her head. The TV was off and a book lay on the table next to her, but when he entered the room, she was staring out the window.

"It took you long enough to visit," she said by way of greeting.

"Good morning. How are you feeling?"

"I've had a heart attack and I broke my hip. How do you think I feel?"

"But your spirit remains intact."

She glared at him. "I've spoken with the doctors. I should be leaving here in a few days. Apparently there is no way around two weeks in a skilled nursing facility. But once the break heals enough, I'll be going home."

"So he told us. Reid is already looking into hiring private duty nurses."

"Reid," she said with a sniff. "How wonderful. I'll have attendants with large breasts and no brains. That should speed my recovery."

He smiled for the first time that morning. "Reid

will choose competent people," he said, thinking they would also have to be patient and thick-skinned to deal with Gloria for eight hours straight.

"What's happening at the company?" she asked. "What changes are you making? I know you are, so don't try to deny it. You won't be able to resist meddling."

"Business is great," he said easily, ignoring the insult as he pulled up a chair and sat down. "No one has quit in nearly a week."

"You say that like it's a good thing. If they're too feeble to handle the pressure, they should go."

"Why do you feel compelled to frighten your staff?" he asked conversationally. "Who does it help?"

"I don't frighten them. I have high standards."

"You have a love of terrorizing."

"What do you know about business? You've been playing soldier for the past fifteen years."

More than playing, he thought. But he wasn't going to get into that with her. Despite the tough words, she looked…frail. Not a word he would have ever used to describe Gloria. But it was true. She was pale and without her carefully applied makeup, she seemed much older. Her white hair hung limp and even in what he would guess was a designer nightgown, she appeared small and helpless.

"You're not still seeing that woman, are you?" she asked. "She's a complete waste of your time."

All his worry for her evaporated. "Not your business," he told her, not willing to give her the pleasure of saying he wasn't. Not in the way Gloria thought.

"I forbid it," she told him.

"By what power? Are you going to fire me?"

"I'm your family. You will respect me and do what I say."

"Not so much," he said as he stood. "I'm going to head to the office now. I'm sure Cal and Reid will be by soon."

"As they should," she told him. "But not Dani. Tell her I don't need to see her. She's not family."

CHAPTER THIRTEEN

ELISSA TOSSED ASIDE the tiger's eye she'd been working with. The small stone bounced on the desk and came to a stop by a few freshwater pearls.

Nothing was going the way it should tonight, she thought irritably. She felt more restless than creative. How had everything gotten so out of hand so quickly? Her life used to be relatively simple. Sure, it was a financial struggle, but everything else was fine. Suddenly she was dealing with family and Walker and too many orders for her jewelry. Although based on how Walker had bolted after taking her tire in to be fixed, she had a feeling he was going to be less of an issue in the future.

Which was starting to piss her off. How dare he do that to her and then disappear? It wasn't polite. It wasn't reasonable. Why did he get to decide?

Zoe was already in bed, so when Elissa heard Walker drive up, she hurried to her front door and stepped out into the night. She waited until he was nearly at the stairs leading up to his apartment, then said, "I'd like to talk to you."

He didn't appear startled, which probably meant

he had known she was there all along. Had he planned to just walk past her without stopping?

She motioned to her open front door, then waited until he'd gone inside to follow him. But once they stood facing each other, she suddenly didn't know what to say.

"How was work?" she asked, feeling stupid.

"Good. Busy. I stopped by to see my grandmother and that always puts things in perspective."

Gloria Buchanan was not a topic to make Elissa sleep better that night.

"I… I'm sorry you had to come to my parents'," she said, which wasn't at all what she'd planned but now seemed appropriate. "It can't have been comfortable."

He shrugged. "It wasn't that big a deal."

"I hadn't realized they wouldn't accept my statement that we were friends. My father admitted he grilled you."

"It's a guy thing."

It was a waste of time. She wasn't looking and he wasn't interested. She got that. Well, part of her did. Her body continued to ignore the message.

"Thanks for talking to Zoe," she said. "I don't know why I thought I could reconcile with my family and not fight with my mother. It's scary the way we've picked up right where we left off. Shouldn't the eight years apart have made a difference?"

"It will. Give it time."

She motioned to the sofa. "Want to sit down?"

She thought he might refuse, but then he surprised

her by taking a seat. She sat across from him in the club chair.

"She won't believe anything good," Elissa told him. "I explained that while I was with a rock band and even sleeping with a member of the band, I didn't get into drugs. She'll accept that I slept around and didn't mean to get pregnant, but she won't believe me about the drugs. She kept asking if I was still using and did I want Zoe exposed to that. I hated it."

"Maybe she's trying to help."

"Could she do it in a less annoying way?"

"Maybe she doesn't know how."

"I hate it when you're reasonable." But this wasn't what she wanted to talk about. "Why did you do it?"

He drew in a deep breath. "Can't you accept it and let it go?"

"Not really." She opened her mouth, then closed it. "I don't know what to think. We're neighbors and you've been great. You've helped me and Mrs. Ford, and Zoe likes you. I know you're worried about getting too close to her and I appreciate that. You've made it clear you're not interested in anything with me and I have a plan to avoid men for another thirteen years, so I'm okay with that. But something has happened here and not talking about it isn't going to make it go away."

"Are you angry? Do you want me to apologize?"

"No to both. I just want to know why."

He was quiet for so long, she began to think he wouldn't answer. She had the feeling he was going to simply walk out and she would never see him again.

But finally he said, "I didn't plan on leaving the Marines when I did. I was going to stay in until they kicked me out because I was too old. But one day I woke up and I couldn't do it anymore. I couldn't kill, I couldn't send men off to die. There was already too much blood. So I left and I came home. Only there isn't a home anymore. I have my brothers and Dani, I have money, but there's nothing else. Nothing permanent."

His emptiness burned her with an aching cold.

"I do it on purpose," he continued. "I stay away, disconnected. It's my choice. But sometimes there are temptations I can't resist. Like you."

Elissa thought of herself as many things, but never a temptation. "Me?" she squeaked.

He shrugged. "The way you move, the way you smell, how you never give up. I knew better but I wasn't willing to act on that. I made love to you because I needed to, Elissa. I needed to kiss you and touch you. I wanted to know what you felt like. How you tasted."

She felt herself blushing and getting aroused. His words were as powerful as his touch had been.

"Then why did you stop there?" she asked.

"Have you ever been in love?"

The question came out of nowhere. "I… No. I thought I loved Neil, but I loved what I wanted him to be."

"I have. Once."

Unexpected pain cut through her. Something dark tightened her chest. "Who is she?"

"Her name was Charlotte and she was my high school girlfriend. I took one look at her and knew I was going to spend the rest of my life with her."

Elissa got a bad feeling inside. She wanted to stop him talking, but at the same time she was desperate to know what had happened between them.

"She transferred in my junior year of high school," he continued. "She was beautiful. Tall with red hair and the biggest green eyes I'd ever seen. I introduced myself and I guess she felt it, too, because we were together every minute after that."

"Sounds nice," Elissa managed through a very dry throat.

"It was. I knew she was the woman I was supposed to marry. We decided to go to college in California together and then get married after graduation. I never had to propose, we both just knew. We were each other's first time, the night she turned seventeen."

Elissa had to force herself to sit still. She wanted to curl up in a ball and press her hands to her ears. She wanted to order him out of her apartment and demand he never return.

Instead she listened.

"One afternoon when we were making love, I felt something in her breast. It hadn't been there before. I told her and she told her mom and she went to the doctor. It was cancer. Breast cancer."

Elissa blinked. "But she was too young."

"That's what we all thought. But there are about five hundred cases every year in women under twenty.

Charlotte was one of them." He shifted so he sat on the edge of the sofa and rested his elbows on his knees.

"She had a lumpectomy. Because she was so young, the doctors didn't want to take her breast. No one knew, except me. I remember walking next to her in the hallways, careful to keep on the side where she'd had her surgery so no one would bump her. I remember how she cried the first time we made love afterward, how she was afraid I wouldn't still love her and how long it took for her to believe that I would never stop."

Elissa drew in a shaky breath. She didn't know what to think, what to feel. The knot in her gut told her the story wouldn't end well.

"It came back," he said flatly. "By April of our senior year they realized their mistake in treating the cancer so conservatively. It was back and it was everywhere. She was given less than six months to live."

He stared at the floor. "She couldn't tell me herself. She had her mother do it. I was scared, so scared. I didn't want to believe it and then I knew I couldn't do it. I couldn't watch Charlotte die. She knew it, too. When I went to go see her, she saw it in my eyes. She cried and I cried and she told me to go away and never come back."

"But why? To spare you?"

He nodded. "I knew she needed me. I knew she wanted me to stay. But I pretended her words made it okay and I ran." He raised his head and looked at her. "I told everyone I went into the Marines to screw with Gloria, but that's not true. I went in because I couldn't stand to watch Charlotte die. I disappeared the day after graduation. I never called, I didn't leave a note. I just walked out on her."

Elissa hadn't seen that coming. She stiffened in surprise.

"Her mother called me," he said. "She begged me to come home. She said Charlotte needed me. It would just be for a few more weeks. That this was her baby and she would do anything to convince me. She asked for herself. Charlotte never said a word. I joined the Marines and went to boot camp."

"When did she die?" Elissa asked softly.

"August. She wrote me a letter saying she loved me and knew I loved her. I couldn't bring myself to read it for a year. I never saw her family again. They moved away."

He stood and moved toward the door. "That's who I am, Elissa. I'm the guy who couldn't be there for the woman I loved. I would have died for her, but I didn't have the balls to watch *her* die. Don't trust me with anything important because there are better than even odds I'm going to let you down."

He stepped out into the night and was gone.

Elissa let him go. She sat alone in her living room and cried. Whether it was for herself, Walker or a brave young woman who had faced too much too early, she couldn't say.

"WE'RE HAVING an intervention," Mindy said the following Tuesday when she, Elissa and Ashley had locked the front door of the diner. Frank had already left to go to the bank and the cleaning crew wouldn't be there until later, so it was just the three of them.

"For who?" Elissa asked, although she had a good idea.

"You."

Ashley nudged her onto a stool at the counter, then crossed to the ice-cream freezer and grabbed a scoop.

"You're not yourself," Ashley said. "It's been coming on for a while, but in the past couple of days, something's gone very bad."

Elissa winced. "I'm sorry. I didn't mean to make it so obvious."

"And yet you did," Mindy said with a grin. "Come on. You know we love you. Tell us what's wrong."

Elissa hesitated more because she didn't know where to start than because she felt like keeping secrets.

"It's that guy," Ashley said. "Isn't it?"

"Partly. It's also about my family. My parents. They live here in Seattle."

Both women stared at her openmouthed.

One of the things Elissa had liked best about working here was the lack of questions about her past. It was understood that everyone had secrets and they weren't expected to share them. Now she gave her friends the Cliff Notes version of her past, starting with her running away and finishing with her Sunday-morning visit with her folks.

"I don't know what I think about any of it," she admitted. "I'm confused. On the one hand, it's nice to have family again, but on the other, I don't know. Now they know I'm here and we're involved and

I'm the one who ran away so why am I so angry with them?"

Mindy moved next to her and gave her a hug. "Because they went on to have lives that didn't include you. Because they didn't suffer enough."

Elissa had a feeling she was right. "I hate thinking that. It's shallow and selfish."

"It's human. You went away and the world went on. Look how much you changed. They changed, too. It's going to take time to figure out this new relationship."

Elissa nodded, then accepted the chocolate milk shake Ashley passed her. "I'm just so confused. It's not just them. It's Walker."

Ashley and Mindy exchanged a glance. "I knew it had to be a guy," Mindy said. "He seemed the likely candidate." She dipped a spoon into her milk shake. "He's good-looking, has money and is single. What's the problem?"

"I would just like to make it clear that this is a theoretical discussion. I'm not actually interested in a relationship."

Ashley rolled her eyes. "Of course you're not."

Elissa ignored that. "He's emotionally unavailable. He's told me and told me and now I'm thinking maybe he's telling the truth."

"If you don't want a relationship, that matters why?" Ashley asked.

Elissa winced. "Did I say theoretical?"

"I don't think it's a theory anymore," Mindy told her. "Do you?"

Elissa didn't know how to answer. A week ago she might have admitted interest. But now…

Hearing about Charlotte had changed everything. He'd abandoned the one person he claimed to love. That scared her.

"I want someone who's going to be there," she said slowly, more to herself than them. "I've done the narcissistic, self-absorbed guy relationships already. I don't want that. I want…"

"You want it all," Mindy said with a sigh.

"Don't we all?" Ashley said. "Someone who makes us laugh, who is supportive and willing to be there through the tough stuff. Why is that so hard to find? I'm willing to do the same for the guy in my life." She sipped her milk shake. "Is it guys or is it us?"

"It's a pain in the ass," Mindy said. She looked at Elissa. "How bad is it? Are you completely in love with him or can you still escape, emotionally I mean?"

Elissa dropped her spoon into the glass. She felt her eyes widen and her mouth drop open. "I am *not* in love with him."

"Uh-huh." Mindy shook her head. "Whatever you do, don't sleep with him. Women tend to bond when they do that. I hate it, but it's true. God knows when I sleep with a guy, everything changes. I think it's hormones—some biological need to mate. I read about it once. Whatever it is, avoid it." She frowned. "You haven't slept with him, have you?"

"Of course not," Elissa said hotly, confident that

what they had done didn't count. At least not technically.

"I told you," she continued, "I'm not getting involved."

Ashley smiled. "I hate to be the one to break the news, but you *are* involved and it doesn't seem to be getting any better. You're going to have to deal with it, and him."

"There is no us. There's barely a him," Elissa insisted.

"Keep saying that," Mindy told her. "Maybe one day it will be true."

WALKER PARKED IN FRONT of The Waterfront. The restaurant wouldn't open for several hours, but he was there for a meeting with the new general manager.

As he stepped out of his SUV, his cell phone rang.

"Buchanan," he said.

"Hi, it's Vicki. I'm sorry to bother you but you had a call from a gentleman named Bob Rickman. He says you'll know who he is." She read off the number.

"I'll take care of it," he said and hung up. He hadn't talked to Bob in a couple of years, not since he'd left the Corps to start his own security company.

Walker punched in the number and asked for his friend. He was put through immediately.

"I heard you were out," Bob said, his voice hearty and loud. "I thought you'd be in until they carted you away in a box."

"Me, too, but things changed."

"Apparently. Hey, what are you doing with yourself?"

"Running the family business."

Bob laughed. "That won't last. I have a better offer. I'm expanding, Walker, and I need good people. People like you. I'm talking big bucks and international security in some pretty dangerous places. Long hours with plenty of compensation. Island vacations, hot-and-cold running babes, you name it. You could make a fortune working for me."

"Or get dead," Walker said easily. Death was the downside. The upside was when he saw men with guns, they would be real.

Bob laughed. "Sure, nothing's free, but you're smart. You know how to keep your head down. Besides, it's not as if you're going to make it where you are. Come on, Walker. I know guys like you. Hell, I used to be one. The civilian world is all well and good, but we're not like them. We live on the edge. This is where you belong."

"I don't think so."

"Don't say no," Bob told him. "Think about my offer. You have my number."

"I'm not going to change my mind."

"Give it time. You'll get bored and I'll be waiting."

Walker disconnected the call. Maybe Bob was right—maybe he never would fit in here, but he wasn't going back.

He crossed the walkway and entered the restaurant. It was cool and dark inside. He could smell garlic and something simmering that made his mouth water.

But instead of thinking about food, he found himself thinking about Elissa. He hadn't seen her in several days, and he didn't expect to for a long time. Not after what he'd told her. Now that she knew the truth, he understood she would want to keep her distance from him.

He made his way to Dani's office. The door was partially closed. He pushed it open without knocking and saw his baby sister locked in the arms of the new general manager.

"I must be early for our meeting," he said wryly as they both turned to stare at him.

"Sorry," Dani said with a grin as she stepped away from Ryan.

Walker ignored his sister and kept his attention on the other man. Ryan straightened and offered his hand.

"Walker," he said.

"Ryan."

They shook. Walker wanted to squeeze until he heard bones pop, but he resisted the momentary pleasure.

Ryan and Dani exchanged a glance. "It'll be okay," she told him. "Give me a minute."

Ryan nodded and left her office. Dani turned to Walker.

"Don't yell at him."

"Interesting behavior."

Her humor faded. "I mean it, Walker. Okay, yes, you're right. This isn't something we should be doing at work, but we were and so what? It doesn't hurt anyone." She paused and her smile returned. "I like him. He thinks I'm sexy and after what happened with Hugh, I deserve that."

He could have resisted almost anything but Dani's smile. "Is it going anywhere?"

"I don't know. I want to say yes, but we haven't known each other for very long and I'm still going through my divorce. So I'm not sure. But given my choice, I'd want it to be."

"Don't get hurt," he told her.

"I won't. This time I'm keeping my heart out of play until I'm sure. But what we're doing is really nice."

"I don't want details."

"Are you sure?"

"Oh, yeah."

It was good to see Dani happy again. Hugh had been a real bastard, first asking for a divorce—after Dani had nursed him and supported him for ten years—then blaming the breakup on Dani. That was bad enough, but finding out he was cheating on her, as well, had made things really tough.

"I should let you get to your meeting," she said.

"It should be your meeting."

"No, I don't want the job. I mean it," she told him. "When Penny's back, I'm leaving. Right now it's fun to thumb my nose at Gloria. I know it makes her crazy to have me here, but eventually, I'm going to want to get back to my actual career."

"Anything I can do to help?"

"Not at the moment. You'll always be there for me. I appreciate that." She smiled. "Don't get mad at Ryan for being involved with me. It's not his fault. I'm just too darned irresistible."

SATURDAY MORNING ELISSA checked Zoe's small suitcase three times.

"I have everything," her daughter told her patiently.

"I know. I just want to be sure." Elissa ignored the fact that anything forgotten could be delivered in less than thirty minutes—much like a pizza. "You're going to have a good time," she said, much more for herself than for Zoe.

"I know." Her daughter beamed. "Grandma and Grandpa are taking me to the zoo this afternoon. And we're making cookies and then we're watching TV tonight. It's gonna be really, really fun."

"It is."

Elissa had been looking forward to the time alone. She could use it to work on inventory for the craft show. But now that it was actually time for Zoe to leave, she didn't want her to go.

"This is your first sleepover," she said. "It might seem strange at first."

"Mommy, I'm five. I can do this."

Before Elissa could answer, her mother pulled up. Zoe ran to the front door and flung it open.

"I'm ready," she called.

Elissa moved more slowly, trying to think up excuses to keep Zoe home. Unfortunately, nothing came to her.

She walked to the open door and smiled. "Hi, Mom."

"Hi, girls." Her mother turned to Zoe. "Are you ready?"

"Uh-huh. I'm packed. I even brought my sleep teddy."

"Good for you."

Elissa picked up her suitcase and then put it down. "It's her first time away from home," she said. "She's only five."

"She'll be fine. Don't worry. I've raised children of my own."

"I know. It's just…"

Her mother waited patiently, but Elissa couldn't say what it was. So she shrugged and carried Zoe's suitcase to the car.

Zoe followed with her worn bear and placed it carefully on the backseat. Then she ran back to the house.

"I'm going to say goodbye to Mrs. Ford," she yelled.

"Okay." Elissa crossed her arms over her chest and waited until Zoe disappeared into the house before turning to her mother. "She likes a glass of water before bed. Not a big one, or she'll have to get up. And sometimes she doesn't eat all her dinner, which is fine. I never make her finish it."

"I know all this," her mother said. "It's what I did with you."

"Okay. Right." Elissa couldn't shake her feeling of dread. "Look, I think it's too soon. Zoe's too young and we need more time for her to get to know you."

Her mother's hazel eyes narrowed. "More time? You mean the time I would have had if you'd come home when you'd found out you were pregnant? The time I would have had if you'd never run away in the first place?"

Elissa took a step back. "What?"

"I've done my best to be patient and understanding," her mother said in a low angry voice. "But don't push me, Elissa. I'm hanging on by a thread."

"*You're* hanging on? What have you got to be upset about?"

"What? How about the fact that my daughter disappeared for eight years? *Eight* years. We didn't know if you were dead or alive. One day you were simply gone. Do you have any idea what that was like? Do you know how many nights I waited, desperate for a phone call or any word at all, yet terrified of what it would be? I half expected them to find your body. But they didn't and in a way the not knowing was worse."

Her mother's voice was heavy with emotion and she looked as if she were going to cry at any moment. At that point, Elissa didn't much care. It was all she could do to ward off the unexpected attack.

"All this time you were fine," her mother continued. "Completely and totally fine and you couldn't be bothered to let us know. Do you know not a day has gone by that I haven't thought about you, prayed for you, wondered where you were and what you were doing? Do you know what your incredibly selfish disappearance did to our family? To your brother? He lost his childhood. We were so busy looking for you that we couldn't spend time with him."

"I called," Elissa said quietly, unable to deal with her mother dumping on her this way.

"Talking to a thirteen-year-old boy doesn't count," her mother yelled. "Why didn't you talk to me or your father? Why didn't you call back? Do you know the pain you caused us? Do you know what it was like to take your picture to the police, to put up posters, to offer a reward? Do you know that they told us you were probably dead and that we should try to get on with our lives?

"I could have forgiven you," her mother said. "With time. But you have a child, Elissa. You know what it's like to love a baby, to hold her in your arms. You know how big that love is and how it never goes away. You knew and you still didn't call me. You still left me in pain."

Something inside of Elissa burst open and years of pain flew out.

"You stopped looking," she screamed back. "You stopped looking! I've been here for *five* years and it took that same teenage boy to find me. I was right here but you had already stopped looking. You stopped caring. You went on with your life. I would *never* stop looking for Zoe. Never!"

Her mother stared at her. "You say that now, not understanding what I've been through. Do you know why I stopped? I had to. I had a breakdown. Your father came home one day and found me curled up in the corner. I couldn't deal with losing you anymore. So I went away and they medicated me and I learned not to hurt so much."

"By giving up," Elissa said bitterly. Her worst fears had been confirmed. She wasn't sure whom she hated more—herself for making this all happen or her mother for not being strong enough to keep looking no matter what.

Her mother's mouth tightened. "You're right. I gave up."

Zoe bounced through the front door and ran toward the car. "I'm ready," she yelled.

"I'll have her back tomorrow by six," Elissa's mother said, then she helped Zoe into the car and fastened the seat belt.

Elissa felt as if she'd been hit with a steel beam. Even her bones hurt. Emotionally, she was an open, raw wound. She could barely wave back when Zoe called "Goodbye."

The small Lexus backed out of the driveway, then drove down the street. Elissa felt herself begin to tremble. Her muscles gave way and she would have fallen, except for a strong pair of arms that caught her.

She recognized the scent and feel of the man, even as he picked her up and carried her into her apartment. When Walker put her gently on the sofa, she allowed herself to lean against him.

"You heard," she whispered.

"The whole block heard."

"I live to entertain my neighbors."

"You've been pretty quiet to date. I think you were due."

She tried to smile, but couldn't. Then she raised her face and stared into his dark eyes. "Why does it hurt so much?"

"Because life's a bitch."

"I don't know what to do. I don't know how to make it better."

And then the man who had warned her he couldn't be trusted bent his head and kissed her.

CHAPTER FOURTEEN

ELISSA KNEW THIS was a bad idea. The last time she and Walker had started down this path, things had gotten out of hand and she'd ended up feeling hurt.

But he kissed her so gently, so carefully, that she wasn't sure how to resist. Still, when he drew back slightly, she opened her eyes and said, "Don't be a jerk again."

One corner of his mouth curved up. "I promise. I'll be a perfect gentleman."

"I'm not sure I want that, either."

"Then what do you want?"

An interesting question and one she didn't know how to answer.

He leaned in and just before his mouth brushed hers he said, "Please, Elissa."

The quiet plea was more than she could withstand. She gave in to both the request and the touch by placing her hands on his chest and parting her lips.

He swept his tongue into her mouth. He tasted of coffee and something sweet. He smelled like soap. He'd obviously recently showered because his hair was damp and his skin freshly shaven.

While his tongue circled hers, teasing, arousing, exciting, she rubbed her palms against the hard planes of his chest. Beneath the worn T-shirt and smooth skin was a layer of muscle that rippled with her every touch.

Suddenly she wanted to be touching that skin. She tugged on the shirt. He broke their kiss long enough to pull it over his head. Then he grabbed her hands and pressed them against his body, as if he needed to feel her caressing him as much as she wanted to be doing it.

As she explored his chest, his shoulders and arms, he bent over her. He kissed her jaw, then along her neck. One arm came around her. He rested his other hand on her belly, then moved it slowly up to her breasts. Her nipples tightened, her insides grew heavy and between her legs she felt both heat and moisture.

Then his mouth was on hers again. Deep kisses took her breath away. She lost herself in the sensations he created. He used his hand to lazily explore her breasts. He brushed against her nipples, one at a time.

Fire shot through her. Fire and need and a desperation that made her feel both weak and powerful.

"I want you," he breathed. "Elissa. I want you."

They were words to soothe a battered soul. She nipped his lower lip, then stood and held out her hand. He rose and allowed her to lead him down the short hall to her bedroom.

She hadn't bothered to make her bed, but the tangle of sheets and blanket didn't seem to be a problem. The second they came to a stop, Walker sat down and pulled off his athletic shoes and socks. As she watched, he unfastened his jeans, then pushed them and his boxers down and stepped away from his clothing.

He was the most beautiful man she'd ever seen. His chest was smooth and highly defined by muscle. Several scars, some old and faded and some still angry and red, marred his warm skin. His chest tapered to a narrow waist that naturally led the eye to a very impressive erection jutting toward her.

Her insides tightened in anticipation. It was all she could do not to rip her clothes off and beg him to take her right there. She'd been without for so long, she could barely remember what it felt like to have a man inside of her, filling her over and over again until she had no choice but to surrender.

And while that was her goal, a woman had to be practical.

"Condoms," she said as she ripped open her nightstand drawer and started rooting around.

Behind her, Walker swore. "I didn't think to bring any. I have some upstairs."

"I think I have some, too."

She could practically hear him raising his eyebrows. "What happened to the no-man plan?"

"It's a goal, but I'm human. I can be weak from time to time. In case that happened, I wanted to be prepared. Aha."

She drew out a small box from under a tube of hand cream and held them up.

He walked toward her, relieved her of the box and put the condoms on the nightstand.

"Only three," he said. "Not nearly enough."

If he'd been trying to impress her, he'd done a fine job. While she was still absorbing his complaint, he drew her T-shirt over her head and made quick work of her bra. Even as he bent down and drew one hard nipple into his mouth, he unfastened her shorts and pushed them off, along with her panties.

She clutched his head, not wanting him to ever stop that delicious sucking. With every tug, a ribbon of need spiraled from her breast to between her legs. She was already swollen and wet and the hunger he'd satisfied the last time they'd been together returned full force.

"Walker," she breathed. "I want you inside."

He raised his head and looked at her. "Now?"

She nodded. "It's been a long time."

He eased her toward the bed. She stretched out on the mattress.

"How long?" he asked as he put on a condom.

"Since before Zoe was born."

He knelt between her thighs. "You meant what you said, then. About avoiding men and relationships."

"Oh, yeah."

She expected him to ask her why she'd changed her mind and was grateful when he didn't. Instead of speaking, he slipped a finger inside of her.

Instantly her entire body tried to tighten around that single finger. Wanting made it nearly impossible to breathe.

He slid out and then pushed in two fingers. She felt herself stretching slightly. He frowned.

"I thought having a baby made things looser."

"They, ah, sewed me up afterward." Something she hadn't considered. "This could be interesting for both of us."

He smiled. "I like interesting."

He bent over her and kissed her. As his tongue danced with hers, he reached for one of her hands and drew it to him. She caressed his erection, then spread her legs and guided him to her.

She was slick and wet and ready, and incredibly tight. Even as she fought against the need to come right that second, she felt herself stretching as he slowly filled her. The pressure was nearly unbearable, in the best way possible.

He broke the kiss and swore softly. "You're killing me."

"Is it uncomfortable?"

"Not in the way you mean. How the hell am I supposed to keep from coming?"

"Think of England."

He gave a strangled laugh that was part groan, then pushed in that last inch.

She rotated her hips and consciously contracted, then relaxed her muscles. When he withdrew and pushed in again, this time she took him more easily. By the third thrust, she gave herself over to the desperate screams of her body and grabbed him by the hips to pull him in deeper. He gave a hard push and she felt the first rippling surrender of her release.

"Oh, yes," she cried as her orgasm claimed her.

He groaned. She felt him get harder, but he continued to fill her over and over again, pushing her through waves of her release. She clung to him, lost in the pleasure, begging him to continue until he gave a cry of his own and stiffened.

WALKER LAY ON HIS BACK and pulled Elissa against him. She rested her head on his shoulder and lightly traced one of the scars on his chest.

His heart had finally slowed to normal, something he hadn't been sure would happen after he'd lost control. His plan had been to last longer. His plan, like hers, hadn't amounted to much.

"That was nice," she said.

"Ouch."

She raised her head and smiled at him. "Is this a guy ego thing? Should I gush?"

"Gushing would be nice."

"It was great."

"Closer."

She put her head back down and moved her fingers to another scar. "It's been so long, I wasn't sure I'd remember where everything went. Thanks for helping with that."

He smiled. "You're welcome. Are you going to ask?"

"About?"

"The scars. Do you want to know what happened?"

"No."

"Are you sure?"

She raised her head again. "Let me guess. Your other women were all aquiver to hear how close you came to death." She drew in a breath and spoke in a high-pitched voice. "Oh, Walker, this one looks nasty. Tell me every little detail about what you went through."

"So you're *not* interested."

"We just shared one of life's greatest intimacies. Why would I want to break the mood by asking about a time when you were in horrible pain and nearly died?"

"Most women find it romantic."

"Then you need to move in another circle, big guy."

He chuckled. "I like your style." He liked a lot more than that, but he didn't want to get into that now. Instead he said, "Turn over."

She narrowed her eyes. "Not even for money."

"I've already seen it."

"Then why do you need to see it again?"

"I'm curious."

"It was a mistake."

"It's cute. Come on. I'll show you mine."

"You don't have one to show."

He touched her nose. "I have other things I could show you."

She sighed and shifted away so she could flop on her stomach. "Fine. Just don't make any cracks and don't comment on my ten extra pounds."

Why did women worry about crap like that? "There aren't any," he said, then leaned over until he could stare at the tiny red heart and the single tear below it on her hip.

"Why this?" he asked.

"It was right before I knew I was pregnant but after I'd finally come to realize Neil would never love anyone but himself and that he couldn't even love himself as much as his next fix. It was a metaphorical statement, I guess. I thought I loved him."

"You didn't?"

"No. Not even close." She turned onto her back and smiled at him. "I didn't really know what love was until I had Zoe. She changed everything. I'm not even sure why I had her. Neil pressured me to get an abortion. I hadn't thought about having kids, but when I found out I was pregnant, I just couldn't get rid of the baby. So I took what money I'd managed to keep hidden from Neil and ran away."

He stroked her hair, then rested his hand on her bare belly. "Where did you go?"

"A halfway house. I got a job cleaning and doing laundry. They let me stay while I had Zoe, then I saved enough for a bus ticket and came back here. I think, in the back of my mind, I figured if I moved to Seattle, my parents would be able to find me. I wanted them to still want me."

"They did. Bobby lied, remember?"

"They had a funny way of showing it. Anyway, I got a job and a studio apartment. I've worked my way up to this place."

"You've kept it all together. You should be proud of that."

"I am. I like my life. Mrs. Ford is great. She's made a big difference for Zoe and me."

"You've made a difference for her. You're family."

She'd filled in what was missing all by herself. He admired that…and her.

"What happens now?" he asked. "With your mother."

"I don't know. She has to be furious and I'm still pretty pissed off myself. I guess we'll deal with it as it comes."

As she spoke, she stretched. Her body arched and her breasts rose toward him. Not one to refuse that kind of an invitation, he bent down and took one nipple in his mouth. She moaned. Wanting grew inside of him as his dick went from zero to sixty in less than two seconds.

He released her and stood. "Come on," he said, pulling her to her feet.

"Where are we going?"

"The bathroom."

Two minutes later they stood under the hot spray. He positioned her so the warm water raced down her body, then picked up the bar of soap and rubbed it between his hands. When he'd built up enough lather, he put his hands on her breasts and circled them. He brushed her nipples with the center of his palm, then with his thumbs. She trembled and let her head fall back.

After the water had washed away the soap, he leaned in and licked her nipples over and over, then lightly bit down, making her gasp. At the same time, he lathered up again, then slid one hand between her legs. The slippery soap allowed him to slide over her most sensitive area, rubbing it, then circling it. She parted her legs and reached out to brace herself on the shower walls.

But he wasn't done with her. Once again, he allowed the water to wash away the soap, then he dropped to his knees and eased between her legs.

His erection pulsed with each heartbeat, but he ignored the pressure to take her again. That would happen, he was sure of it. This was about pleasing her.

He used his fingers to part her swollen flesh, then pressed his mouth to the very heart of her. As his tongue stroked her, he felt her tremble. He opened his mouth and sucked, then licked, repeating the actions until her breathing was ragged and she seemed close to losing control. Only then did he settle into a rhythm designed to *make* her lose control.

Back and forth, back and forth, with the flat part of his tongue, then the tip. Her center engorged, then the first shudder of her release struck. She cried out as her whole body convulsed.

When she was done, she collapsed next to him in the tub. Her eyes were dilated, her skin flushed. Water rained down on them.

"Your turn," she breathed, her hand reaching between them to close around his erection.

He held in a moan. "What did you have in mind?"

She smiled. "Stand up and find out."

He rose and stepped under the shower. Elissa knelt in front of him and licked the very tip of his arousal. Instinctively he flexed and surged toward her before he could stop himself. He wanted to bury his hands in her wet hair and pull her closer. He wanted her to suck as hard as she could until he exploded.

Instead he braced himself against the wall and did his best not to act too aggressively.

She circled him with her tongue, then opened her mouth and took him inside. The wet heat combined with the pounding of the shower to create an other-worldly experience.

Suddenly she stopped and stepped out of the shower. A minute later, she returned, condom in hand.

"You're holding back," she said simply. "This way you don't have to."

He was surprised she'd noticed and grateful for her actions. After he slipped on the protection, he turned her so her back was to the tile wall.

"Gonna be cold," he said.

She grinned. "I can handle it."

She only shrieked a little as he raised her up against the tiles. Then she moaned and wrapped her legs around his hips when he thrust inside of her.

She was hot and slick and already contracting around him. In a matter of seconds he was hanging on by a thread and a few seconds after that, he just didn't give a damn.

"I HAVE TO GET TO WORK," Elissa said two hours later when they'd moved back to the bedroom and used the last condom. "I'm supposed to spend the weekend working on my jewelry. The craft show is in a couple of weeks and I'm not close to ready."

Walker leaned over and kissed her shoulder. "I'll help."

She blinked at him. "I'm sorry, what did you say?"

He rolled onto his back and pulled her with him so she stretched across him.

"What's so hard to believe?" he asked. "I'll go out and get supplies, then come back and help. You can tell me what to do and I'll do it."

Just like that, she thought. A couple of days ago, she'd assumed they would never speak to each other again. Suddenly they were lovers and he was implying they would be spending more time together. Was that what she wanted? Was that the safest route?

She already knew the answer to that last question, but in that moment, she didn't care.

"You don't have to go to the store," she said. "I have enough food for us."

"I wasn't talking about food." He leaned over and shook the empty condom box.

"Oh," she said. "You really think you're going to want to do that again?"

He cupped her face and kissed her firmly. "You can bet on it."

"HOW HARD COULD IT BE?" Walker asked when Elissa sat him down at the kitchen table and gave him detailed instructions on how to wrap the wire around the pale blue topaz.

"It takes practice," she told him, not sure if she should be insulted by his assumption that what she did was so easy.

She returned to her worktable and began sorting stones. She had ideas for several matching sets, which would be her most expensive items, along with lots of different styles of earrings, rings, bracelets and necklaces.

She'd already made a list of the different designs to help her keep on track. Another sheet held her completed inventory list. If she really focused she could—

"This isn't right."

Walker stood next to her and handed over a mess of twisted wire and barely visible stone.

"Are you asking me or telling me?"

He set the object on the table. "This isn't my thing. Why don't I make labels or put stuff in boxes?"

She held in a smile. "But you said it was so easy. You said it wouldn't be a problem. You said—"

"I was wrong." He spoke between gritted teeth.

"Really? You? Wrong? Color me astonished."

"It's not easy," he grumbled. "Is that what you want? Is that enough crawling?"

"Nearly," she said brightly. "I think another minute will do it."

"Fine. You have talent and I don't. You were right and I was…"

He paused and she held a hand up to her ear. "Yes?"

"Wrong."

She sighed. "What a beautiful sound. The *w* word. I rejoice for all women everywhere."

"You're taking this a little too much to heart. I can think of only one way to shut you up."

Then, before she could react, he pulled her to her feet and kissed her thoroughly.

"I have to work," she protested.

He put one hand on her breast and slipped the other between her legs.

"What was that?" he asked against her mouth.

"Nothing. Nothing at all."

BY LATE SUNDAY AFTERNOON, Elissa had made progress on her inventory and Walker had, knowingly or not, made inroads into her heart. Her friends had been right—sleeping with the man meant bonding with him and no matter how much she told herself to keep her distance, neither her brain nor her heart were listening.

He put the last label on the box, then stacked that container with the others. After glancing at his watch, he said, "Zoe will be home soon. I should go. You don't want to have to explain me to her or your mother."

"Right."

She'd forgotten about the fight she'd had with her mother. All her anger and confusion returned in a rush.

He kissed her once and left. It was only after he was gone that she realized he hadn't said anything about seeing her again. Did he plan to? Had anything changed for him or was this just the long version of a one-night stand?

She hated the questions nearly as much as she hated herself for asking them. If she wanted to know, she should be a grown-up and ask. But before she could, she heard a car in the driveway.

By the time she got to the door, Zoe was already out and racing toward her.

"Mommy, Mommy, I had the best time," her daughter yelled. "I have so much to tell you!"

Elissa crouched down and held out her arms. Zoe rushed into them. Elissa glanced over her daughter's head and saw that her mother wasn't alone in the car. Elissa's father was with her.

Had he come along to say goodbye or was he to provide a buffer between the two women?

Elissa straightened as her parents got out of the car and walked toward her.

"Hi," she said, not looking at her mother. "It sounds like Zoe had fun."

"I did!" her daughter said. "I want to stay over again."

"If that's not a problem," her mother said stiffly. "We'd love to have her."

"Sure. That would be great. We'll have to work something out."

Her father handed her Zoe's small suitcase and kissed Elissa's cheek. "You know we love you, Elissa, don't you? You understand things happened?"

Meaning what? They were allowed to be pissed she'd left but she wasn't supposed to care that they'd stopped looking?

"Of course." She forced herself to smile.

"Good."

She could tell he thought everything was fine now, but she knew differently and from the way her mother avoided her gaze, she, too, understood that all was not well.

"We won't keep you," her father said. "Let's talk soon."

"Sure."

She and Zoe waved while her parents drove away, then she led her daughter into the apartment.

"All right," she said with a smile. "Start at the beginning and tell me everything you did."

Zoe threw her arms around her. "I missed you, Mommy, but I had really, really big fun."

"Did you? Tell me."

"First, we went shopping. Grandma said I could pick out new sheets for my bed there. So we got pink sheets with princesses on them. Then we went home and we made cookies. Then in the afternoon…"

Zoe kept talking, but Elissa found it difficult to concentrate. She kept thinking about the fight she'd had with her mother and wondering if they would ever come to terms. She also kept remembering her time with Walker and wishing he were with her now.

While she loved Zoe with all her heart, for the first time in a long time, she felt lonely and out of place.

CHAPTER FIFTEEN

LORI JOHNSTON WAS everything Reid didn't like in a woman. Disapproving, plain and completely uninterested in him. She glanced around the sports bar with the same lack of enthusiasm she'd shown at being introduced to him.

"We should go into my office," he said over the yells of the afternoon crowd in for a Mariners game, then took her total lack of response as agreement.

Once there, he motioned for her to take the seat opposite his desk while he settled on a corner. Not so much to look down on her, he told himself, as to, well, maintain control of the interview process.

She adjusted her glasses before handing him a copy of her résumé. "The agency recommended me for this assignment because I've had a lot of experience with difficult patients. I've been doing private duty nursing for two years. Before that I was on the orthopedic ward. I've worked with several heart patients recently. I believe those are the two issues your grandmother will be facing—recovery from both a heart attack and a broken hip?"

She spoke the way she looked, sensibly and with

nothing wasted on the frivolous, which made him uncomfortable.

"I could put the game on here," he said, jerking his head toward the TV in the corner. "The Mariners are tied."

She blinked at him. "I don't follow sports."

Why was he not surprised? "So you don't know who I am."

"Should I?"

Ouch. "Sure. I'm a famous major league pitcher."

"Then why do you work in a bar?"

"I blew out my shoulder."

"Given the effort and daily stress necessary in that line of work, I'm not surprised. The body has limits, Mr. Buchanan. No matter how much we would like that reality to be different, it simply will not change."

She reminded him of every teacher he'd never liked, all self-righteous and…and…priggy, he thought with no idea of where the word had come from.

She wore a long-sleeved shirt tucked into a boring skirt that fell well below her knees. Her shoes were ugly, she didn't wear jewelry or makeup and if she narrowed her eyes at him any more, she was going to go cross-eyed. Her only redeeming feature—thick reddish-gold hair that she'd pulled back into a horrible braid—was wasted on her.

He wanted to tell her she wouldn't do, except she was the most qualified applicant he'd met and from her work history, the most likely to be able to handle Gloria's day shift.

"The agency said you want three nurses working

eight-hour shifts," she said. "We get paid a twelve-hour shift, regardless of the hours we work, so you're really wasting money."

"You haven't met my grandmother," he told her. "Eight hours is going to be difficult enough."

"I see. Is the family close?"

"No."

"Perhaps if you'd spent more time with her before her heart attack, she would have been easier to deal with."

"What makes you think I didn't?"

She smiled coolly. "With your very impressive baseball career, I'm sure you were on the road a lot."

She was being sarcastic. Her tone gave nothing away, but he knew it down to his bones.

"Gloria isn't like other grandmothers," he said. "She runs an empire."

"Perhaps, Mr. Buchanan, but everyone gets lonely. Especially the elderly. Many of them are in the position of having friends and loved ones gone. Does your grandmother have any contemporaries?"

"You mean friends?"

"Yes. People her own age with whom she has close attachments."

He wanted to tell her he wasn't a moron, but to what end? She wouldn't believe him. "I don't know."

"I see."

There were miles of disapproval in her voice.

"Are your parents still alive?" she asked.

"Ah, no."

"So your grandmother has no friends you know

about and she lost at least one of her children. Do you know what it does to a parent to outlive a child?"

He slid off the desk and stepped around it. "I haven't done anything wrong."

"I'm sure you haven't done anything at all."

"Hey, I'm not the bad guy here. If you don't want the job, just say so."

"I am interested in the job, Mr. Buchanan. I suspect your grandmother needs me."

That made him smile. "If you're thinking you're going to rescue her from her uncaring relatives, you're in for a shock, lady."

Lori did not look convinced.

She would be, though. A few minutes in Gloria's company and she'd come begging to apologize for what she'd said and assumed. He found himself looking forward to that.

"The job is yours if you want it," he said.

"Thank you. I require regular meals, which means time to eat them. I am happy to do so in the company of your grandmother. I have low blood sugar and can't go long periods without eating."

"Not a problem. Do you bring your own food or would you prefer that we provide it?"

"I bring my own. I would also like to meet the other nurses you've hired."

Reid had a feeling she wasn't going to approve of anything about Sandy Larson.

"No problem." He gave her the start date.

"Excellent." She stood and held out her hand. "Thank you for your time, Mr. Buchanan. I'll go back to the agency and fill out the paperwork. I'm looking forward to meeting your grandmother."

"Me, too," he said smugly. "Me, too."

WALKER LOADED the last box in his SUV while Elissa hovered nearby and shifted nervously from foot to foot.

"I don't like this," she said. "I'm just not comfortable. What if something happens?"

When it had become obvious that her inventory and supplies wouldn't fit in her small car, he'd insisted she use his.

"But it's so expensive," she'd protested.

He'd pointed out that's why he had insurance. Necessity had forced her to agree, but he could tell she didn't like it.

"I'll be extra careful," she promised.

He put an arm around her. "You don't have to be. Relax. This is going to be a good weekend for you."

"Maybe. I hope so." She drew in a breath. "No, you're right. It's going to be great. If only it weren't so early."

He glanced at his watch. It was barely after six, but Elissa had to get to the craft fair in time to set up.

"What if no one buys my stuff?" she asked in a panic again. "What if I sit there for three days and don't sell anything? I can't do this."

He had a feeling once she came uncorked she was never going to recover so he did the only thing he could think of to silence her. He kissed her.

She stiffened, then melted into him. Her arms

came around him and he felt the familiar heat and need that were always lurking when he was near Elissa.

Between her work schedule, his work schedule and her frantic efforts to build enough inventory for the craft fair, they hadn't seen much of each other in the past week, so there hadn't been a repeat of their previous weekend.

He missed having her in bed, but knew it was probably for the best to let things cool off.

She drew back and stared at him. "Wow. That's better than coffee. I'm totally awake now."

"But are you more calm?"

"In some ways, yes. In others, not so much."

She smiled as she spoke and he found himself leaning toward her. As always, everything about her drew him to her, even though he knew it was not a place he should go. So he wasn't disappointed when a familiar low sports car pulled into the driveway.

Reid got out of his Corvette and walked toward them.

"Do you know what time it is?" he asked by way of greeting. "Do you know how late I was up last night?"

Elissa glanced between the two of them. "Hi, Reid. What are you doing here?"

"Helping," he said, then stretched, before slapping Walker on the back "You owe me."

"Put it on my tab."

"I don't understand," Elissa said.

"You can't set up alone," Walker told her. "You can barely handle one table and there are four. I'm staying here with Zoe until she and Mrs. Ford wake up. Then I'll bring them along to the fair. In the meantime, Reid is going to help you set up."

"No." She took a step back. "I couldn't."

"Sure you can," Reid said easily. "It's not like I have anyone waiting for me at home."

Walker raised his eyebrows. "A slow night?"

"I guess. I haven't been in the mood lately. I met the most annoying woman a couple of days ago and she's put me off my game."

"Not possible," Walker said with a grin.

"It is." Reid looked and sounded both bitter and unhappy. "She didn't know who I was and she sure as hell wasn't pretty. She actually said that the reason Gloria is so difficult is because I don't spend enough time with her."

"Gloria's problems started long before we were born."

"I know, but she went on about Gloria needing contact." He shrugged. "I don't remember it all. I got bored. She really pissed me off."

"So what did you do?"

"I hired her to be Gloria's day nurse."

Even Elissa chuckled at that. Walker guided her toward the driver's side of the SUV and insisted she get inside.

"You'll be fine," he told her. "I'll bring the girls later this morning."

"But…"

He pressed a finger against her mouth. "Go," he told her.

"I'll follow you," Reid said. "Hey, there's lots of women at these things, right? Maybe I'll hang around and meet a few of them."

"Get the taste of the uncooperative one out of your mouth," Elissa said.

Reid grimaced. "I didn't kiss her. Why would I want to? So what if she doesn't appreciate me? She's not my type. Now that I've hired her, I don't have to have anything to do with her. I'll never see her again, which is a damn good thing, let me tell you."

Elissa looked sidelong at Reid. "For a man who's not interested in this woman, you're sure talking about her a lot."

Reid narrowed his gaze. "You remember that I'm helping you, right?"

She grinned. "Oh, yeah." She rolled down the window and then closed the driver's door. "See you there," she told Walker. "And wish me luck."

"You're not going to need it, but good luck anyway."

BY MIDAFTERNOON, Elissa was so happy she thought she might float home. She was doing great. Sales had been brisk from the moment the fair had opened. If this kept up, she would exceed her ambitious hopes for the weekend and be able to put at least three thousand dollars away in the bank.

Just thinking about that massive number made her light-headed. It meant not having to sweat every grinding noise in her car. It meant a new winter coat for Zoe wasn't a reason to panic. It meant peace of mind.

She helped a woman choose a pair of earrings for herself and a bracelet for her sister, then counted back the change.

She grabbed her water bottle and took a long drink. She hadn't eaten all day, but she was just too excited to think about food. She felt as if her life had suddenly taken a turn for the positive. That things were seriously looking up.

She didn't want to think Walker was responsible, but she couldn't help giving him a little credit. He'd been good to her and for her. When she thought about what he'd told her about his girlfriend, she had trouble reconciling those actions with the man she knew. She knew he believed what he'd done meant he couldn't be trusted with the big stuff. That both she and Zoe were at risk. But her gut told her otherwise.

He'd been a kid, she reminded herself. He was talking about something that had happened a long time ago. Sure, what he'd done had been awful, but she could also understand his fear.

"How's it going?"

She looked up and saw Cal and Penny standing by her booth. "Hi." She stood and glanced at Penny's huge belly. "How are you feeling?"

"Awful. The baby's due any day now. I thought walking around might help." She put her hand on her stomach. "Walking very, very slowly."

"You're doing great," Cal said, then kissed her cheek. "It will be over soon."

"Not soon enough." Penny sighed. "So where's Zoe?"

"She was here earlier. She's spending the rest of the day at a friend's house."

"Lucky girl. She's having fun." Penny rolled her shoulders. "I used to have fun."

Cal seemed to be hiding a smile. "You will again."

"I don't think so. I think I'll always be this huge." She glanced down at the jewelry. "I want some new earrings. My clothes are all massive and I deserve something pretty."

"Pick as many as you'd like," Cal said.

"Yes, please," Elissa said with a grin. "I'll even give you a discount."

"I don't think so," Penny told her. "Friends don't let friends lose money. We'll pay retail."

She pointed to a pair of earrings, then another. Cal collected them and handed them to Elissa who rang up the total.

"Where's Walker?" Penny asked while Cal counted out the money.

Elissa felt her cheeks flush at the assumption she would know where he was.

"He's, ah, bringing my neighbor, Mrs. Ford, to the fair. She's meeting up with some of her friends here and they're heading off to a movie."

"Good for them. I want to be like that when I get old," Penny said. "Assuming I don't simply pop like a balloon, with all my insides spilling out."

Cal took the bag Elissa gave him and put his hand on the small of Penny's back.

"On that happy visual, we're going to go," Cal said

firmly. "Come on, Penny. Let's find the car. I'll take you home and rub your feet."

"Okay."

He glanced over his shoulder. "Dani said to tell you she'd be by later."

"Oh, good. Thanks. Feel better, Penny."

"Not possible. I'm never going to feel better."

An older woman laughed softly. "I felt the same way with all three of mine," she said with a sigh. "Of course that was a long time ago. You have a lovely family."

Elissa opened her mouth to explain they weren't her family, then she decided to just smile and say, "Thank you."

WALKER MOVED SLOWLY beside Mrs. Ford.

"I don't usually bother with this," she said as she leaned on him and steadied herself with a cane. "I was concerned with the crowd and getting jostled." She gave him a teasing smile. "I knew if I asked you to protect me, innocent people would be risking life and limb. You're just so strong."

"Are you flirting with me?" he asked.

"Maybe a little. Although I know where your real interests lie, don't I? With our pretty neighbor."

"Elissa and I are friends," he said, ignoring what had happened the previous weekend and how much he wanted to be with her again.

"Good friends." Mrs. Ford sighed. "I used to have friends like that when I was younger. But after eighty, it's nearly impossible to get a man. Still, I'm happy with my life. Not everyone can say that."

He kept his left hand on her elbow and offered as much support as he could. It was warm and crowded and he didn't think this was a good place for a woman well into her nineties. But Mrs. Ford had insisted and arguing with her was like reasoning with a tornado.

"Maybe if you weren't so closed off emotionally," she said. "I can certainly understand why it would happen. You've seen some horrible things. War has a way of changing a man."

Honest to God, he didn't know what to say to her.

"I'm only afraid that you'll miss a perfectly wonderful opportunity with Elissa. She's not like other women. You're not likely to do better."

"I'm not interested in doing better."

"Then what's the problem? You should have had her in bed by now. There's nothing like a fabulous few days in bed to turn a woman into putty."

He swore under his breath. "Did you want to do any shopping?" he asked, motioning to the crowded booths on either side of them.

She glanced at a display of kites. "I don't think so, but you're very sweet to offer. I know shopping is rarely a man's first choice as a way to spend his free time. Do you think it's a traumatic event from your past, or the way your mind works, or do you simply prefer being single?" She glanced at him. "I can't imagine it's being single. You strike me as someone who cares about family."

"I..."

Words failed him. Until this moment, he'd always really liked Mrs. Ford. This was the first time she'd tried to interrogate him. And as they hadn't even reached Elissa's booth, he was well and truly trapped.

"I'm not going to go running to Elissa, if that's what you're worried about," Mrs. Ford said with a smile.

"I…"

Just then he spotted Dani with Ryan and called out to them. Dani turned and smiled. As they approached, Walker noticed they were holding hands. Apparently things were progressing.

He wasn't sure how he felt about his sister getting involved so quickly after the end of her marriage. Not that it was his business or that she would listen to anything he had to say on the subject.

"Mrs. Ford, this is my sister, Dani, and her friend Ryan. This is Mrs. Ford, one of my neighbors."

"Hi," Dani said. "Nice to meet you."

"And you, dear." Mrs. Ford eyed Ryan. "What do you do?"

"I'm the general manager of The Waterfront," Ryan told her.

"Your restaurant," Mrs. Ford said to Walker. "Dani, do you work there, as well?"

"Yes. That's where Ryan and I met." She looked at Walker. "Now it's your restaurant?" she asked, her voice teasing.

He groaned. "Give me a break."

"How lovely." The old lady sighed. "An office romance. I always wanted an office romance. Of course I never really had a job, which made the situation more challenging. Oh, I worked on an assembly line during World War II, but there weren't very many men around and as my husband was off serving his country, an office romance would have been unpatriotic, don't you think?"

"Are you enjoying the craft fair?" Dani asked Mrs. Ford.

"Very much. Walker is quite patient with me."

"Really?" Dani eyed her brother. "Lucky you. Ryan only recently moved to Seattle. This is his first time here."

Mrs. Ford turned to Dani's date. "What do you think of our city?"

"I like it," Ryan said.

Dani released his hand and stepped close to Walker. "This is new. I don't remember you volunteering with seniors before," she said in a low voice.

"She wanted to come see Elissa's booth."

"Uh-huh. You'd better be careful or we'll all think you're turning into a nice guy."

"Anything but that," he muttered. "So how's the new guy?"

"Good. I'd thought I needed time to get over my divorce, but maybe not."

Walker looked at his sister. "It's serious?"

She smiled, then blushed. "Maybe. I don't know. I really like him and he's a good guy. I know this is fast and I want to stay detached, it's just…I can't seem to."

He wanted to tell her to be careful, but who was he to give advice about personal relationships?

"I'm glad you're happy."

"Really? You're not going to warn me or anything?"

"Nope."

She grinned and leaned against him. "Did I ever mention you're my favorite brother?"

She and Ryan said goodbye, then strolled off. Mrs. Ford watched them go.

"Now where were we?" she asked as they once again started for Elissa's booth. "I believe we were discussing your inability to commit. Do you have any thoughts on why that is?"

BUSINESS CONTINUED to be good, Elissa thought happily Sunday afternoon as she made change, then bent down to collect more inventory. She was still selling at a brisk pace and this was only day two. Tonight she would go over her receipts and figure out if she could actually increase her profit estimate. The thought of how much easier life would be with a bit of a financial buffer in the bank nearly made her giddy.

She straightened and put a dozen or so boxes on her table, then froze as she heard a familiar and incredibly unwelcome, "Hey, babe."

Despite the near ninety-degree temperature, her entire body went cold. She felt her breath catch in her throat and a shriek building up inside as she fought against the need to scream against the unfairness of it all.

She turned slowly, hoping she was wrong, then nearly collapsed in disappointment when she saw the tall, painfully thin, shaggy-haired man standing in front of her booth.

"Neil," she said, wondering if this was going to be a never-ending nightmare. "This is an unpleasant surprise."

CHAPTER SIXTEEN

"WHAT ARE YOU DOING HERE?" Elissa asked, keeping her voice calm. Neil was like an injured wild animal—dangerous when cornered and sensitive to any sign of fear.

"I came to see my girl," he said with an easy smile. "A buddy I know got a bunch of gigs here and in Portland. His bass player couldn't make it, so I said I'd fill in. I knew it was a chance to catch up with you." He moved closer and his smile turned more predatory. "You're looking good, Elissa. It's been a long time."

Over two years, she thought bitterly. He'd come into town, threatened her, then left when she'd cleaned out her meager savings account.

"I went by where you work and some guy there told me I could find you here." He frowned. "Do you really wear that uniform? I don't know about the chicken, Elissa. Still, the place was busy and the tips must be good."

Oh, Frank, she thought desperately. *Don't try to be so helpful.*

"Did you tell him you were my brother?" she asked.

"Cousin. What with us not looking anything

alike." He picked up a pair of earrings. "Nice little setup you've got here. I didn't know you were so talented, but then you've always been good at keeping things from me."

She snatched back the earrings. "The only reason you don't know that I could do things like this is because that would have required us having a conversation about something other than you. Something you never saw the value in."

He smiled. "You're still a fireball, Elissa. I like that."

She couldn't believe she'd ever thought herself in love with him. Mitch had been bad enough—foolish, self-centered and unfaithful, but compared to Neil, he'd been a candidate for boyfriend of the year.

Neil moved closer to the table and reached across it. She stepped out of reach.

"I've missed you, baby," he said. "We had something good together."

"We had shit," she said flatly. "The only reason you kept me around was because I could hold a job, which meant money coming in. You needed that money to stay stoned."

"You always did take care of me," he reminded her. "Still do. That's why I'm here, Elissa. For my little something. But now that I've seen how well you're doing, I'm thinking it should be more than a little."

Why now? she thought desperately. Why today? The only thing that kept her from getting lost in panic was the knowledge that Zoe was safely away.

It was as if he could read her mind. He looked around, then back at her. "So where's the kid?"

She wanted to scream at him that he had no right to any contact with her daughter. He didn't care about Zoe. She would bet her entire day's sales that he couldn't remember if she was a boy or a girl.

"She's at a birthday party."

"Too bad. I would have liked to meet her." He shook his head. "I don't know why you insist on keeping us apart. She's as much my child as yours."

"She's not your child. She's not your anything. You don't care about her. She's just leverage."

"You're right. You should have had me sign off on the kid," he told her. "Funny you didn't, because you were always so good at the details. Could it be you secretly wanted to keep me in your life? Am I the one who got away?"

He asked the question sincerely, as if he truly believed it was possible she missed him. As if she didn't regret every second spent with him.

She wanted to scream that he was nothing but a druggie loser. That if she had her way, he would be sent to an island and never rescued. That the only reason she hadn't gotten him to sign a release for Zoe was because she'd left with almost nothing and she couldn't have afforded a lawyer.

"Go away," she said. "Just go away."

"I will, Elissa. But first you have to give me what I want."

Money. It always came down to money.

Thank God she'd taken home her earnings from the day before. Still, she hated handing over her cash box, knowing how much was inside.

She reached for the small metal box and opened it. Before she could figure out a way to conceal the amount from him, he grabbed it and fingered the thick stack of bills.

"Sweet," he said as he pulled out all the tens and twenties, along with more than half the fives. "I'll leave you some change." He pocketed the money, then handed her the box. "In case you get any ideas about calling the cops on me and claiming I stole the money, remember this. I know where you live, Elissa. That means I know where the kid is. I could come in the night and steal her away. Just like that." He snapped his fingers. "Then you'd never see her again. You know I'd do it. So think of this as cheap insurance."

He gave her a grin, then sauntered away.

Elissa stood staring after him. Now that she was alone, fear crashed into her, with panic not far behind. He knew where she worked and he claimed to know where she lived. How was she ever going to keep Zoe safe?

If Neil thought he was onto a good thing, he might not go away this time. He might keep coming back until there wasn't any more money, then make good on his threat. She had to stop him. She had to find a way.

Elissa desperately wanted to leave. She wanted to be home with her child, with the doors locked and the blinds closed. She wanted to hide out until all this was over.

But she couldn't do that. She could only figure out a way to get enough money to hire a really good attorney who would make Neil go away forever.

DANI ROLLED OVER and smiled at Ryan. "I have to go," she said, wishing that weren't such a true statement. In a perfect world, she could stay in bed with him forever.

He glanced at the clock on the nightstand and sighed. "I'm not due in until four. Can you wait until then?"

It was just after two on Sunday, which meant brunch was winding down. "Everyone's pretty crabby after brunch," she said. "I need to go smooth feathers."

"Agreed." He fingered the ends of her hair. "Our customers love brunch and the staff hates it. Okay. I'll let you go…this one time."

"How brave of you." She leaned over and kissed him. He moved against her and she felt his leg slip between hers.

The fact that he could move independently still startled her. She'd enjoyed their lovemaking, but in truth some section of her emotional self had stood apart, openmouthed and hyperaware of how *different* it all was.

"What are you thinking?" he asked.

"Nothing."

"You don't have a nothing face. What is it?"

She hesitated, then sighed. "I'm thinking about Hugh."

"Wow." He sat up and leaned against the padded headboard. "Okay, should I worry that you're thinking about your ex-husband while you're in bed with me?"

"No. I don't miss him or any of that. It's just…" She sat up, careful to cover herself with the sheet. "I told you that he was in a wheelchair."

Ryan nodded, his blue eyes focused totally on her face.

"We'd been lovers before that happened. Hugh was only the second guy I'd been with. After the accident, it was never the same. I mean we did stuff, but traditional sex was out of the question."

She bit her lower lip, not sure how much to share or even how much she needed to share. "I was fine with that. I read some books and talked to his doctor and physical therapist. We would have needed help for me to get pregnant, but that seemed a long way off. I don't mean to sound disloyal or like a horrible person, but being intimate was always work. Physical work for me. There were things I had to worry about. But with you, it's easy. Your legs move. You can feel what I'm doing. Is that awful?"

He gathered her into his arms and kissed her. "Dani, the man left you and then you found out he was cheating on you. You owe him nothing. I think he was damn lucky to have you and an idiot to leave you. I'm glad you enjoyed being with me. I'm glad it was easy. You've earned that."

The combination of his strong arms and supportive words made her heart flutter. How had she gotten so lucky so soon after her divorce and how did she make sure this never, ever ended?

"Thank you," she whispered.

"You're welcome." He kissed her. "Okay, you either have to get out of bed right this second or brace yourself to be taken again."

She laughed. "As much as I want to be ravished,

I have to get to the restaurant." She touched his cheek. "See you at four?"

"I'll be there."

She dressed quickly, then retouched her makeup. Twenty minutes later she entered the restaurant to find them clearing away brunch.

Edouard met her with a growl. "It is ridiculous," he told her by way of greeting. "Do you know who I am? I am a famous, incredibly talented chef. I am gifted. You had me spend the morning supervising cooks making omelets and Belgian waffles. I am insulted."

"Sounds like trouble in your personal life to me," Dani said, unfazed by his complaints.

"My personal life is fine. It is excellent. It is much better than yours."

She wanted to tell him he was wrong. That Ryan did things to her body that might not be legal in some states and that until doing the wild things with him, she hadn't known she was a screamer. But sharing that kind of personal information would make her vulnerable and right now she needed to keep control of the kitchen.

"If you're so happy, then handling brunch should be easy," she said. "It's only one Sunday a month. You know we rotate the assignment."

"It is torture and I hate you for making me do it."

She smiled. "Good to know."

He narrowed his gaze, then walked away. She wanted to call him back and give him a big hug. Or break into song. The sun was shining, the sky an amazing shade of blue and her life was perfect in nearly every way.

She walked to the front of the restaurant and saw there were only a few customers lingering over coffee. The buffet stations had been broken down and stored until they would be needed next week. She was about to return to her office, when she saw a young woman carrying a little boy walk into the restaurant.

The hostess was long gone and most of the servers were in the back. Dani didn't see anyone else who could help her, so she walked to her and smiled.

"Hi, we've stopped serving brunch. Sorry."

"That's okay. I'm not here to eat. Is Ryan around?"

Ryan? Dani looked from the woman to the toddler, then back. "Ah, no. He's not due in until four."

"Huh. I just called his apartment and he didn't answer. Still, it's a beautiful day so I'm sure he's out somewhere. I wonder if I should try to find the apartment or wait here."

Dani didn't know what to think. She almost said that Ryan had probably been in the shower and the woman should try again, but she didn't. Her body felt as stiff as wood and she wondered if she would be able to speak.

Fortunately it wasn't an issue. The other woman kept chattering away. "I know I'm just dropping in. It's a surprise. I told him I'd be staying with my mother another week, but she was making us both crazy. It's the grandma thing. Nothing I did was right, which is always the case, but I'm not usually living with her. I would have come up sooner, but I had to finish my orals." She smiled shyly. "I'm getting my Ph.D. in nutrition with an emphasis on eating disorders."

She stopped and shook her head. "My God, listen to me talking and talking. It's just for the past three days it's been me and Alex here. I'm so excited to see another adult."

The toddler stuck his fingers in his mouth.

The woman was tall and thin. Pretty in a sensible sort of way. Dani's gaze dropped to her left hand and the diamond band on her ring finger.

The cold inside started to hurt. She told herself it wasn't possible, but she couldn't make herself believe it.

"I'm Dani Buchanan," she said. "I work here with Ryan. He didn't mention any visitors."

"Like I said, I'm a surprise. Alex and I weren't due here for a few more days." She held out her free hand. "I'm Jen, Ryan's wife."

WALKER PARKED in front of Cal's house, then hurried inside. Reid's car wasn't there, meaning Cal hadn't been able to get a hold of him. Which was fine—Walker was ready to take care of this himself.

Anger burned hot and bright inside of him. With Hugh, beating the crap out of the guy hadn't been possible, but shit-bastard Ryan wasn't in a wheelchair…yet.

He walked in without knocking and saw Dani on the sofa, curled up and leaning against Penny's shoulder. His sister looked up when he entered.

Her face was wet and flushed, her eyes swollen. "He's m-married," she said on a sob. "He's married and he never told me, never hinted. He never said anything.

I can't believe it. Even when we talked about how Hugh had cheated, he never said a-anything."

As he moved toward her, she rose and stepped into his embrace. He held her tight, rocking her.

There weren't any words. Nothing he could say would make this right. He hated that Ryan had done this to her right after Hugh's rejection and betrayal.

He glanced at Cal, who looked as if he wanted to put his fist through something. Penny had obviously been crying.

"This just sucks," Penny murmured. "I hate him."

"Me, too," Dani murmured against Walker's chest. He felt her tears dampening his shirt. "He has a kid. A little boy. How could he have slept with me while he has a kid? That's so wrong." She raised her head and stared into his eyes.

"It hurts," she whispered. "Make the pain go away."

He kissed her forehead, then drew her against him again. "I can't. I want to, but I can't."

If only he could tell her things would get better. He knew that they would, eventually, but the words were a cold comfort to her now.

He hated how much she hurt. She was his baby sister and he'd always felt the need to protect her. He told her he wanted to find Ryan and beat the shit out of him, wait for him to heal, then do it all again.

"I'll join you," Cal said quietly.

Penny looked between the two of them. "You can't beat up Ryan," she said. "He'll have you arrested and I'm due to give birth at any minute. Neither of you can be in prison then."

Dani drew in a shaky breath. "She's right. I'd love to watch you pound him into the ground, but you can't."

"Maybe not," Walker admitted, although in his mind the idea was still worth considering. "But I can fire him."

One corner of Cal's mouth turned up. "Perfect. Let him try to get a job in this city without a reference from us. He'll starve."

"No!" Dani stepped back and glared at them both. "You're not going to fire him, Walker."

He couldn't believe it. "You still care about this guy?"

"What?" She wiped her eyes with her fingers. "No. Of course not. I want him roasted on a spit. But I went into this relationship on my own. No one made me. I'm the one who didn't pay attention or ask the right questions. I have to take responsibility for that."

"Dani, he tricked you," Penny said.

"I know that, but I refuse to give him all the power. I am *not* some spineless female who is going to be rescued by her big, bad brothers. Ryan stays. I'll get through it."

Walker appreciated her attempts to be strong, even though he still wanted to hit something...or someone. "If I don't fire his ass, he's going to show up every day. You're going to have to deal with that. Can you?"

She straightened her back and squared her shoulders. "Bring it on."

THE CONCEPT HAD SEEMED simple enough at the time, Walker thought the next day, as he waved to Mrs.

Ford and one of her friends. The two old women drove away, leaving him alone with Zoe and all the potential things that could go wrong. All he had to do was watch the kid for a few hours until Mrs. Ford finished with her Labor Day Seniors Picnic. As it was adults-only, Mrs. Ford had been unable to take Zoe along, and for reasons still not clear to him, he, Walker, had volunteered.

"Brain injury," he muttered to himself as he stepped into Elissa's apartment. "Must have been a blow to the head I don't remember."

He'd left Zoe on the floor watching something on Nickelodeon, but when he returned, the TV was off and she'd spread out several articles of clothing on the sofa.

"I start school tomorrow," she told him with an expression that was both hopeful and terrified. "Mommy and me are still talking 'bout what I'm wearing." She fingered a T-shirt with a crown on the front. "This is pretty."

"Very nice," he said, wondering how the hell he was supposed to fill a whole day. Mrs. Ford wouldn't be back until after dinner. Even though the craft fair ended relatively early, he didn't expect Elissa until six. Sure he could take Zoe to the fair, but that was only going to burn two hours. Plus, what about meals? He'd said he would take her out, but that meant sitting across from her and thinking up things to say. What if she choked or something?

Despite the heat of the morning, a cold sweat broke out on the back of his neck.

"Did you see what Mommy got me for my lunch?"

she asked suddenly, then raced into the kitchen. She came back with a brightly colored lunch box.

Zoe opened it and showed him all the wonders of a space for a juice box, a plastic container for a sandwich and fruit, along with a special pack that would keep everything cold.

"It's the best," she said reverently as she closed it, then ran her hand along the top.

He glanced at his watch. Great. Two minutes down, four hundred and eighty to go.

"Want to ride your bike?" he asked, thinking at least that would tire her out. Did kids her age take naps?

"Okay."

But instead of running toward the front door to get to the garage, she raced down the hall, only to return with a large bottle of sunscreen. After handing it to him, she stood patiently, as if waiting for him to apply it.

"Right," he said slowly. "You don't want to get a sunburn."

"Mommy says it's important to protect ourselves." She held out one impossibly small, skinny arm.

Walker squirted sunscreen into his left palm, then used his right hand to rub the lotion onto her skin. He could encircle her upper arm with his thumb and forefinger and he had a bad feeling that he could have snapped any bone in her body just as easily. If she was this little now, what had it been like when she'd been born? Elissa had to have been terrified, but she'd handled it all on her own. She hadn't bolted or even tried to get away.

Unlike him.

He ignored the ghosts from his past and finished applying the sunscreen, then followed Zoe outside.

"Stay on this side of the street," he said.

Zoe sighed. "I know. Mommy always tells me where I can ride. I'll be good."

After opening the garage, he helped her put on her helmet. Then she climbed on her bike and set off down the sidewalk. The small training wheels gave her balance and she rode with a purposeful confidence. Walker watched her for a couple of seconds, then glanced around for something to do while she burned off energy.

He saw several gardening tools in a corner of the small garage and remembered noticing Elissa weeding flowers in the front bed. As busy as she'd been getting ready for the craft fair, he would guess she hadn't had time to keep up with her outside chores. Weeding he could handle.

He collected the tools, ignored both the gloves and some kind of squishy mat to protect his knees, grabbed a bucket and went to work.

The sun was hot, the day already warm. He attacked weeds and anything questionable looking, then dumped them into the bucket. Every now and then, he glanced up and checked on Zoe. She continued to ride back and forth, waving as she passed.

About fifteen minutes into her ride, she was joined by the girl from across the street. Walker couldn't remember the kid's name but she was a year or so older and seemed okay. They rode together for a few minutes, then collapsed on the lawn in the shade.

"I'm comin' back," Zoe yelled as she raced into the house.

Before Walker could get up and go after her to find out what she was doing, she'd returned with an armful of toys. The other girl did the same and they settled on the grass for a serious session of…whatever it was girls that age did. He reached the corner of the house and started down the side.

He worked the earth, not noticing when spade became shovel and the hole got big enough for a body. *Digging graves,* he thought grimly. *Digging…*

He jerked back, willing the image to fade. It did and there were plants again. Sweat dripped down his back. He didn't belong here, he thought. He couldn't do this—couldn't be normal. He—

He heard voices. Too many voices for just Zoe and her friend. Walker stood and hurried to the front yard. When he stepped around the house, he saw Zoe standing up to a boy several years older than her. The boy pushed her lightly. Zoe shoved back. The boy pushed harder. Zoe went down on the cement sidewalk.

Walker tore across the lawn and grabbed the kid by the shirtfront. He was about to shake him like a dog when he heard Zoe start to cry. When he glanced down, she had tears on her face and blood on her shirt.

"Don't hurt me! Don't hurt me!" the boy cried.

Walker narrowed his gaze. "There won't be a next time, will there?"

The terrified boy shook his head. Walker released him and crouched by Zoe.

"Let me see," he said.

Her girlfriend had disappeared, as had the other boys. Walker examined Zoe's scraped knee and the bit of skin missing at the base of her palm, then picked her up in his arms and carried her inside.

He set her on the counter and made quick work of her injuries, careful to use the nonstinging antiseptic Elissa had on a shelf with different sizes of bandages. When he was done with the patching up, he got a paper towel, dampened it, then wiped her face.

"What happened?" he asked.

She hiccuped another sob, then sniffed. "Those boys came by and said we were playing baby games. I said we weren't."

"You stood up to him," Walker said. "Your friend didn't."

"Natalie got scared and ran home. I was scared, too, but we weren't stupid and those boys were wrong. Sometimes they boss other kids around. I don't like it."

The boy had to be at least two or three years older than Zoe, but she'd been fearless. So what was the lesson? Did he tell her that it was good to stand up for herself, but then she had to face the consequences? Was it better to warn her to play it safe?

He stared into her big eyes and didn't have a clue. How the hell did Elissa always know the right thing to say?

He wanted to be anywhere but here. Still, he stayed. Right now he was all Zoe had. He would face all the demons for her, real or imagined, and survive.

She held out her arms and looked expectant.

"What?" he asked.

"You need to give me a hug and then kiss it all better."

Feeling both stupid and awkward, Walker wrapped his arms around her. He was careful not to squeeze too hard. Then he kissed the bandages.

When he was done, Zoe smiled. "Want to go to a movie? We could go to the mall and have lunch at the food court, and go shopping and go to a movie."

It was his idea of the seventh level of hell. But who was he to refuse a five-year-old girl with the heart of a warrior?

CHAPTER SEVENTEEN

AFTER THE FAIR CLOSED on Monday, Elissa packed up the last of her supplies and carried them to Walker's SUV. One of the guys in a neighboring booth had helped her with the tables she'd rented.

"See you next year," he called as she climbed into the driver's side.

"Sure. Congratulations."

She waved, then closed the door and started the engine.

Home, she thought wearily. She just wanted to be home. Home where she could be quiet and finally think. Or maybe not think. Maybe what she needed was to sleep.

Because she hadn't the night before. Long after she'd gone to bed, she'd lain awake in the dark, staring at the ceiling, wondering what to do about Neil.

He hadn't said how long he was going to be in Seattle, but she didn't think he would make the trip for just a few nights of work. Which meant weeks, maybe even a month in the area. He could show up at any time, demanding more money, insisting she pay or he would want to see Zoe.

Her stomach clenched at the thought. Zoe thought her father was dead and that was better for everyone. But if things got ugly, Elissa could find herself having to tell Zoe about Neil—and she would do nearly anything to avoid that.

The fear grew until it was hard to think about anything else. She briefly considered running—packing up a few suitcases, grabbing Zoe and going. But where? And what would happen when they got there? Unless she figured out how to get a fake name and identification, Neil would eventually find her. How would she explain the situation to Zoe? Plus she hated the idea of running—it was too much like letting him win.

The most logical solution was to go to a lawyer. Something she should have done years ago. Neil was not a good influence for a small child. Surely the courts would see that. If she could work out a deal, pay Neil off and get him to sign a release of some kind, that would be the best solution. Only what would motivate him? She didn't have enough money to give him a lump sum large enough to satisfy him.

A loan, she thought. Not from a bank, but maybe her parents or Frank. Even with her and her mother at odds, surely her parents would help her keep Zoe. Walker had the cash, but she wasn't comfortable discussing Neil with him. Besides, she wasn't sure any of them would approve of her decision to pay a drug addict to stay away from his child. What if they wanted her to be more reasonable, to let Neil have the chance to prove himself as a good father? Neil was a great manipulator. He'd had a lifetime of practice, using people. What if he convinced them he deserved a chance?

She eased the large SUV into the driveway and put it in park. Walker stepped out of her apartment and crossed toward her.

It was almost dark and he appeared to be more shadow than man. Yet she felt drawn to him. She wanted to jump out of the SUV and throw herself into his arms. She wanted to confess everything and have him hold her and tell her it was going to be all right. She'd been on her own for eight years and she was tired of being the only one responsible.

"Good day?" he asked, moving to the rear of the vehicle and opening the hatch. "Make millions?"

She managed a smile. "Close. We were busy right up to the end. I sold nearly everything I had."

"Good for you. Are you tired?"

She nodded. Bone weary, and for reasons she realized she wasn't going to explain. She might be able to handle a lot in her life, but she couldn't face Walker looking at her with pity or scorn. Only an idiot would have gotten involved with Neil in the first place and only a fool would keep on paying him now.

He collected her few remaining boxes of supplies, then closed the back. "I'll return the tables in the morning."

"You don't have to do that. I was going to take them in after work." Which would have meant borrowing his SUV again.

"It's on *my* way to work. Don't sweat it."

She'd prepaid for the tables, so that wasn't a problem. "Okay. Thanks. They have a deposit check they'll return."

He followed her into her apartment and set the boxes on her worktable.

"How was Zoe?" she asked.

"Good. She went to bed right on time and was asleep in thirty seconds. We went to the mall, saw a movie, then had dinner at the food court."

Somehow Walker didn't strike her as the mall type. "Was it horrible?"

"I survived."

She winced. "Why do I know the movie was pure torture?"

"At least it was short."

They stood on opposite sides of the sofa. The last time they'd been alone in her apartment, they'd been making love. Everything was different now. Not only weren't they alone—even though Zoe was in bed asleep—she felt as if their intimate experience had happened to someone else.

Even as her body cried out for him, her brain knew that getting involved—more involved—was dangerous. Not only for her own sense of self-preservation, but because having Neil around changed everything. If Walker knew about him, he would, in typical macho guy fashion, want to fix the problem. That could only lead to trouble.

While she didn't doubt Walker could take care of himself in a fair fight, Neil was never fair. No, telling

Walker about her problems with her ex would definitely mean trouble.

Before she could figure out a polite way to ask him to leave, he gestured for her to take a seat on the sofa. Given all he'd done for her, she owed him at least that. So she would talk for a while, then claim tiredness and get him out of here.

"I'm glad your booth was a success," he said. "Does that mean you'll get asked back next year?"

"I hope so. I liked watching people look at my designs. I could ask them questions and figure out what was selling best and why." She glanced at him. "Your entire family came by. That was really nice of them. They certainly didn't have to, but I appreciated the support."

"They like you," he said, then exhaled slowly. "Dani found out Ryan's married."

That got her attention. "What? Are you kidding?"

He shook his head. "His wife came by the restaurant yesterday. He'd never said a word about her. There's a kid, too."

Betrayal was never easy, she thought sadly. "How's Dani holding up?"

"She's tough. She'll get through it. But having this happen only a couple of months after Hugh walked out on her and then turned up a cheater isn't helping."

Apparently Elissa wasn't the only one with sucky taste in men. "Tell her I'm thinking of starting a club for women who've given up on men."

His gaze snapped to her face. "I will."

She realized what she'd said and wasn't sure how to recover. "It's just, before you… I've had issues. You know. In the past, I mean."

He nodded without speaking. Silence filled the room. At last he said, "Something's wrong. What happened?"

"Nothing. I'm fine. Beyond tired. This was a tough three days, but really worth it."

His gaze didn't waver. He studied her with an intensity that made her shift on the sofa.

"I'm fine," she repeated firmly.

"There's something. I can see it in your eyes."

"You're wrong. Let it go."

Walker knew he probably should. She'd made it more than clear she wasn't interested in telling him. But she looked…defeated. He'd never seen that in her before. Everything about her was tough and capable. What could have brought that on?

"Were you robbed?" he asked sharply.

"What? No. Of course not." She pulled a wad of bills out of her jeans pocket. "I made a ton of money."

"Did your mother stop by and harass you about Zoe?"

She actually rolled her eyes. "Will you stop? I'm good."

She wasn't. The more she protested, the more he was sure.

"Elissa, I can help."

"You're not going to let this go, are you?"

He wasn't sure. His gut told him there was something serious at stake. That her defeat had come from a place of fear. But who could scare her and why? If she—

She slid across the sofa and straddled him. Before he could react, she put her hands on his shoulders and kissed him.

Her mouth was hot and aggressive. Her tongue darted into his mouth, claiming, teasing, arousing. While his brain knew this was nothing more than a distraction, his body was willing to play the game.

Still, he fought the sudden rise of both his need and his erection right up until she grabbed his hands and placed them on her breasts.

The soft curves beckoned him. He found himself exploring them, squeezing gently, then moving his thumbs across her tight nipples. He dropped his hands to her waist, then moved them up again, under her T-shirt. After unfastening her bra, he returned to her breasts, this time touching bare skin.

She was hot and demanding, rubbing herself against his arousal, kissing him deeply, then pulling back to nip on his jaw and neck and ear. She jerked his T-shirt over his head, then pulled off her own. Then she rose up on her knees and leaned forward so her nipple brushed against his mouth.

He had no choice but to wrap his arms around her, holding her close as he sucked and licked. Wanting pulsed through him, burning him with its intensity. He moved to her other breast. She clasped his head and whispered for him to take her.

"I want you," she breathed.

Then she was gone. She stood and walked across

the living room without once looking back. But at the entrance to the hall, she paused and kicked off her sandals, then pushed off her jeans and panties. The invitation was clear.

In deference to a small child living in the house, Walker kept his jeans on until he reached Elissa's bedroom. Then he shut the door and gazed at the naked woman waiting for him in bed.

She lay on her back, a condom dangling from one hand. Her smile of invitation was all he needed. He shed the rest of his clothes and joined her on the bed.

She slid the condom onto him, then pushed him onto his back.

"I want to be on top," she told him. Once again she straddled him, only this time there weren't any layers between them. As she eased down on him, he pushed inside of her.

He felt the heat and dampness of her body as he entered her. She slid down slowly, claiming him in an erotic dance that made his body surge. Her breasts hung tantalizingly in front of him. He reached for them and rubbed her nipples.

She closed her eyes and groaned. As she rose and fell on him, her body contracted around him. The position meant she controlled both speed and depth, which meant she could push him too close too fast.

"Slow down," he breathed, wanting to make sure she was as far along.

But she ignored him. Up and down, taking him deeper and deeper, drawing him in, tightening around him. He started to lower his hands to her hips, to make her stop, but she cried out.

"Touch me," she breathed.

He returned his hands to her breasts.

She moved faster and faster until he reached the point of no return. Until he had to give it up with a shuddering moan. Pleasure shot through him, as he pushed into her and came.

When he was finished, he opened his eyes. "Elissa?"

"That was great," she said as she moved off of him. "I'll sleep tonight."

Would she? Or was that as much a lie as the sex had been. Because what she'd just done hadn't been about connecting or even getting off. Not for her. It had been about distracting him. He'd been had.

She walked to her closet and pulled out a robe, then yawned broadly. "Thanks, Walker. I'd ask you to stay, but with Zoe and all." She looked at her clock radio. "Wow, when did it get so late? You must be exhausted from your day. Don't let me keep you."

"I HAVE TWENTY-SEVEN hundred dollars," Elissa told the female attorney sitting across from her, wishing she'd had that money five years ago and had taken care of this then. "I'm not kidding about that. When that's gone, I'm lucky to scrape together twenty-five dollars a week."

Sally Chasley smiled. "Don't worry, Elissa. We charge fees on a sliding scale basis. Right now the most important issue is dealing with your problem. You said you're being harassed by your ex-husband."

"No. Neil and I were never married. We were living together, with me paying for everything. He uses drugs, sometimes heavily. It gets expensive. Anyway, I got pregnant and he wanted me to have an abortion. I refused and I left." Ran was more like it, Elissa thought grimly. She'd run for her life and Zoe's.

"And then?" Sally prompted. "Did you get in touch with him after the baby was born?"

Elissa shook her head. "I saved money until I had enough for a bus ticket, then I came here."

Sally frowned. "You didn't discuss the baby with Neil? You didn't talk to him about child support or getting involved in his daughter's life?"

"I told you, Neil wanted me to have an abortion."

"I know, but a lot of men panic at the thought of a baby. Especially a first child. But once that child is born, many of them change their minds. They want to be fathers."

"Neil is only interested in his next fix."

"Has he physically threatened you?"

Elissa didn't like the direction of the conversation. "He beat me up when he found out I was pregnant." Would that be enough? "He finds me and demands money. If I don't pay him, he says he's going to insist on being in Zoe's life. Isn't that extortion or something?"

Sally sighed. "Elissa, the law takes the rights of both parents seriously. Neil reacted badly one time. He hit you one time. It happens."

Elissa couldn't believe that. "How many times does he get to hit me before it's not okay? What about his chronic drug use? I don't want Zoe exposed to that."

"Nor should she be. However, Neil still has the right to see his child. You could make a case for supervised visits. He would have to earn your and her trust."

"I'll never trust him," she said flatly. "He doesn't care about Zoe. He's using her to get money from me."

"You're letting him," Sally told her. "Stop paying. If what you're saying is true, he'll go away. If he pursues his parental rights, then perhaps you're misjudging him. The bottom line is you can't prevent a parent from seeing his or her children without cause. Not liking him isn't sufficient grounds."

It was her worst nightmare come true, she thought bitterly. No doubt the very sensible and clueless Sally would refuse to help her draft documents offering Neil a large sum of cash to relinquish his rights as a father.

"Thank you for your time," Elissa said and stood. "If you'll just tell me your hourly fee, I'll pay you for your time."

"Elissa, don't go. Let's talk about this more."

"I don't have anything else to say."

ELISSA DROVE HOME Thursday after work feeling as if she'd been drop-kicked off a cliff. Both her body and her spirit ached and she suspected she only had herself to blame.

The meeting with the lawyer had been a disaster. Sally had offered nothing constructive. The idea that Neil was actually interested in Zoe was beyond stupid and it terrified her that a reasonably intelligent professional would even consider it. Did that mean the courts would lean that way, as well? If push came to shove, could Neil get visitation rights?

If only he would go away for a few years, she thought. He was known to disappear for months at a time, but she didn't think she was going to get that lucky. Him finding her at the craft fair meant he suspected she had resources and therefore cash. If anything, his appearances might become more frequent.

She pulled up in front of her apartment and climbed out of her car. Zoe came running toward her.

"Mommy, Mommy, I love school so much!! We made a little book about our summer and I brought mine home to show you. And I brought my lunch today but tomorrow is tacos. Is that okay? Can I buy lunch tomorrow?"

"Of course."

Her daughter flung herself at her. Elissa caught her and held her close. Okay, whatever else might be screwed up in her life, Zoe was exactly right. She was worth any price, any hardship and there was no way in hell Neil was getting his hands on her.

"So you had a good day, huh?" Elissa asked as they walked toward the apartment. "Were you good for Mrs. Ford?"

"Oh, she's not here," Zoe said happily. "She's playing bridge. Walker is with me."

Elissa stopped on the bottom step of her small

porch. Shame and embarrassment rose up inside of her. Her face burned, her throat got tight and she wanted to curl up in a ball and disappear.

She hadn't seen him since Monday night when she'd used sex to shut him up and get him out of the apartment.

After he'd left, she'd felt awful. Cheap and mean and disgusting. Seven years ago, she'd used her body to get a job after she and Mitch broke up and afterward, she'd felt so horrified with herself she'd vowed to never do anything like that again. But when backed into a corner, she'd taken the easy way out.

She hated herself for what she'd done and she was terrified to know what he must think of her. Sure, she'd known there could never be anything between them—he'd made that clear on multiple occasions—but she'd liked knowing they were friends and that he at least respected her. Now all that was gone.

"Come on, Mommy," Zoe said, tugging on her hand.

Elissa couldn't think of a way to avoid the encounter, so she sucked in a breath and stepped into the apartment.

Walker stood in the center of the room. A half-finished puzzle sat on the coffee table next to a couple of juice boxes.

He'd been in her house before, but this time was different. She felt exposed and embarrassed.

"I, ah, want to thank you for looking after Zoe," she said, refusing to raise her gaze above the center of his chest. "I'm sorry Mrs. Ford bothered you. It's the middle of your workday."

"Not a problem."

That couldn't be true, she thought, wishing she could think of a gracious way to end the conversation.

"I need to get changed," she said, motioning to her uniform, then practically running toward her bedroom.

She closed the door behind her and did her best to avoid looking at the bed. After changing, she wished she could hide out forever, but that wasn't an option. She would have to face him sometime. Maybe it was better to get it over with sooner rather than later.

Or maybe he'd just left, she thought hopefully. Maybe he didn't want to see her any more than she'd wanted to see him. But she had a feeling her luck wasn't that good.

Sure enough, when she returned to the living room, she found Zoe engrossed in a video and Walker standing in the entrance to the kitchen. While she longed to settle next to her daughter, she knew Walker deserved an explanation, so she entered the kitchen and carefully closed the door behind them.

Once they were alone, she braced herself for the attack, but what he said instead was, "There's an opening for an assistant manager at Buchanan's. It's the lunch shift, but you'd need to work a couple of nights a week. Maybe one weekend night. We have full benefits, including matching on the 401K. Management also has a profit-sharing plan, but that wouldn't kick in for six months." He named a salary that made her knees shake. "You interested?"

"Are you offering me a job?" she asked, not able to believe it.

"Yes."

"You don't know anything about me."

He folded his arms over his chest. "I know plenty."

If possible, her blush deepened. "I meant you don't know anything about my work life. If I show up on time, what kind of work I do. I have no management experience and I've never worked in a restaurant other than Eggs 'n' Stuff. Why would you think I'm qualified?"

"I've seen you work until your fingers are swollen. You're always out of here plenty early, so I know you get to your shift on time. The job is considered entry level management. You'd learn as you go."

It was a terrific opportunity. So why did she have a knot in her stomach?

"I like the job I have," she told him.

His gaze narrowed. "This one's better."

"I don't want to work nights. I'm not willing to give up my time with Zoe."

"We're talking one or two evenings."

"I don't…" She swallowed. "I won't work for someone I've slept with."

There. She'd said it. Now he was going to pounce all over her and want to know why things had gone the way they had.

"Dammit, Elissa," Walker said, careful to keep his voice low, which she appreciated. "What the hell kind of game is this? You know it's a good job. Why won't you consider it? If your reasons are about me, don't worry. I'm a temp."

"You think things are going to be better when

your grandmother comes back? You think she won't fire me that first day?"

"We do a contract. She won't be able to."

"Oh, great. So the president of the company will be stuck with me. That should be fun."

"I'm trying to help."

"This isn't helping. Besides, I'm fine."

"You're not fine." He paused and drew in a breath, as if trying to control his temper. "You're not fine," he repeated. "Something is wrong. Do you think I'm stupid? Whatever it is had to be pretty damn big for you to go to that kind of extreme just to change the subject. What is it?"

"Nothing I want to talk about with you."

"Look around. You don't have anyone else. You need me."

She didn't need anyone. Never had, never would. "Talk about an ego," she told him, stepping forward so she could make her point without raising her voice. "I was doing just fine before you came along."

He made a sound that was suspiciously like a growl. "I'm not talking about money or the fact that I can unfasten lug nuts. I'm the one person you can talk to. Who else are you going to tell? Mrs. Ford?"

"I don't make it a habit of talking about my problems."

His gaze narrowed. "So there *is* something wrong."

"No. I meant in a general sense. Look, Walker, if you want to make a complaint, put it in writing. Otherwise—"

He dropped his hands to his sides. "Do *not* tell me to leave."

"It's my house."

She could feel the frustration building up inside of him. Despite his physical presence and strength, she wasn't afraid. He would never hurt her.

"Something happened at the craft fair," he said. "I know and you know. So can we please stop playing this game so you can tell me what the hell it is?"

She opened her mouth to tell him no, but suddenly she couldn't. He was right—she didn't have anyone else in her life.

"Zoe's father showed up on Sunday," she said quietly. "He's in Seattle with some band. He wanted money. It's the same thing every time—either I pay him off or he's going to become a part of Zoe's life."

"Did you give him money?"

"All I'd made that day."

"And you think he'll be back?"

"I know he will."

Instead of speaking, Walker moved close and put his arms around her. She resisted the embrace.

"I'm fine," she insisted. "I can handle this."

"No one doubts that, but even the Marines sometimes call in reinforcements."

He pulled her against him and she gave in because she didn't have the strength to keep standing on her own.

"I'm so scared," she whispered.

"I'm right here. We can handle this. I'll help."

She wanted to make him promise that he meant what he said. That he wouldn't change his mind.

She was a woman who didn't trust men in her life and he was a man who didn't trust himself. But her gut said to go with him. Despite everything, Walker was turning out to be the best kind of hero.

CHAPTER EIGHTEEN

DANI SPENT SO MUCH TIME on her hair and makeup that she felt like a beauty contestant. Ryan, aka the weasel loser, had called in sick for the past couple of days, but he was expected back and she needed to be braced to face him. Hence the extra time spent on her appearance, along with the decision to dress in a killer pair of black slacks and fitted silk blouse. If there was any kind of spillage from the kitchen, she would be crushed, but the risk was worth it. She wanted Ryan to regret what he'd lost. She wanted him to pay.

Unfortunately she'd yet to find out a way to make that happen, but she was working on it. Eventually something would come to her.

She got into work at her regular time and noted his car wasn't in the parking lot yet. Good. She could load up on coffee and brace herself.

About a half hour later, while she was editing Edouard's suggestions for specials, she heard familiar footsteps in the hallway. She didn't glance up, but she took a second to brace herself to confront the lying cheat.

"Dani," he said, his voice low and seductive. "Hi."

She looked at him, at the handsome face, the killer eyes and knew she'd been duped by a master. "Ryan."

"How are you? I've been worried about you."

Had he? Oh, goody. Her life was now complete due to his amazing concern.

"Why?" she asked.

He stepped into the room and shut the door behind him. "Because of what happened. Jen coming here like that." He sighed. "I really didn't want you to find out that way."

Oh. My. God. His words were so familiar, it was almost eerie. Were all men chronically unable to take responsibility? Hugh had said the same sort of thing to her, saying he felt so awful about her finding out about his affair but never apologizing for actually cheating, the bastard.

Like Hugh, Ryan wasn't sorry for what he'd done, he was just upset about being caught.

"How did you want me to find out?" she asked cheerfully. "Or were you hoping I never would?"

"I, ah…" He looked startled, as if he hadn't expected the question. "Dani—"

She cut him off with a flick of her fingers. "Here's my question. Have you ever been faithful to your wife? Did you at least wait a couple of months before starting to cheat? Because there's no way in hell I'm the first time. You're too smooth at the lies."

He stiffened. "I love my family."

"Of course you do. I can see it in every move you

make. Sleeping with me was such an incredible act of love. Is Jen grateful?"

"Are you threatening me?" he asked. "Are you going to tell her?"

"Honestly, the thought never crossed my mind. I think you're hurting her enough for both of us, so I don't need to. Now that I realize what an asshole you are, I would like to tell her the truth, but I suspect she wouldn't believe me. I'm sure you've convinced her you're all things wonderful. It's funny. When I first found out I felt really sorry for myself, but I don't anymore. I feel sorry for her. I'm in a position to walk away and never look back."

He swallowed. "You're going to have your brother fire me, aren't you?"

"Not necessarily. You're a decent general manager and with Penny out on maternity leave, the restaurant can't handle any more changes right now. So as long as you don't piss me off, you're safe. But you will play it straight with every single woman who works here and every woman I may ever encounter. You'll start the conversation by announcing you're married and not even think about flirting. Do I make myself clear?"

"You're still angry."

She considered the statement. "You know, I'm not. I thought I would be, but I feel oddly cleansed by this conversation. Maybe because I finally get that I didn't do anything wrong. That was the thing I hated, that I'd made such a lousy choice. But I didn't. You set out to convince me you were exactly what I was looking for. I had no reason to mistrust you. *You* lied, I didn't. Thanks to Al, our fabulous cat, you're the only rat in this building, and I can live with that."

WALKER STAYED for dinner. Elissa found it interesting that her once-reserved neighbor was now comfortable with her five-year-old. Zoe and Walker chatted easily and even had a couple of shared jokes from their day at the mall.

He was so different from any man she'd ever known. Some of it was her life circumstances. She'd gone from being a kid in high school to a runaway on her own. Being on the fringes of the music business in L.A. hadn't exactly put her in the path of very many guys who could be considered normal. Then she'd gotten pregnant and returned to Seattle where her lifestyle didn't lend itself to meeting a lot of single men.

So Walker was quite the change. But it was more than that. Some of the differences came from who he was. She had trouble reconciling a man who would carefully and patiently play cat's cradle with her daughter with an eighteen-year-old who had abandoned his dying girlfriend.

So what had happened in the fourteen plus years in between? Was it just a matter of growing up? Or was it deeper than that? He'd run from Charlotte to avoid death and pain, yet he'd planted himself right in the middle of a war. He'd sent men into battle and some of them had been killed. And what about his quest for Ben's Ashley? How much of that was guilt about Ben taking a bullet and how much of it was about his leaving Charlotte?

Walker was a complex man, she thought as she sipped her wine and listened to her daughter laugh. But a good man. She didn't like that he'd run out on his girlfriend, but she also didn't like several pieces of her own past. Everyone made mistakes. The measure of a person was what happened afterward.

Later, when Zoe was in bed, Elissa returned to the living room and settled on the sofa. Walker had produced another bottle of wine which, given her exhaustion and stress level, might be considered dangerous. On the other hand, alcohol would make it easier to talk about Neil, who happened to be her big mistake.

"Neil's come after you before," Walker said by way of introduction.

She nodded. "He often travels with bands. It's easier than putting his own together—that might require actual work, something he really hates. He's been through twice before. I don't know how he got my phone number, but he did. He would call and say we had to meet. If I refused, he threatened me. When I showed up he would start talking about Zoe and how he doesn't ever see her. It was always some version of that. I would give him whatever money I had and he would go away."

"Have you ever talked to him about signing a release?"

"No. Why would he agree when he can just step up to the money train anytime he's in town?" She sipped her wine. "Neil is a gifted musician and songwriter. When he's clean, he's brilliant. Still an ass, but brilliant. When he's on drugs, all he can do is play guitar and try to get through a day."

"Legally what he's doing is blackmail," Walker told her. "There are laws against that."

"I know, but if I push things legally, it could get ugly. He could tell the courts he desperately wants to see his daughter. He's a good liar. He could also say I've been keeping her from him, which is true. I saw a lawyer today."

"From the look on your face, it didn't go well."

"Not even close. She wasn't very sympathetic. Her feeling was supervised visits wouldn't be such a bad thing. Neil had never been emotionally or physically abusive, so Zoe's not at risk. The fact that Neil told me to get an abortion didn't seem to matter, either. She feels that many men react badly to an unexpected pregnancy and that I shouldn't hold that against him."

She clutched her glass in both hands. "The thought of getting involved in the legal system terrifies me. What if he were to win the right to see Zoe? Neil doesn't care about her. He would use that right to get money from me. I can see him running off with her and then holding her hostage while I begged or borrowed more money."

Her eyes began to burn. She drew in a breath and concentrated on staying in control.

"I would do anything to keep Zoe safe. I've even thought about running away. I just didn't know if I could start over again. And she would hate it."

"Running is a temporary solution. You need something permanent."

His words were cold and flat and for the first time since getting to know him, she remembered that Walker was a man capable of killing.

"What are you thinking?" she asked, not sure she really wanted to know.

"That I want to find him and beat the shit out of him. That I want to teach him a lesson he'll never forget and make him understand that if he ever gets near you or Zoe again, it would be the last thing he did." His mouth twisted. "Scared?"

"Of you?" She shook her head. "No. You wouldn't hurt me or Zoe. I'm not even sure you'd hurt Neil. I believe you'd want to, but I don't know that you could just walk up to him and beat on him."

"Want to bet?"

She smiled. "I don't think so."

He stared at her for a few seconds, then said, "You need to talk to a lawyer."

"I just did. It was awful."

"I'm talking about a specialist. Someone who will take your side and get the job done. Someone brutal."

"Someone expensive," she said, thinking of her pathetic twenty-seven hundred dollars and knowing a lawyer like that would suck it up in a week.

"Experienced," he said. "I want to do some research and find the right person. I'll pay for it and before you get all emotional, let me say this is a loan. You can pay me back over time."

"I don't get emotional," she told him, even as she

considered his offer. In her heart she knew that continuing to pay off Neil would only lead to trouble. If she could find someone who would *really* help, then she could keep Zoe safe.

"You do," he said. "Okay. Have at it. I'm braced for the fight."

She smiled. "There isn't going be a fight. Thank you for the offer and yes, please, find someone to help me."

He opened his mouth, then closed it. His expression of shock made her giggle.

"I had all my arguments lined up," he said with a frown. "They were pretty good."

"You can still use them if you want. I'll just sit here and listen, and then I can applaud."

He reached across the sofa and touched her cheek. "Better," he said. "I like the attitude. It's been missing lately."

She covered his fingers with her own. "You've been so good to me and I've…" Oh, God. She had to apologize, but just thinking about what she'd done made her want to crawl under a rock. "I wanted to tell you I was sorry. About what happened. About what I did. It was wrong and I feel awful. I panicked and reacted but that's no excuse."

"It's okay."

"No, it's not. I hate that I went there. It makes me feel as if I haven't grown at all. I just kept thinking I had to distract you."

"You did a hell of a job." He leaned in and kissed her. "Here's an idea. You quit beating yourself up, I'll accept your apology and we'll call it a day."

He was making it easy on her. "Thank you," she said. "Was it too awful?"

He kissed her again. "Emotionally it sucked but physically, let's see. I had a beautiful woman desperate to have her way with me. Every guy should be so abused. And just as a heads-up, you're never allowed to tell anyone I care about emotions during sex. I have a reputation to think about."

The last of her guilt and shame faded away as she studied his face.

"Your secret is safe with me," she promised.

"Good. Now..." He took the wine from her and set both their glasses on the coffee table. "The way I see it, you owe me and I think it's time to collect."

Her first instinct was to protest. Not because she didn't want to make love with him, but because she felt foolish and awkward.

"I'm nervous," she admitted.

"Nervous as in no?"

She stared into his dark eyes. He would stop if she told him to. He would walk away and never blame her.

"Nervous as in 'Oh, God, what does he really think of me'?"

He leaned in and kissed her. "That kind of nervous I can handle."

WALKER DRESSED while Elissa stepped into the shower. It was still dark outside and not much past four in the morning. They'd stayed up way too late making love and he knew she was going to spend her day exhausted. But based on the way she'd moaned and writhed beneath him, he was willing to bet she'd think the night had been a fair trade for sleep. Besides, it was Friday and the end of her workweek.

He considered going upstairs and sleeping for another hour, but then decided to get an early start on his day. He could—

His cell phone rang. He grabbed it, then studied the caller ID. Cal. Which meant…

"Hello?" he said. "Cal?"

"Penny's in labor," his brother said, sounding both excited and terrified. "We're at the hospital. It's going to be a few hours yet, but I wanted you to know we're here."

"Want me to come in now or wait?"

"You can wait. I'm staying pretty close to Penny, so you'd just be hanging out by yourself. But check back with me."

"Will do. Tell her good luck and that I'll be thinking about her."

"Sure. I'm gonna call Reid. See you soon."

Cal hung up. Elissa walked out of the bathroom, her hair pulled back and a large chicken staring at him from the front of her apron.

"Everything okay?" she asked. "Is it your grandmother?"

He hadn't given Gloria a single thought. "No, Penny's in labor."

Elissa grinned. "At last. I know she was ready to have the baby out. Are you going to the hospital?"

"They just got there. Cal said I should wait. I thought I'd go by this afternoon."

"First babies can be slow. I was lucky. Zoe only took about six hours, but I've heard horror stories of long deliveries. Can I call you later and find out how she's doing?"

"Of course. Do you want to come by the hospital after work?"

"I'd like to but I don't want to get in the way."

"You won't. Phone me and I'll let you know if we have a kid yet or not. How's that?"

"Perfect." She raised up on her tiptoes and kissed him. "Want coffee?"

"I'd rather have you, but I'll take what I can get."

WALKER ARRIVED at the hospital shortly after one in the afternoon. Cal had called to say Penny was ready to deliver, so by the time Walker arrived, Reid was standing in front with good news.

"A girl," Reid said with a grin as he pounded Walker on the back. "She's kinda red and squashed, but Penny and Cal think she's beautiful so don't say anything."

"You seen Penny yet?"

"For a couple of seconds. She's tired but happy. There's some test for newborns and the baby did great, so that's good."

Walker knew both Cal and Penny had to be relieved. Penny had miscarried their first baby years ago.

"Dani's here," Reid told him as he led him to the elevator and pushed the up button. "She was the standby coach in case Cal couldn't do it, but he managed. Said he nearly passed out a couple of times." Reid grimaced. "I never much thought about having kids. Now I'm thinking I won't."

"Based on Cal's one experience?" Walker asked. "You might want to come up with a better reason."

They stepped onto the elevator. "Do I need one?" Reid asked. "Do you?" He narrowed his gaze. "It's Elissa, isn't it? Her daughter's getting to you."

Walker wasn't about to admit that. "Zoe's a good kid, but that doesn't mean I'm ready to be a father."

He'd never thought about having a family because he'd long ago decided he would never get married. Connections weren't for him. He couldn't be trusted.

Except the familiar litany no longer had such a ring of truth. After all these years, was he willing to let the past go? Was he willing to forgive himself?

They stepped off the elevator and onto a long corridor. The maternity ward was bright and airy, but the underlying smell of hospital was still there. Walker flashed back to visiting soldiers in makeshift wards after a battle and then he remembered visiting Charlotte after her first surgery. How she'd been scared and he'd promised she would be fine.

He'd been wrong. And then he'd left. He swore silently as he remembered her tears when she figured out he was leaving, that he wasn't going to stick around and watch her die.

He should have stayed. He should have been there for her. They'd been in love, and when the going had gotten tough…

So did he have the right to forgive himself? Did he have the right to acknowledge the mistake and move on? She had told him to. Maybe that's what made this all so difficult—that she'd been able to see what no one else had. His coward's heart.

He'd faced death, had sent men to die. He'd been wounded, taken prisoner for an ugly three weeks and had lived to tell the tale. But did that change who he was inside? He wasn't as concerned about anyone else trusting him as he was about trusting himself.

"Hey, big guy."

Walker turned at the sound of the familiar voice. But the woman walking toward him wasn't exactly the tall, brunette bombshell he remembered. She still wore leather pants and come-fuck-me boots, but her walk, her smile, everything else was different. Softer. Happy.

"Naomi."

She smiled, shrugged, then moved toward him and hugged him. "In the flesh, so to speak."

"You look good," he said.

"I feel good," she told him as she stepped back. "You're still hot."

"I do okay." She linked arms with him. "Have you seen the baby?"

"No."

"Then let me show you. She's beautiful." She led him down the corridor. "How are you doing? Penny told me you've taken over Buchanan Enterprises. I would never have predicted that happening."

"Me, either. But there wasn't anyone else."

"There's always someone else. But I'm sure they appreciate you stepping up and saving them from the job."

They stopped in front of the nursery. Naomi glanced around. "Oh, they're still fussing with her. She'll be along in a few minutes. So are you happy?"

"Are you?" he asked, sidestepping a typically blunt Naomi question.

She smiled. "Yes. Blissfully so. My husband and I are back together. The old fool didn't bother to fall out of love with me, which makes no sense."

"You'd be hard to replace."

"Aren't you sweet for saying that." She sighed. "We have a lot of work to do on the relationship, but we're determined. We're also going to adopt a little girl from China. We've sent in the paperwork and we're very hopeful."

He knew about the loss of her son and how she'd nearly lost herself in the grief. "Good for you."

"Have you found Ashley?"

He didn't want to think of failing Ben, but he was running out of names on the list. "Not yet. I'm beginning to think she doesn't exist."

"She does and you'll find her," Naomi told him. "Have faith."

"There's not a lot of that going around."

"There should be." She faced him and took his hands in hers. "You're a good man, Walker Buchanan. One of the best I know, and I've known plenty. Don't give up on yourself or the world and don't stop saving people, especially yourself."

"I haven't saved anyone," he said gruffly, not believing a word of it, but also unwilling to get trapped into an emotional moment.

"You saved me," she said quietly. "You saved my life in more ways than you can know." She raised herself onto her toes and lightly kissed his mouth. "For old times' sake, whatever the hell that means."

He touched her cheek. "I'm glad you found your way."

"Me, too. I wish you could—" She sighed, then swore. "Okay, there's a very attractive woman in her midtwenties glaring at me like I'm the devil with boobs. I'm guessing you know her."

Walker held in a groan as he turned and saw Elissa standing about six feet away. She'd obviously gone home and changed because she wasn't wearing her chicken uniform. She also didn't look all that happy.

He stepped back from Naomi, but knew it was too little too late and that he was going to have a hell of a lot of explaining to do. Before he could figure out how to start or what to say, Naomi released his hands and walked over to Elissa.

"Hi, I'm Naomi," she said with an easy smile. "I'm an old friend of Penny's and a friend of the family. I mean that. I've even seen Cal naked—which is a fascinating story, if I do say so myself. I'm happily married and Walker never really saw me as anything significant anyway, but I will admit to trying."

Too much information, Elissa thought, feeling both embarrassed and exposed. She felt as if she'd walked in on something intimate and she didn't like being the outsider.

"Nice to meet you," she said, forcing herself to smile and hoping she looked pleasant instead of shell-shocked. She'd known Walker had flaws, but she hadn't considered kissing other women would be one of them.

"Okay. I'm going to go check on Penny," the other woman said and strolled away.

Elissa watched her go. Naomi was everything she wasn't—tall, elegant, confident and beautiful. Worse, Elissa could imagine Walker with her. They would have made a stunning couple. Both fiercely sexual and larger than life.

"Elissa," Walker said awkwardly. "Naomi and I are friends. Nothing more."

"Now," Elissa murmured as she fought the sudden wave of nausea that swept over her. "Before you were a whole lot more."

"We weren't romantically involved," he said. "I want you to know that."

"But you *were* lovers."

She didn't mean to say that. The words simply popped out on their own.

He was silent for a long time, then admitted, "Once."

Great. Once as in "one time" or once as in "once upon a time but it lasted for weeks and weeks?" Not sure she could handle the truth, she drew in a deep breath.

"No biggie," she said, lying and hoping he couldn't tell.

"It's not," he told her, moving close and gazing into her eyes. "I could have said we weren't lovers, but I don't want to lie to you. It was one time. We were lost souls looking for a little peace, nothing more."

He was both making the situation better and worse, she thought, wishing she could see the humor in it. Maybe later, when she didn't feel so raw. Intellectually she knew that his wanting to clear the air was a good thing. It meant his relationship with her was important. But why did he have to have slept with an Amazon beauty? Why not some silly mousy blonde with the personality of a cucumber?

"Are we all right?" he asked.

She nodded, then pointed as "Baby Buchanan" was placed in her bassinet.

They turned to stare at the infant. Walker said something about Reid saying she wasn't all that much to look at but he thought she wasn't so bad. Elissa may have responded. She wasn't completely sure. Mostly because her brain had frozen, just like a computer in the middle of a glitch. There was only one thought in her head and it played over and over again until it had burned itself into her neurons or synapses or whatever it was in her brain.

That she could never be beautiful and amazing like Naomi or any of the other women Walker rescued. That she was just a lost soul, too, and wasn't this a hell of a time to realize she was in love with him?

CHAPTER NINETEEN

ELISSA FOUND HERSELF somewhere she wasn't sure she was ever going to be again…standing in front of her parents' house. She hadn't meant to drive here. Somehow her car had gotten on the freeway and this was where she'd ended up.

Her whole body hurt and the list of reasons why seemed to stretch on forever. Just a few weeks ago, she'd felt really good about her life. Suddenly everything had changed and not necessarily for the better. She'd thought she was handling it, the stress of Neil, building her jewelry business, watching her baby grow up and start school. But seeing the stunning brunette in Walker's arms had created the last crack in her already crumbling facade.

But to run here? Her last encounter with her mother had been less than friendly. To be honest, she wasn't sure they were even speaking. This was crazy.

She turned to leave, then stopped when the front door opened. Her mother stood there.

"I thought I heard a car pull up," she said, her expression unreadable. "Elissa. Are you all right?"

Elissa opened her mouth, closed it and stunned them both by bursting into tears.

"I'll take that as a no," her mother said, stepping out onto the porch and putting an arm around her. "Come on inside, honey. Whatever the problem is, I know we can fix it."

Elissa allowed herself to be led into the house. It felt good to relinquish control of her life, even for a few minutes, to pretend to be that young girl who had always run home when there was trouble.

Why hadn't she done that when she'd found out she was pregnant? Why had she taken the word of a thirteen-year-old?

"I was afraid you'd stopped loving me," she said with a sob. "That's why I believed Bobby. I knew I'd hurt you and I knew you'd be so mad. I thought you'd want to punish me and I was afraid if I came back you would tell me to go away."

"Never," her mother said, rubbing her back as she guided them into the kitchen. "You're my daughter, my firstborn child, Elissa. I love you. I'll always love you. There's nothing you could ever do to change that." She sighed. "I'm sorry I got sick. I'm sorry we stopped looking."

Elissa sank into a kitchen chair and looked at her. "That's not your fault. I'm sorry I ran away, Mom. I'm the reason you got sick."

Her mother sat next to her and reached for her hand. "You were a kid. I wish I'd been stronger. If we'd just kept looking a little longer, we would have found you." Tears filled her mother's eyes. "You could have come home."

Home. That sounded nice. Except this wasn't

her home anymore. She had her own family and her own life.

"I really blew it," Elissa said and wiped her face with her free hand. "Really bad." She swallowed. "I don't know how to tell you, even."

"Just start at the beginning and go until you're done."

Which sounded so easy. She drew in a deep breath. "Zoe's father isn't dead. He's alive and currently here, in Seattle. His name is Neil."

She explained the ugly truth about him, about their relationship and how stupid she'd been. She detailed the drug use, the blackmail and how he'd found her at the craft fair.

"I know he's going to keep coming after me for money," she said. "I went to a lawyer and she was pretty useless. Basically she tried to convince me there was nothing wrong with Neil wanting to see Zoe. Only I won't let that happen. I can't. Do you know what he'd do to her? What he'd expose her to?"

"Of course you're not going to let him see her," her mother said firmly. "My God, that woman was an idiot. Neil isn't interested in his parental rights. No one has the right to use a child like that. You need a different lawyer."

"That's what Walker said," Elissa admitted. "He's going to help me find someone who can take on Neil and win." Walker. She didn't want to think about him now, but how could she not.

"He's been so good to me," she murmured. "So *there.* No guy's ever been there like him. He's strong and caring and really amazing." The tears started up again. "And that sounds really perfect, doesn't it? But it's not perfect. Because finally, after all the losers I got involved with and promising myself I'd never fall for anyone again, I did. I fell for him. I love him and he doesn't love me."

She hiccuped and brushed away her tears again. "I know he likes me, but that's not love. He won't let himself love. He feels guilty about some stuff that happened a long time ago and while I understand that, I don't think I can get him to realize it's time to let the past go. He thinks he's not good enough or worthy or something. But I think he's worthy. I get that what he did happened a long time ago. He was really young and he needs to give himself a break. And maybe he would, except there's Naomi who's so tall and beautiful and about as far from average as anyone could get. How am I supposed to compete against that?"

Fresh sobs broke free. Her mother moved closer and hugged her tight.

"You have a lot on your plate."

"I guess," Elissa said, fighting back tears. How long could one breakdown take?

But her mother didn't pressure her to stop or straighten up or be strong. Instead she held her, rocking back and forth.

When Elissa finally felt able to get a little control, she straightened. "So, Mom, how are you?"

The two women laughed.

"The way I see it," her mother said a few minutes

later over coffee and cookies, "you need to prioritize. Neil has to be dealt with first. Walker's right. You do need a good lawyer. One who'll kick Neil's ass."

Elissa raised her eyebrows. "I don't remember you ever saying 'ass' before."

"I kept that sort of thing from my children," her mother said primly. "But you're an adult now. I also say 'damn,' but that's about all. Your father uses the really dirty words."

Information she did not need, Elissa thought wryly.

"Anyway," her mother said. "Back to the lawyer. We can help with the money."

"You don't have to do that."

"I want to and your father will, as well. Besides, the money's actually yours. Your college fund," she said, then shrugged. "It's just been sitting there compounding. We always wanted you to come home and learn you had a nest egg waiting. I was thinking you'd use it for a down payment on a house, but this is more important. Let's skin the weasel."

Despite everything, Elissa laughed. "Go, Mom!"

"I can be tough," her mother said.

"I know you can." She hesitated. "I'm sorry I got weird before…about you seeing Zoe. I was upset and confused. I want you to be a part of her life. I want her to know how amazing you and Dad are."

"I know, honey. You shouldn't worry about that. We have a lot to deal with and a lot of catching up to do. That's going to take time and cause a little stress, but we'll get through it. I've been thinking about that lately—all you did. How you made it on your own with a baby. You had no job skills, no education, nothing but determination. I'm not sure I would have been so successful."

"You would have," Elissa said softly. "You would have done it for me or Bobby."

"The power of loving a child." Her mother pushed the plate of cookies toward her. "All right. We've reconciled, we have a plan for Neil, so what about Walker?"

Elissa bit into a cookie and chewed. "I don't know what to do. I don't know how to get through to him."

"Tell him the truth," her mother advised. "Tell him you love him."

"What? I can't say that."

"Why not? What's the worst that will happen?"

What would be the worst? "I'll never see him again. He'll run and I'll be alone."

"You've been alone before. So that's survivable. And if he runs, then he's not the man for you. Loving someone is a gift and if the guy in question is too stupid to realize that, then you're better off without him. Wouldn't you want to know that sooner rather than later?"

Elissa thought about the wonderful times she and Walker had shared. The way he was so patient with Zoe, how great he was in bed. "I prefer later."

Her mother raised her eyebrows. "Are you sure about that?"

Elissa sighed. "Okay, not the mature answer, I know. You're right. Find out now and then I can get started on getting over him. How's that?"

"Better," her mother said. "Besides, don't you want him to know? Even if it doesn't work out, wouldn't it be better to tell him so you don't spend the rest of your life wondering 'what if?'"

"You're using logic in a matter of the heart. I'm not sure that's even legal."

"Trust him to do the right thing," her mother said. "If you can't do that, then trust yourself to survive whatever happens."

WALKER SCROLLED through the August numbers. Business was up, which was what he liked to see. Apparently the employees liked having more responsibility and they were proving it in a tangible way. If this kept up another month, Buchanan Enterprises was due for its best year yet.

A fact that would fry his grandmother, he thought cheerfully. Maybe knowing he was doing a damn good job would encourage her to get better more quickly.

His phone buzzed. "A Mr. Dalton on line one for you," Vicki said. "He won't tell me what it's about."

Walker frowned as he picked up the receiver. "Buchanan," he said.

"Good afternoon, Mr. Buchanan," the man on the other end said. "I'm Jonathan Dalton. My firm specializes in placing highly qualified candidates in growth opportunities. If you have a few minutes, I'd like to tell you about just such an opportunity because you're exactly the kind of candidate we're looking for."

It took him a second to realize the guy was a headhunter. "What's the business?" he asked and braced himself for a detailed explanation of gunrunning, security or straight-out black ops.

"A small chain of restaurants in Idaho. They're not The Waterfront or Buchanan's," Dalton said heartily. "But that's our client's goal. To grow the business. To reach a higher level of quality and service, not to mention appeal. The salary is generous and there is ownership potential. Let me tell you a little bit about the company."

Dalton continued to talk, but Walker wasn't listening. Restaurants? The guy was calling him about restaurants? Not war or danger or death?

"Are you familiar with my background?" Walker asked. "You know I was in the Marines for nearly fifteen years."

"Of course. Our client believes that kind of experience builds leadership. Now you have hands-on in the restaurant business, which makes you the perfect candidate."

Walker doubted that a few weeks of running the family company qualified as "hands-on experience" but it was good to hear someone else did. Until that moment, he'd never seriously considered he might have a career outside of something military.

"I appreciate you thinking of me," he said, "but I'm not interested. I'm going to be tied up here for several more months." Then he didn't know what he was going to do, but there seemed to be dozens of possibilities.

Mr. Dalton sighed. "I was afraid you were going to say that. All right. I understand. But I'd like to send you some information on our firm. You're exactly the kind of person we like to offer our clients. Perhaps you could send me a résumé when you have time."

"Sure thing," Walker said, thinking now he'd have to write one.

He finished with the call, then walked to the window and stared out at Gloria's view.

A few weeks ago, he'd felt as if he didn't have any choices. Running the company had been a job he'd taken on by default, yet he'd quickly found himself enjoying his work. Was he a tycoon in the making?

The thought made him smile. Maybe not a tycoon, but there were other things he could do. Other jobs, other careers. He still had his ghosts, but they came less frequently. The dreams were still there and would be until he found that one person who cared.

After fifteen years in the Corps, he should know how to move on. He had known, until Ben. Until that kid had gotten under his skin. He, Walker, had vowed to keep Ben alive and he'd failed.

He wouldn't fail again.

"I *WAS* ON THE ROAD A LOT," Reid said, annoyed with himself for even bothering to explain to someone who wasn't interested.

Lori Johnston stood in the center of Gloria's large library and stared at him blankly. "I have no idea what you're talking about."

Of course she didn't, he thought irritably. She'd passed judgment on him and then had dismissed him. Just as he should have dismissed her. But he hadn't.

No matter where he went or what he did or who he was with, he kept remembering her comment about him ignoring his grandmother and that being the reason she was so difficult.

"She doesn't like people," he said.

"Who?" Lori asked in the kind of tone usually reserved for dealing with the mentally disabled.

"My grandmother. She's not a people person."

"I haven't met her yet," Lori said, obviously not the least bit interested in the conversation. "I'm sure she's perfectly lovely."

"She's not. She difficult and demanding. She has her grandchildren followed. Walker's seen the reports. She actually hires private investigators to find out about our lives."

Lori's steady, cool gaze drilled into him. "Perhaps if her grandchildren were more interested in her well-being than in their own, she wouldn't be forced to resort to such drastic measures."

"Forced? No one's forcing her. She's doing this all on her own and do you know why?"

"Because she's lonely and you're the only family she has in the world and you're too busy for her?"

He wanted to hit something or strangle something. His gaze zeroed in on her neck. "You haven't even met the woman. Why are you taking her side?"

"In my experience, the elderly are often abandoned or at the very least, shuffled aside. You yourself said you were on the road all the time. What does that say about your relationship with your grandmother?"

His fingers twitched. "I played baseball. Of course I was gone. That's what the job involves. Traveling from city to city."

"For a season," Lori said. "How long is that? Five or six months? What about the rest of the year?" She walked to the tall windows and pulled open the drapes. Sunlight spilled onto the hardwood floor. "You're trying to convince me of something, Mr. Buchanan, but I can't figure out what. My advice is that you stop trying. Seriously. You and I don't need much more than a very casual relationship for me to do my job." She smiled. "It's not as if we'll be seeing a lot of each other."

He got that—the little jab as she implied he wouldn't be visiting. The whole damn thing was annoying, he thought. He wanted to tell her that he'd been the only one of the grandchildren willing to take on the task of lining up home-care nurses for Gloria. That he'd been to the hospital three times and that he *had* visited the old bat in the off-season.

But before he could explain, Lori was talking again.

"I think this room is perfect," she said. "Have the desk removed and those two chairs. Leave the recliner. She'll like that. The area rug is fine, as well. The hospital bed and table will be delivered tomorrow. I confirmed with them before I came over. Someone will be here to let them in?"

She raised her tone as if she were asking a question, but Reid knew she was giving an order. As in someone *would* be waiting for the delivery people.

"I've made arrangements."

"Good." She picked up her purse. "Thank you for your time, Mr. Buchanan. I've spoken with the doctor. Your grandmother should be ready to come home in about a week. I'll check in on her a few times before then so we can get acquainted."

"It's Reid," he said. "Call me Reid."

"All right. Anything else?"

He shook his head. She left and he was alone in Gloria's large, empty house. Much as his grandmother had been.

"BUT I DON'T HAVE any homework," Zoe said. "Why can't we have homework like the big kids?"

Elissa laughed. "I want you to write that down, Zoe. Write down that you want homework and then give the paper to me."

"Why?"

"So that a few years from now when you're older and complaining about how much homework you have, I can pull it out and remind you this is exactly what you wanted."

Zoe thought for a moment. "Okay."

She ran off to get paper. Elissa grinned. What a fabulous kid. She'd sure gotten lucky with her.

Someone knocked on the front door. Elissa looked up and her heart quickened. Walker? She hadn't seen him since Penny had her baby and she missed him. There was also the possibility of her confessing her feelings, which kept things interesting.

She crossed the living room and pulled open the door.

But it wasn't Walker. Instead, Neil stood there. Or swayed there. He was unsteady on his feet and there was something about his eyes that chilled her.

"Neil, what are you doing here?" she asked as she glanced back over her shoulder and prayed Zoe would take her time getting the paper.

"You know why I'm here," he told her. "I'm here for my money."

"I gave you money," she whispered, suddenly afraid. She tried to push the door closed, but he'd already stepped inside.

"Not enough," he told her. "I know you made more that weekend. I want it. I want it all. If you don't give it to me, I'm going to take the kid."

"Never," she said, standing her ground.

"You always say no," he told her. "Then you give me the money anyway. It's a little game we play. You like playing games with me."

"You're so wrong," she said, disgusted and afraid at the same time. "Neil, you need to go to your place and come down from whatever you're on."

"I'm flying, baby, and flying is the best."

"Get out before I call the police."

He laughed. "I've done nothing wrong. That's how good this is. You pay me to stay away. Nothing wrong with that."

"You threatened me," she said, remembering her baseball bat and inching toward the kitchen. If she could get the bat, she might be able to force him to leave. "I'm done paying you. You're not going to threaten me anymore."

She turned and lunged for the broom cupboard but before she could get there, Neil grabbed her by the arm and spun her toward him. Then he punched her hard in the face.

Pain exploded. She staggered, then collapsed against the couch and tasted blood.

"Mommy, Mommy!" Zoe flew to her side. "Go away! Don't you hurt my mommy. Stop it. You're a bad man and I'm telling Walker."

Neil grinned, but there was no humor or joy behind the movement. He looked dark and evil and the fear inside of her exploded until it consumed her.

"Now look at you," he said to Zoe. "Aren't you a pretty little girl. Do you know who I am? Do you want to come play a game with me?"

CHAPTER TWENTY

WALKER CONCLUDED the meeting and returned to his office. He'd thought about discussing his new ideas for employee profit sharing, but then had decided to wait until everything was in place. He would make a general announcement at that time, then implement the plan as each employee came to his or her anniversary date. Restaurants worked better without a lot of staff turnaround.

He also wanted to do something special for the corporate staff. Although he'd managed to convince them there wouldn't be executions at dawn, they still jumped every time he walked into a room. Gloria had sure as hell played out her quest for glory with a lot of innocent people. He was starting to think it would be better if she never came back.

He crossed to his desk and tossed down the folder, then considered what that meant. If Gloria didn't come back, was he willing to take over the company? Was this how he wanted to spend the rest of his life? Working for the family business?

He didn't have any answers and he wasn't sure this was the –

The skin on the back of his neck prickled. While he hadn't felt that since returning stateside, he was familiar with the sensation. It meant trouble. Bad trouble. More than once that uncomfortable feeling had saved his ass.

He turned slowly in the office, half expecting to find a sniper hiding under a table or lurking behind a desk. But there was no one. No guns, no grenades, no mines, no danger. Did that make the feeling more or less real?

He walked to the window and stared out at the city. The prickling increased and with it came a fear. Not for himself but for...

"Elissa," he breathed.

He grabbed the phone and dialed her number. A quick glance at his watch told him she should be home from work now. He hadn't seen her in a couple of days. Not since Penny had her baby, when Elissa had had to leave to go take care of Zoe.

He let the phone ring until the machine picked up and tried to tell himself she was fine. Only he didn't believe it and suddenly he had to know for himself.

The drive was the longest forty minutes of his life. He wove in and out of traffic as he crossed the bridge. Going south on the 405, he blew past seventy and watched his speedometer hit eighty before he took his exit. He ignored two red lights and a stop sign, then parked directly behind an unfamiliar, beat-up red van.

He ran toward Elissa's door and found it standing open.

"Elissa?" he yelled as he let himself inside.

There was a sound from the kitchen. A moan that made his blood freeze in his veins.

He burst into the room to find Elissa in a heap by the wall. His battle-trained gaze took in the scene in less than a second. The baseball bat by the back door. The blood on her face and the way she cradled her obviously broken arm against her body. Zoe crouched by her mother, a dark bruise already forming around Elissa's right eye.

Walker felt more than saw the movement to his left. He sidestepped the first punch easily and used the second to grab his attacker's arm. Rage filled him, but it was a calm, honed rage used against a thousand enemies. It gave him strength and direction.

He twisted the man's arm behind his back, hit him in the stomach, then tripped him as he started to go down. The man turned and Walker saw the dilated pupils, smelled the stink of something gone bad.

"Neil, I presume," he said, easily wrestling him to the ground and fighting the urge to snap his useless neck like a twig. "You should know better than to mess where you don't belong."

Elissa roused herself. "He's got a knife."

Walker quickly bent his wrist until he released it. "Not anymore."

The drugged-out loser lay on the ground, mewling like a kitten. Walker thought about killing him. It would be so easy. A quick twist of his head and Elissa would never have any trouble with him again.

The need grew until one of his hands reached for Neil's throat and tightened slightly.

"I told you Walker would save us," Zoe whispered as she huddled next to her mother.

The quiet words spoken with such confidence were enough to release his rage. He'd arrived in time—that was going to be enough.

"Do you have any rope?" he asked.

Five minutes later Neil was hog-tied, the police were on their way along with an ambulance, and Walker had examined both Zoe and Elissa for other injuries. The little girl had been punched in the stomach and back, along with the blow to her face. Elissa had been kicked around. The break looked clean. Once he knew what the little shit had done, Walker wanted to kill him all over again.

"How did you know we were in trouble?" Elissa asked as he shifted her into a more comfortable position and wiped her face with a damp cloth. "I thought he was going to…"

Her voice trailed off as she glanced at her daughter, but he knew what she'd been about to say. She thought Neil was going to kill them both.

"I had a feeling," he said. "I couldn't get you on the phone, so I came home."

"I heard the phone ring right after he arrived," she said, her eyes dark with pain and tears. "I thought maybe it was you, but I couldn't pick up and let you know. I don't know what would have happened if you hadn't come when you did."

Zoe watched her mother anxiously. "Don't cry, Mommy. Walker made us safe." She glanced fearfully at a tied and moaning Neil. "The bad man is going to jail."

He was going to make sure of that, Walker thought grimly. He didn't care how much it cost, Neil was going away. But not before he cut Elissa loose, once and for all.

The next couple of hours passed quickly. The police and EMTs arrived at the same time. While Elissa and Zoe were looked over and prepared for transport to a local hospital, Walker explained everything to the police. The officer in charge took him aside.

"You could have killed him," the officer said, glancing at a still-tied Neil.

"No, I couldn't. He's the kid's father. I doubt she'll want him in her life, but I didn't want her to see him die. Not at my hand."

"I know what you mean," the other man said. "I've got kids myself. We'll finish this up at the hospital."

Walker explained everything to a stunned Mrs. Ford who had just arrived home from a bridge party, then followed the ambulance to the hospital. He found both his girls in the E.R.

"Hey," he said, stepping into Elissa's room.

She was white and fading fast. "Where's Zoe?" she asked, barely able to form the words.

"Right next door."

"Stay with her, please. I might have to have

surgery. She'll need you. The nurse is going to call my parents, but you're the one she trusts right now." She managed a smile. "Even when Neil had us both cornered and hit my arm with that damn baseball bat, she said you'd come rescue us." Tears spilled out of her eyes. "She said you were the handsome prince, and that the prince always shows up in time."

His gut twisted and he swore as he took her hand and kissed her fingers. "I'm no prince."

"Tell that to my daughter."

She was bruised and beaten, yet he saw the strength and courage in her eyes. "You would have been a hell of a soldier," he said.

"This feels like war. Everything hurts. They want to check for internal injuries and X-ray the arm to see how bad the break is."

"I'll take care of everything," he said. "Don't worry. I'm not going anywhere. I'll be with Zoe and handle Mrs. Ford and call your boss."

"Work," she breathed. "I forgot about work."

"They'll understand. Just rest. Have they given you something for the pain?"

But she didn't answer. She had faded into unconsciousness.

He called for one of the nurses to come check on her, and was quickly pushed out of the room.

Even as he told himself she was going to be fine, he felt the stiff chill of panic. It was just a beating, he thought, refusing to give in to the need to burst back into the room and take over. It's not as if he knew anything about making her better.

But he'd seen plenty of guys after fights and she was going to be fine, right? It wasn't as if Neil had taken the baseball bat to any other part of her body, had he?

A familiar cry of his name sucked him into the next room, where he found Zoe in tears as a nurse put a bandage on the cut by her eye.

"She's been really brave," the young woman told him, "but she needs a little comforting."

Without thinking, Walker moved to the side of the bed and held open his arms. Zoe dived into them and held on as if she would never let go.

"Where's Mommy?" she asked.

"Getting looked at by the doctor," the nurse said before he could answer. "They want to take pictures of her arm and then she's going to get a cast." The nurse smiled. "I'll bet she'll let you be the first one to sign it. Maybe you can even draw some pictures on it or put on stickers. Stickers make it look really nice."

Zoe sniffed and raised her head, but she didn't let go of him. "We have stickers at home."

"Then we'll use those," Walker promised, hoping Elissa's recovery was all going to be as simple as a cast.

The nurse patted Zoe's back. "You need to stay here, honey, until the doctor releases you, but other than that, you're good to go. The bast—" The nurse cleared her throat. "That man only hit her a couple of times. She's okay."

Thank God.

Walker didn't know if he said the words or only thought them. Either way the relief was instant and powerful. He carried Zoe to the chair and settled her on his lap where he kissed the top of her head and held her securely in his arms.

"Was that man really my daddy?" Zoe asked quietly.

Walker swore under his breath. *Not on my watch,* he thought desperately. He couldn't answer these kind of questions. Not now, not after what she'd just been through. He was the wrong person to help her deal with all this crap.

But there wasn't anyone else, so he cleared his throat and prayed for divine guidance.

"It takes a man and a woman to make a baby," he said, then wondered if he'd just dug the hole bigger. "But making a baby doesn't mean a man is a daddy. Being a daddy is different. It's a name a man has to earn. He has to prove himself by doing the right thing and being there and…" And what else, he thought desperately.

"And loving his little girl," Zoe whispered as she began to cry.

"Right. He has to know her and because he knows her, he loves her. Because she's a very special little girl."

Zoe raised her head and stared into his soul. "So you're my daddy."

From the moment he'd found out Charlotte was dying and had realized he was going to walk out on her, he'd carried around a weight in his chest. It was as if that action had somehow locked his heart in a small box that was both heavy and painful.

Zoe's innocent, trusting, scary-as-hell words had just opened the box—and for the first time in over a decade, it didn't hurt to breathe.

"Yes, Zoe. I'm your daddy."

ELISSA RESURFACED in a hospital room where a brisk, efficient nurse explained she would be kept overnight for observation.

"The doctor will be by later to discuss your injuries," the woman said. "Basically you've got a broken arm and some internal bruising. Nothing's seriously damaged, though. You got lucky."

Lucky was an interesting word for what happened.

"My daughter," Elissa said. "Where's Zoe?"

"I met your little girl. She's a sweetheart. That big handsome man of yours said to tell you he was taking her home to a Mrs. Ford and he would be back later tonight."

Elissa closed her eyes and breathed a sigh of thanks. Zoe must be all right or she wouldn't have been let out of the hospital. Thank God.

"You can have more pain medication now," the nurse told her. "But as it seems to knock you on your butt, you might want to wait until you've seen everyone. Unless you don't want to see them."

Elissa still felt fuzzy. The details of Neil's rampage were still completely clear in her mind, but she was less certain about what had happened after that.

"Everyone?" she asked, shifting, then wincing as waves of pain shot up her arm. She glanced down and stared at the cast covering her left arm from just below her wrist to above her elbow. "I slept through getting a cast?"

The nurse grinned. "Honey, you slept through more than that. Are you up to seeing the herd?"

She had a herd? "Sure."

A few minutes after the nurse left, her parents entered, followed by Bobby. Her mother and father rushed to her side.

"Are you all right?" her mother asked. "I couldn't believe it when Walker called us. Oh, baby, your face."

Elissa touched her swollen lips and had a feeling she looked even worse than she felt. "I'm all right, Mom. Zoe and I survived, thanks to Walker's help."

"I wish he'd killed that bastard," her father said, his gaze intense. "I'd like to do it myself."

Elissa waited for her mother to scold her husband for being so aggressive, but she only stroked the uninjured parts of Elissa's face.

Bobby stepped closer. "You've got a black eye. Cool."

Elissa couldn't help smiling. "Black-and-blue?"

Bobby squinted. "More purple-and-red."

Her mother shushed him. "How's your arm? It must hurt."

It throbbed, but Elissa didn't want to take any pain

medication until the visit was over. Right now the fussing felt really good.

"Knock, knock."

Elissa looked up and saw Dani Buchanan hovering in the doorway.

"Are we interrupting?" Dani asked.

Elissa smiled. "Of course not. Come on in."

Dani entered, followed by Reid and Cal.

"Penny's at home with the baby," Dani said. "Otherwise she'd be here."

Elissa was more surprised that *they* were here. "You didn't have to come to the hospital."

Reid smiled at her parents, then leaned in and kissed her unbruised cheek. "Sure we did. You're Walker's girl."

Tears filled her eyes. She appreciated the sentiment, even if it wasn't true. *Walker's girl.* She liked the sound of that and she would have given a lot to make it happen.

Cal walked over and squeezed her hand. "You don't look so bad."

"Good to know." She introduced the Buchanans to her parents.

After they'd chatted a few minutes, her mother excused herself. "I'm going to go pick up Zoe. Mrs. Ford called me earlier and said she was fine. Still, I want to see for myself." She hesitated. "You don't mind, do you? You're going to be in the hospital overnight so I thought..." Her voice trailed off.

"I don't mind," Elissa told her. "I'm glad you're going to take care of her. I know she'll be safe with you."

"Of course she will be. She's your daughter, Elissa. I would give up my life for her."

"Oh, Mom."

Elissa felt tears on her cheeks. Suddenly she and her parents were hugging. She opened her eyes and saw Dani sniffing and both Cal and Reid clearing their throats.

"Where's Walker?" she asked.

Reid shrugged. "He said he had a couple of things to do, but that he would be back. He said not to worry."

She didn't know what that meant, but she smiled and nodded as if she did. She didn't want anyone to know how much she missed him and wished he was with her. He'd saved her and Zoe. That should be enough.

But it wasn't.

WALKER WAITED until the police officer in the emergency room had stepped out to grab some coffee and then he moved into Neil's room.

Neil lay on the bed, his eyes closed. Two IVs connected to a single line that fed into his arm. Walker moved next to the bed and bent down so his face was close to Neil's ear. Then he placed one hand on Neil's chest and the other over the man's mouth.

"How you feeling?" he asked, pressing against Neil's nose just enough to let him know that breathing was a privilege, not a right. "Coming down from that shit yet? Is your skin crawling or do you still feel good?"

Neil opened his eyes wide. Panic tightened his face and his breathing increased, but he was smart enough not to struggle.

"I'm going to make this real simple," Walker said quietly. "We can do this the easy way or the hard way. Personally, I'm in favor of the hard way. Nod if you understand."

Neil nodded.

"Is there any doubt in your mind that I could kill you if I wanted?"

Neil shook his head frantically.

"You want to live?"

Neil nodded.

"I'm going to send somebody in to see you. He's a lawyer. A real expensive guy in a fancy suit who knows all about the law. He's going to give you some papers to sign and you're going to sign them. Do you understand?"

Neil nodded again.

"Good. Once the police release you, hopefully after some serious jail time, you're going to leave Seattle and never come back. You're going to leave Elissa and Zoe alone. You'll never contact them again in any way. Is that clear?"

Neil nodded again.

"Just in case you think you can get out of our deal, I'll remind you that prison is a scary place.

You're kinda skinny, Neil. Some big guy could make your life there real unpleasant. And I know plenty of big guys. You got that?"

Neil nodded so hard, he nearly banged his chin against his chest.

"I thought you'd see things my way," Walker told him as he straightened, released Neil and left the room.

AFTER EVERYONE HAD GONE and Elissa got her pain medication, she drifted in and out of consciousness for a few hours. When she finally woke up, she saw a very dapper-looking man sitting beside her bed.

"Do I know you?" she asked groggily.

"We haven't been formally introduced. I'm Jeremy Fitzwalter," he said in a faintly British accent. "Walker Buchanan retained my firm to help you with your problem with Zoe's father. I stopped by to give you some paperwork."

He handed her a folder and smiled. "I think you'll like what's inside."

She looked from him to the folder. She remembered talking to Walker about finding a better lawyer, but she hadn't known he'd gone ahead with the plan. "I'm still a little out of it. Could you just tell me what it says?"

"Yes, of course. Under the circumstances, that makes the most sense." He shrugged. "Zoe's father has signed away all rights. He's given up his rights of custody and visitation. In return, you will not seek him out for child support. He agrees not to contact you or Zoe, however if Zoe wishes to get in touch with him after she's eighteen, that's fine with him."

Elissa rubbed her temple and wished her head didn't feel quite so big. Her arm throbbed in time with her heartbeat and her stomach and chest felt as if they were one giant, pulsating bruise.

"Neil won't be back," she said, barely able to believe it. "You're sure?"

"I'm positive. He has no hold over you anymore. He can never get custody of Zoe or even threaten to see her. He also asked me to tell you he apologizes for what happened. The drugs he took really messed him up." Jeremy leaned closer. "You're done with him, Ms. Towers. You're free."

Elissa wasn't sure what to do with that information. She was still trying to figure out how it had all happened when her mother showed up with Zoe that evening.

"Mommy, Mommy, you have a cast!" Zoe ran over and touched the hardened plaster. "Does it hurt?"

"The cast doesn't. My arm is a little sore. But that doesn't mean I don't want a hug."

Her mother lifted Zoe onto the bed, where her five-year-old hugged her as if she would never let her go.

What a horrible experience for her daughter, Elissa thought. Would Zoe have nightmares from this? Should she take her to a counselor of some kind?

"How are you feeling?" she asked tentatively.

"Okay." Zoe showed off a couple of her bruises.

"But Mrs. Ford read me three stories and Grandma and me made cookies. We would have brought them, but Grandma says we should wait until you come home tomorrow. Only maybe we can stay with Grandma for a few days. Wouldn't that be the best? I have princess sheets at Grandma's house."

"I remember," Elissa said as she glanced at her mother.

Her mother shrugged. "You don't have to come stay if you don't want to. I just thought while you were adjusting…"

"It would be great, Mom," Elissa assured her. "Really. Thank you. I didn't know how I was going to cope with one arm in a cast and the pain and everything."

"Good."

Zoe shifted so she could lean against her mother's unbroken arm. "Are you better, Mommy?"

"I will be. What about you? That man…" Elissa wasn't sure what to say about Neil. "He won't be back to bother us again."

Zoe looked up at her. "It's okay, Mommy. I know he's not my daddy."

Elissa held in a groan. How was she supposed to explain the complexities of her and Zoe's relationship to Neil?

"Actually, honey," she started, then stopped. There weren't any words, she thought.

Zoe smiled at her. "That bad man isn't my daddy

because he doesn't love me. Loving a little girl is what makes a daddy. Walker's my daddy now."

Elissa glanced at her mother, who raised her eyebrows. *All yours,* she mouthed.

If the pain hadn't been so bad, Elissa might have found the situation funny. Instead she felt herself wanting to cry.

"Zoe, Walker is a really good man," Elissa said. "He's—"

"My daddy," her daughter said firmly. "I know he is. He told me and daddies don't lie."

THE APARTMENT BUILDING was in the University district, typical for the area. The fall quarter would be starting in a few days and already students' cars lined the street.

Walker parked behind a beat-up truck and set his alarm before walking to the third floor of the building and knocking on the door marked 16.

The second the woman opened the door, he knew she was the one. He'd nearly forgotten that night in Kabul when Ben had gotten drunk and talked about Ashley's hair being the color of a sunset. But now, staring at the auburn-colored strands, he remembered.

"Ashley?" he asked, wanting to hope, but not there yet.

"Yes," she said, drawing out the word. "Do I know you?"

"I'm a friend of Ben's." He held out the picture he always carried. "Did you know him?"

"Ben?" She smiled and took the picture. "Sure.

Wow, I haven't talked to him in a while. Almost, what, a year? Sorry, I'm a little brain-dead. I was in the library all night. I'm working on a final draft of my dissertation, which is a mess. But yeah, I know him."

Walker felt his pulse increase. "You went out, right?"

Ashley's smile widened. "A few times. He was great. A lot of fun. He went into the Marines. We wrote a few times, but then we kind of stopped."

They'd stopped? Because… "You weren't in love with him?"

"What?" She took a step back. "No. I mean I liked him, but nothing really happened between us. I don't even remember if we kissed. Why are you asking me this? Has Ben been saying stuff about me?"

Walker felt the heaviness of defeat rest on his shoulders. He'd tried so damn hard, only to fail right at the end.

"Ben thought you were great," he said quietly. "He told me you were one in a million."

"Yeah. Where is he now?"

"He didn't make it back. He died a few months ago."

"I'm sorry," she said sincerely, but without any pain. "You were a friend of his?"

Walker nodded. "I was looking for his family."

"Oh, right. I don't know anything about them. He never said anything. I'm sorry. I wish I could help."

"You have helped," he told her. "Thanks for your time."

He turned and walked down the stairs. He was done. He'd found Ben's Ashley and he'd still come away with nothing.

ELISSA HAD TO WAIT UNTIL almost nine to see Walker. He finally walked into her hospital room shortly before the end of visiting hours.

She'd just been given another shot for the pain, so the edges of her day were starting to blur. She'd talked to Zoe before her daughter had gone to bed, then had chatted with her mother. Leslie had promised several days of rest punctuated only by large amounts of her favorite foods.

Despite the broken arm and the bruises, Elissa felt cared for and safe for the first time in a long time. The only tiny cloud on the horizon had been Walker's absence, and now he was here. He looked tired and mussed, but she could live with that.

"I'm sorry I'm late," he said as he approached her and took her uninjured hand. "I had some things to do. How are you feeling?"

"Better."

What to say to this man? How could she thank him for all he'd done for her?

"You saved our lives," she told him. "Thank you doesn't come close."

"It's enough."

She thought about what he'd said to Zoe. Had her daughter misunderstood?

He released her, pulled a worn envelope from his pocket and turned it over in his hands. "I found her."

With her brain fuzzy, it took her a second to figure out what he meant. "Ashley? You found Ben's Ashley."

He nodded.

The fact that he still had the letter made her chest tighten. "What happened?"

"I shouldn't have been surprised," he said, not looking at her. "Ben was great, but geeky and not really the kind of guy women go for. He would have grown out of it and found someone who appreciated him but…" He shrugged.

Elissa's heart began to ache. "She wasn't in love with him."

"No." He stared at the letter. "All I wanted was for his family to know how great he was. I just wanted there to be one person who had loved him, who would miss him and know the world was a better place for him having been in it."

Walker's pain filled the room and pressed in on her until she found it difficult to breathe. It wasn't the sort of ache that could be helped by a shot or a pill and she didn't have the words to release him from his burden. Unless…

She took the envelope from him and opened it. She scanned the typed contents, then began to read.

> "I met Ben the first day he landed in Afghanistan. If ever a new recruit had been out of place, it was him. But in less than a week, Ben was the guy everybody knew and every-

body liked. He had the soul of a poet, but the heart of a warrior. He was the bravest man I've ever met."

She read on as Walker's words detailed Ben's service and sacrifice.

"I know this is a time of grief, but I hope you'll eventually be able to see past that to the hero he was. I'll never forget him. He will always be a part of me, just like he's a part of you. He made me proud to be a soldier and a Marine. He made me proud to be an American."

She wiped away her tears and folded the letter. "You can stop looking, Walker. Not because there isn't anyone, but because *you're* Ben's family. You always have been. The person you've looking for…is you."

He stared at her for a long time. Then he bent over and gently gathered her against him as he shook with emotion.

"I miss him," he said, his voice gruff. "Every day."

"Then he's not really gone. He lives in you and through you. He lives in me and everyone else you tell about him."

Walker heard her words and knew she spoke the truth about all of it. He *was* Ben's family. In a way he'd always known that, but he resisted it because he'd wanted Ben to have more. Someone not so flawed and broken.

"I should have—"

She reached up and pressed her fingers to his mouth. "No. No *should haves,* no blaming, no guilt. He was your friend and you loved him. You will mourn him. No one can ask for more."

For the first time in more than a decade, peace settled over him. He felt the loss of Ben, just as he felt the loss of Charlotte. He'd made mistakes, but he'd loved them both. And they'd loved him.

"We're not perfect," Elissa was saying. "No one is. We have to learn to accept our faults and move on."

She was so damn serious, he thought as he bent down and kissed her. He liked that about her. Her serious side and her laughter. How she made jewelry and loved her daughter and took care of Mrs. Ford and stayed strong.

"I love you," he said.

She stared at him. "What? I had a whole speech prepared."

He smiled. "About what?"

"I can't remember now. You love me?"

"Totally. And Zoe."

"She said you were her daddy."

"I am by every definition but biology." He touched her cheek. "Although I should have talked to you first."

She looked dazed. "No, this is fine. You really love me? This isn't the painkiller talking?"

He kissed her, careful to be gentle against her bruises. "I love you, Elissa. I've been locked up tight for so long, I barely remember what it's like to live, but I want to learn again. I want to be with you in every sense of the word. I don't know if this is right for you or just scary. I don't know anything except you're the most amazing person I've ever met and that I want to spend the rest of my life with you."

She blinked several times. "You love me and you want to marry me?"

"Absolutely."

"Okay."

He looked at her. "Okay?"

She grinned. "Okay."

"So you love me, too?"

She sighed. "You're not too bad. Decent in bed, handy around the house. Sure, you'll do."

He growled. "I was hoping for more."

She leaned back against the pillows and closed her eyes. "I knew you were special from the first moment I figured out you were too surly to be a serial killer."

This had to be the drugs talking, he thought. "Excuse me?"

"Serial killers. Everyone always says how nice they are. You're not especially nice. You have a temper, you can be distant. But I've seen how you look at Zoe and I know you'd take on the world to protect her."

That was true. "And you."

She sighed. "And me. You make my heart beat faster, just by walking into the room. You're sweet and tender and funny and I wanted to die when I saw you kiss that bitch."

"What—oh, Naomi. Elissa, it wasn't like that."

"Did you or did you not see her naked?"

He swallowed. "Did I mention I love you?"

"Uh-huh. Which is why I'm letting it go."

"Do you want to marry me?" he asked.

She snuggled into her pillows and he knew she was fading fast. "Uh-huh."

"Maybe have a few more kids together?"

She held up two fingers.

He guessed that was a yes and knew he would never know why he'd gotten so damn lucky. "I'll let you get some sleep."

"Don't go," she said, opening her eyes and looking at him. "Don't ever go, Walker."

So he settled on the narrow mattress next to her and she cuddled in close.

"I love you," she whispered. "I have to go stay with my parents for a few days, but then we'll be together. Okay? You won't go anywhere?"

"Not without you. Not ever."

"That sounds nice. Let's always be in love," she said.

"Of course."

And they were.

Turn the page for a look at Susan Mallery's
next BUCHANAN FAMILY *romance*
SIZZLING
coming from HQN Books in 2007

CHAPTER ONE

UNTIL SIX FORTY-FIVE ON THAT Thursday morning, women had always loved Reid Buchanan.

They'd started leaving notes in his locker long before he'd figured out the opposite sex could be anything but annoying. During his sophomore year of high school, his hormones had kicked in and he'd become aware of all the possibilities. Over spring break of that year, Misty O'Connell, a senior, had seduced him in her parents' basement on a rainy Seattle afternoon, during an MTV Real World marathon.

He'd adored women from that moment on and they had returned the affection. Until today, when he casually turned the page in the morning paper and saw his picture next to an article with the headline: Fame, Absolutely. Fortune, You Bet. But Good in Bed? Not So Much.

Reid nearly spit out his coffee as he jerked to his feet and stared at the page. He blinked, then rubbed his eyes and read the headline again.

Not good in bed? *Not good in bed?*

"She's crazy," he muttered, knowing the author had to be a woman he'd obviously dated and dumped.

This was about revenge. About getting back at him and humiliating him in public. Because he *was* good in bed, dammit. Better than good.

He made women scream on a regular basis. They clawed his back—he had the scars to prove it. They stole into his hotel room at night when he was on the road, they begged, they followed him home and offered him anything if he would just sleep with them again.

He was better than good—he was a god!

He was also completely and totally screwed, he thought as he sank back into his chair and scanned the article. Sure enough, the author had gone out with him. It had been one night of what she described as nearly charming conversation, almost funny stories from his past and a so-so couple of hours naked. It was all couched in "don't sue me" language. Things like "Just one reporter's opinion" and "Maybe it's just me, but…"

He studied the name of the reporter, but it meant nothing. Not even a whisper of a memory. There wasn't a picture, so he grabbed his laptop and went online to the paper's Web site. Under the bio section he found a photo.

He studied the average-looking brunette and had a vague recollection of something. Okay, yeah, so maybe he'd slept with her, but just because he couldn't remember what had happened didn't mean it hadn't been incredible.

But along with the fuzzy memories was the idea that he'd gone out with her during the playoffs, when his former team had been fighting for a chance to make the World Series and he'd been back in Seattle, in his first year of retirement. He'd been bitter and angry about being out of the game. He might have been drunk.

"I was thinking about baseball instead of her. So sue me," he muttered as he read the article again.

Deep, soul-shriveling embarrassment chilled him. Instead of calling him a bastard to all of her friends, this woman had chosen to humiliate him in public. How the hell was he supposed to fight back? In the courts? He'd been around long enough to know he didn't have a case, and even if he did, how was he supposed to win? Parade a bunch of women around who would swear he made the earth move just by kissing them?

While he kind of liked that idea, he knew it wouldn't make a difference. He'd been a famous baseball player once, and there was nothing the public liked more than to see the mighty fall.

His friends would read this. His family would read this. Everyone he knew in Seattle would read it. He could only imagine what would happen when he walked into the Downtown Sports Bar today.

At least it was local, he thought grimly. Contained. He wouldn't have to deal with hearing from his old baseball buddies.

The phone rang. He grabbed it.

"Hello?"

"Mr. Buchanan? Reid? Hi. I'm a producer here at *Access Hollywood.* I was wondering if you'd like to make a comment on the article in the Seattle paper this morning. The one about—"

"I know what it's about," he growled.

"Oh, good." The young woman on the other end of the phone giggled. "How about an interview? I could have a crew there this morning. I'm sure you want to tell your side of things."

He hung up and swore. *Access Hollywood?* Already?

The phone rang again. He pulled the plug and thought about throwing it against the wall, but the damn phone wasn't responsible for this disaster.

His cell rang. He hesitated before picking it up. The caller ID showed a familiar number. A friend from Atlanta. He exhaled with relief. Okay, this call he could take.

"Hey, Tommy. How's it going?"

"Reid, buddy. Have you seen it? The article? It's everywhere. Total bummer. And for the record, dude, too much information."

IF LORI JOHNSTON HAD BELIEVED in reincarnation, she would have guessed she'd been a general, or some other kind of tactical expert in one of her past lives. There was nothing she liked more than taking a few unrelated elements, mixing them together and creating the perfect solution to a problem.

This morning she had to deal with hospital equipment arriving the day *after* it was supposed to and a catering service delivery with every single entrée wrong. In her free time, she had her new patient to meet and safely deliver home, assuming the ambulance driver wasn't late. Where other people would be screaming and threatening, Lori felt only energized. She would meet this challenge as she met all others and she would be victorious.

The delivery men finished assembling the state-of-the-art hospital bed and stepped back for her inspection. She stretched out on the mattress to check for bumps and low spots. What might just be annoying to someone healthy could be impossible to endure when one had a broken hip.

When the mattress passed inspection, she worked the controls.

"There's a squeak when I raise the bed," she said. "Can you fix that?"

The men shared an exasperated glance, but she didn't care. Trying to get comfortable while in pain was bad enough, but an annoying noise could make things worse.

She checked out the table on wheels, and it was fine, as was the wheelchair and the walker.

While they dealt with the squeak, Lori hurried into the massive kitchen where the catering staff sorted through the meals they'd brought.

"The chili?" a woman in a white uniform asked.

"Has to go." Lori pointed to the list she'd posted on the refrigerator. "This is a woman who is in her seventies. She's had a heart attack and surgery on a broken hip. She's on medication. I said tasty, but not spicy. We want to encourage her to eat, but she may still have stomach issues from all the medication.

She doesn't need to lose weight, so that's not a problem. Healthy, tempting dishes. Not chili, not sushi, nothing fancy."

She'd been so specific on the phone, too, she thought with minor exasperation.

"You could beat them. That would get their attention."

That voice. Lori didn't have to turn around to know who was standing in the doorway of the kitchen. Amused, no doubt, because, God forbid, he should have an actual meaningful thought or do something constructive.

She braced herself for the impact of the dark, knowing eyes, the handsome-but-just-shy-of-too-handsome face, and the casual slouch that should have annoyed the heck out of her, but instead made her want to melt like a twelve-year-old at a Jesse McCartney concert.

Reid Buchanan was everything she disliked in a man. He'd always had it easy so nothing had value. Women threw themselves at him. He'd had a brilliant career playing baseball, although she'd never followed sports and didn't know any details. And, he'd never once in his entire life bothered with a woman as ordinary as her.

"Don't you have something better to do than just show up and annoy me?" she asked as she turned toward him.

The impact of his physical presence was immediate. She found it difficult to breathe, let alone think.

"Annoying you is an unexpected bonus," he said,

"but not the reason why I'm here. My grandmother's coming home today."

"I know that. I arranged it."

"I thought I'd stop by to visit her."

"I'm sure knowing you stopped by four hours before she was due home will brighten her day so much that the healing process will be cut in half."

She pushed past him, ignoring the quick brush of her arm against his and the humiliating burst of heat that ignited inside of her. She was pathetic. No, she was worse than pathetic—one day she would grow enough to achieve pathetic and that would be a victory.

"She won't be here until this afternoon?" he asked as he followed her back into the library.

"Unfortunately, no. But it was thrilling to see you. So sorry you can't stay."

He leaned against the door frame in this room. He did that a lot. He must know how good he looked doing it, Lori thought grimly. No doubt he practiced at home.

She knew Reid was shallow and selfish and only interested in women as perfect as himself, so why was she attracted to him? She was intelligent. She should know better. And she did…in her head. It was the rest of her that was the problem. She was a total and complete cliché—a smart, average woman pining after the unobtainable. The bookstores probably contained an entire shelf of self-help books dedicated to her condition. If she believed in self-help books, she'd go get herself healed.

As it was, she was stuck with enduring.

"Don't you have to go away?" she asked.

"For now, but I'll be back."

"I'll count the hours."

"You do that." He stayed where he was, apparently unmovable.

"What?" she asked. "Are we waiting for something?"

He smiled, a slow, sexy smile that caused her heart to actually skip a beat. It was a new low.

"You don't read the paper, do you?" he asked.

"No. I go running in the morning and I listen to music."

The smile brightened. "Good. I'll see you later."

"You could wait until the evening nurse shows up and visit then. Wouldn't that be a great plan?"

"But then you'd miss me. Snarling at me is the best part of your day. Bye, Lori."

And then he was gone.